SEAL TEAM 666

SEAL TEAM 666

WESTON OCHSE

THOMAS DUNNE BOOKS ✈ St. Martin's Press, New York

This is a work of fiction. All of the characters, organizations, and events portrayed in this novel are either products of the author's imagination or are used fictitiously.

THOMAS DUNNE BOOKS.
An imprint of St. Martin's Press.

www.thomasdunnebooks.com
www.stmartins.com

Design by Steven Seighman

Library of Congress Cataloging-in-Publication Data

Ochse, Weston.
SEAL team 666 : a novel / Weston Ochse. — 1st ed.
p. cm.
ISBN 978-1-250-00735-3 (hardcover)
ISBN 978-1-250-01346-0 (e-book)
1. United States. Navy. SEALs—Fiction. 2. Special operations (Military science)—Fiction. 3. Demonology—Fiction. 4. Cults—Fiction. I. Title.
PS3615.C476S43 2012
813'.6—dc23

2012034563

First Edition: November 2012

10 9 8 7 6 5 4 3 2 1

For our Wounded Warriors

ACKNOWLEDGMENTS

Many people helped to make the book you're holding (or viewing or listening to) and I owe them all a sincere thanks. Thanks first to Brendan Deneen for his trust; and to think I almost passed up the email because I thought it was another Bin Laden gag photo. Thanks also to Peter Joseph, Margaret Smith, Nicole Sohl and the rest of the Thomas Dunne/St. Martin's Press Team, including Tweetmaster Paul. Thanks to Thirdy Lopez for your invaluable Tagalog language help and to Chris Fulbright for the hookup. Thanks to Ma Tai Tai for teaching me Chinese. Some of it stuck. Thanks to Dick Couch and Mir Bahmanyar, whose work I relied on for my initial research, as well as all my friends on the teams. You know who you are, especially Brian and Tommy. My gratitude includes Drew Williams for early reading, Dave Lake for a solid heart, Brian Wallenius for a solid ear, and Eunice and Greg Magill for your invaluable reconnaissance. Thanks of course to my agent, Robert Fleck. Shout-out to the bands Justice, Creed, the Eagles of Death Metal, Guns and Roses, and QOTSA for rocking me through the writing process. And thanks most of all to Yvonne, without whose support, wisdom, and love none of this would be possible.

SEAL TEAM 666

Prologue

EARLY MORNING. PAKISTAN. MAY 2, 2011.

DON'T TRY THIS AT HOME was stenciled on the side of the first of two Blackhawk helicopters assigned to the 160th Special Operations Aviation Regiment, aka Night Stalkers. They were en route from Jalalabad Air Base in Afghanistan to the sleepy residential section of Abbottabad, Pakistan, where a million-dollar compound rested a mere eight hundred meters from Kakul military academy, one of Pakistan's premiere army officer training schools.

SEAL Team 666 rode in the first helicopter. Comprising only five men and a dog, they were different in form and function from all other special-operations units. They wore black camouflage fatigues with dark gray Rhodesian combat vests. On their heads were Protec skate helmets modified for multiband inter/intra team radio (MBITR) headsets and microphones. Atop each helmet was a mount that held a pair of night-vision goggles (NVG). All but one of the SEALs wore gray ballistic face masks. Designed to protect the wearer from 9mm and shotgun hits, the masks produced a likeness similar to a hockey goalie's.

On board the second helicopter, eleven members of SEAL Team 6 were ready to provide backup if necessary. Dressed similarly to the SEAL team in the first helicopter, none of them wore face masks and they did not have a dog.

"Five minutes," the pilot announced over the radio system. The crew chief and his gunner prepared the doors and checked the M60 machine guns they could employ if necessary.

SEAL Team 666 heard the announcement through the MBITR and performed a last-minute weapons check. All five SEALs carried SIG Sauer 9mm automatic pistols. In addition to the 9s, two SEALs carried Heckler & Koch (HK) MP5s, two SEALs carried M4 Super 90 semiautomatic 12-gauge shotguns, and the fifth SEAL carried a Stoner SR-25 sniper rifle.

The dog was a Belgian Malinois and lay panting at the feet of the sniper, her mouth open in what could be considered the canine equivalent of an anticipatory grin. She wore a canine tactical assault vest. Spare ammo clips were tucked into compartments, as was a first-aid kit. The word HOOVER was stitched across the back of the vest.

SEALs lowered the NVGs into place, turned them on, and watched the world transform into a realm of phantom green. They postured, ready to deploy through the side doors. The dog stood, prepared to leave last.

The Blackhawk's doors opened, letting in the cool Pakistani mountain air. The triangular compound came into sight in the SEALs' green-tinged vision. The Blackhawk was coming in fast, just beginning to flare. But as the helicopter passed over and started to land, the green vision flashed white and all systems blacked out.

"Hold on," shouted the pilot. "We're going down."

"Force field," grunted one of the SEALs. "Does it every time."

The SEALs held on to the static bars affixed to the ceiling and ripped their NVGs free, now useless since the force field had fried the electronics.

The pilot managed to autorotate the Blackhawk to a clear

piece of ground outside the twelve-foot wall skirting the compound. The other helicopter landed nearby, steering clear of what took down the lead chopper.

One member of SEAL Team 666 vaulted out of the Blackhawk and placed a shape charge on the wall. He stepped aside while a man-sized hole blew through it with a dull *whump.* Then the two SEALs with the HKs deployed into the breach, weapons sunk deep into their shoulders, barrels leading the way. The SEALs with the shotguns came next, followed by the sniper and the dog.

The sniper set up in a corner of the yard where he had a field of fire that included the main entrance to the compound, the front door, and windows on all three floors. Outside the wall, SEAL Team 6 would ensure that no one got in, especially if anyone was planning on coming to the rescue of those they were about to kill. Ultimately, it was up to the sniper to ensure that no one got out. Hoover waited with him until the others gave the all-clear.

The other four slammed through the front door, pouring through in a routine that had been drilled into them so many times it had become second nature. Every corner of the entry room was controlled by the four SEALs and their weapons. When a bleary-eyed guard stepped into the room from a hallway, a 12-gauge slug disintegrated his face. The sound of the explosion in the tight quarters was stunning, but a thousand hours of close-quarters battle (CQB) training enabled the SEALs to ignore it.

With the communications gear fried as well, they had to resort to hand signals. The fact that the gear no longer worked meant two things, however. One, it meant that the monitoring from the White House Situation Room, Coronado, Dam Neck, and a dozen other places could no longer be conducted, meaning any chance of a flag officer or politician trying to use a ten-thousand-mile screwdriver to fix something they didn't like was impossible. And two, it meant that their target was most likely here, unless someone else had the capability of constructing a force field large enough to make a platoon's worth of twenty-first-century electronics worthless.

One of the SEALs made a hand motion to the sniper and Hoover. The sniper returned the gesture and spoke a few words. The dog shot across the ground until she was inside and with the SEALs.

They cleared the first floor, shot three more guards, and cut the power and telephone lines.

The two SEALs with the MP5s stacked up the stairs. They paused at the landing between the first and second floors. A hand signal to the others indicated there was a door at the top. After ensuring the stairs weren't booby-trapped, the lead SEAL gestured for Hoover to check out the door. The dog padded silently up the stairs and sniffed at the space between the bottom of the door and the floor. It didn't take long for the dog to turn rigid, then glance worriedly at the SEAL beside her.

The SEAL gave a hand signal to the others. The other SEALs responded immediately, pressing themselves against the walls as they waited for the door to open. Then the SEAL gave another signal to the dog. They were now hair-trigger ready.

The SEAL posted nearest the door pointed his Super 90 toward the spot where the locking mechanism met the doorframe, then pulled the trigger three times. Amid the explosion of sound, light, and wooden splinters, he shoved the door open and flattened himself against the stairs.

The door opened into a hallway, where three men and something dark had been waiting. The men hesitated, still stunned by the explosion. The lead SEAL double-tapped all three, putting two in each chest. They didn't have a chance, and as they sank to the floor, he could almost see the disappointment in their eyes.

But the thing behind them showed no sign of being stunned. It stepped forward. Glowing eyes. Taloned hands. Dark skin stretched tightly over elongated bones.

Demon.

The next SEAL in line emptied his MP5 into the creature. But it wasn't enough. The demon roared as it advanced. Pieces of its face had been blown away, revealing old black and brown pitted bone. An eye had disappeared in a burst of dust along with a batlike pointed ear. But even as the lead SEAL watched, the face began to re-form. First the cheek, then the eye, and soon the rest would be as it had been.

The SEAL who'd breached the door dropped to his knees and emptied his shotgun in the direction of the creature's legs.

The other two SEALs ran forward. The other MP5 opened up, sending fifteen 9mm rounds into the thing's face. The Super 90 unleashed seven 12-gauge shotgun slugs toward its knees. This combination was immediately duplicated by the first two SEALs, who'd had a moment to reload.

Under the combined damage of fourteen shotgun slugs and thirty 9mm rounds, the demon had no choice but to fall to its back as its soulless body fought to re-form.

Hoover knew what to do. She launched forward, landing on the demon's chest. Digging herself in place with the claws of her back feet, she opened her mouth wide, then snapped it shut on the demon's throat.

Behind her, the lead SEAL let his MP5 drop on its sling and pulled his MK3 knife free from the sheath on the side of his right thigh. He knelt on the demon's outstretched right arm and began to saw madly at the wrist. The hand came away just as Hoover jerked the jugular free like a dirt-encrusted vine. While one of the SEALs opened a canteen filled with holy water and poured it in the empty space in the demon's neck, another pulled out a flare and jammed it in the center of the unholy beast's chest. A platoon of Vatican exorcists couldn't have done a better job.

As the SEALs and the dog worked their way back down the hall, the demon burst into flame and was soon consumed, turning to an ashy reminiscence of its former shape before dissolving into nothing.

They cleared the rest of the second floor with no further interaction.

Outside, they could hear reports of gunshots from SEAL Team 6, as well as those of their sniper, but they couldn't concern themselves with that at the moment. Whatever was happening outside would be taken care of by those assigned to that mission. For now, all they had to worry about was their target on the third floor, someone the entire world had been searching for over the past ten years.

They repeated the same method for breaching the third-floor door as the second, but the door swung open to an empty, dark hallway. They stepped carefully into the hall, hugging the walls and wishing their NVGs were still working. Only two doors exited off the hallway. From the week of practice they had in the mock-up, constructed based on intelligence from the interrogation of an informant at Bagram Air Force Base Detention Facility, they knew the one on the right was a storage room. Their target was through the door on the left. Still, the storage room had to be cleared. Two of the SEALs did so, while the remaining SEALs and the dog made the left-hand door their universe.

Once the storage room was cleared, SEAL Team 666 converged on the last door.

The lead SEAL checked. It was unlocked.

They exchanged glances; then the SEAL turned the knob and pushed the door, which opened into a bedroom suite. The only light in the room came from a fire burning in a brazier on a central table. Behind this sat the man they'd come to kill. But instead of concerned, he appeared unfazed, drinking from a silver goblet.

"Down on the floor!" the SEALs shouted, first in English and then in Arabic.

The man made no move to comply.

Two SEALs moved into the room and searched the corners. They each raised a hand signal that meant clear.

Hoover stalked forward, growling, one stiff leg at time.

The lead SEAL kept his MP5 trained on the man. "If you won't get down, then stand the fuck up."

The man placed the goblet on the table and slowly got to his feet. He was very tall, with a graying beard that flowed to the center of his white-robed chest. His face had an almost cherubic quality that could have inspired a smile had it not been universally known that he was the mastermind of thousands of innocent deaths.

A shriek erupted as a woman charged from the inside of a wardrobe. She struck one of the SEALs in the back with the blade of a knife, but it snapped against his Kevlar body armor. The SEAL spun and caught her on the side of the head with the barrel of his Super 90. She fell to the ground, unconscious.

Another shriek erupted, this time from the other side of the room. Another woman leaped free of a wardrobe. This one took two bullets in the leg. The SEAL who shot her then kicked the knife free from her grip. It skidded across the floor and stopped beneath the bed.

The tall man started to change after the failed attack from the women. His face contorted. His features shifted and reshifted, changing the architecture of the human face into something else entirely.

The lead SEAL opened fire, but the bullets had even less effect on this figure than they'd had on the demon one floor below.

The other SEALs opened fire as well, unloading every slug and round they had into the creature. The MP5s ran out of ammo first. The SEALs let them fall on their slings. They opened metal canisters filled with holy water and doused the newly formed creature.

Where the water hit, smoke rose. A multi-octave scream filled the room, the sound of hundreds in agony coming from the mouth of one.

The lead SEAL knelt and withdrew an ancient blade from where it was secured in Hoover's tactical harness. The blade was black with age. Etchings from a dead language adorned the surface. The shape was a like a tongue of flame, and as he held it toward the creature, the creature recognized the blade and showed fear for the first time.

The SEAL and the beast clashed in a mad jumble of punches, blocks, and kicks. One was fueled by the righteousness of his mission and thousands of hours of practice, and the other was fueled by the infinite darkness that had filled its soul.

The remaining SEALs stood aside as their leader fought. Their hands flexed, each teetering on the balls of his feet, eager and ready. Even Hoover waited, her only dissent a constant growl of frustration for not being allowed to join in.

Somewhere outside, they heard a cry for help, then a gurgling scream. Whatever it was, there was nothing that could be done. Their mission was in this room, and until the beast was down, none of them would leave.

The combatants fell to the ground, but their new position did nothing to halt the frequency of their blows. Then suddenly the fighting stopped. The lead SEAL shot rigid, a taloned hand gripping his neck, his tongue jammed out from blue lips. One of the SEAL's hands came up to pry away the hold on his neck, slipping down to the creature's wrist to try and wrench it free. But the hold was too tight.

The creature climbed stiffly to a standing position, dragging the SEAL with it. As they stood, the SEAL brought his other hand upward, embedding the blade so deeply through the bottom of the creature's chin that the point erupted from the top of its head. It stood for one long, mad minute, choking the life out of the SEAL as tightly as it could, then toppled. As the creature fell, it pulled the lead SEAL with it.

The other SEALs worked to lever open the thing's hand from their team member's neck. It took great effort, but they finally managed, and as they did, the SEAL took in a lungful of air.

"Mother of God," he rasped.

They grabbed a blanket from the bed and rolled the creature into it, then rushed it downstairs and out the door. Bodies littered the yard. By the looks of them, they were reinforcements who'd been trying to assist the creature SEAL Team 666 now carried. The team's sniper lay in the corner. Half of his face had been torn away. His single remaining eye stared into the Pakistani night. Something terrible had happened here and it had happened to one of their own.

But there was no time to mourn. They took him, exiting through the hole in the wall, and crowded aboard the second helicopter. They placed the demon on the floor of the aircraft and strapped their deceased sniper into a harness as the doors snapped shut. One by one, they removed their masks, sweat and grime coating their faces. The members of SEAL Team 6 were eager to assist where they could. With their target achieved, the SEALs rose into the air, leaving the first chopper behind. A hundred meters up and the first chopper exploded, denying it to the enemy. Once SEAL Team 666 returned to Bagram, a joint FBI-CIA forensics team videotaped the creature from all angles and took DNA samples. Afterward, SEAL Team 666 escorted the body to the USS *Carl Vinson* in the Arabian Sea, where they disposed of the demon in a private ceremony.

Only then did SEAL Team 666 appreciate their accomplishment.

Only then did they mourn the loss of their sniper.

Before the next mission, they'd need a new one.

1

KADWAN. SIX MONTHS EARLIER.

The evisceration of the woman was majestic to behold. He'd delighted in her screams, relished the way her mouth opened so wide that it could have eaten the world. Her pathetic gestures as she begged for her life had almost spoiled it. Not that it had evinced any empathy on his part, but it had marred his journey to the spiritual plateau he'd been striving to reach in order to prepare himself for the transformation.

It was at once funny and sad that he'd been living such a life of somnambulant grace, pitifully ignorant of the creatures and beings that coexisted in their shared universe, kept at bay only by a paper-thin film of civilization and ignorance. If he'd only known sooner, maybe he wouldn't have wasted half his life pretending to be someone who cared about his fellow man.

2

CORONADO ISLAND. MORNING.

Petty Officer First Class Jack Walker felt like the crap had just been beaten out of him. Then again, he'd felt like that for the last twenty-one weeks. Since the first moment of Indoc, when Instructor Alberto Reno had slammed the door and commanded them to their feet, through the ten thousand push-ups, the twenty thousand flutter kicks, the one hundred and twenty continuous hours of training in Hell Week with only four hours of sleep each night, to the bone-numbing cold of Coronado Bay, his body had been beaten, cracked, and remolded. The pain was there when he got up in the morning. It was there when he drank his coffee. It was there when he went to bed at night. Walker pretended not to notice it, but the pain was persistent.

Which was what it was doing now—being persistent.

Instructor Kenny ran up to him. "What is it, Walker?"

"Nothing, Instructor Kenny. It's just pain leaving the body."

"If you're going to scream, then do it standing up. Get on your feet, Walker."

Walker crawled out of the sand and onto his feet. He'd just completed the final timed four-mile run. He and the other members of SEAL Class 290 had come in under twenty-nine minutes, and for the first time, they'd all made it. Part of it was that those who couldn't make it mentally and/or physically through the training had either been rolled back or had rung the bell—Dropped on Request, or DOR. Another part was that they were working together as a team. Several of his mates had seen the way he was pulling up and had helped him as the shin splints soared with the pain of running seven-minute miles. And then there was the fact that the end was in sight. He had four weeks before he could finally graduate. One week more of training, then off to San Clemente Island for the final live-fire exercise.

Instructor Howard ran up and got in his face.

"How'd you make it this far, Walker? Did you have sex with the president or did we collectively just forget what it takes to be a SEAL?"

"I didn't have sex with the president, sir."

"Why not? Isn't he handsome enough for you?"

"No, sir. I mean yes, sir."

"Make up your mind, SEAL."

"Yes, sir."

"So answer my question, Walker. Do you know what it takes to be a SEAL?"

"Yes, sir!" The pain laced up and down his legs, digging through his shin and scoring the bone from beneath. He'd lived with it for weeks now and would live with it for four more.

"I don't think you know. I don't think you know anything. I think your body is ready to give up, isn't it Walker?"

"No, sir. This SEAL candidate is fit and fine!"

Instructor Howard leaned in and whispered violently. "What do you think I'm going to say next, Walker?"

Walker paused, then in a voice that was eerily calm said, "You're going to say Hooya, sir, because this candidate is going to be a damn good SEAL."

Howard hid the smirk that flashed across his face. "I don't think that was what I was going to say."

Instead of continuing the conversation, Walker hit the sand and pushed out twenty fast push-ups. When he completed them, he popped back up and said, "Petty Officer First Class Walker requests permission to rejoin the class!"

Walker eyed the others, who were already forming on Stumpy, the seventy-pound log with four handles that had become their classmate, never to be forgotten, never to be left behind. Despite the pain, despite the agony, he wanted nothing more than to stay with his class and put his arms around his best friend, Stumpy.

"Permission granted," Instructor Howard barked.

Walker ran over to the others, happy to be out from under the watch of the instructors.

"Take ten," Kenny called as he turned to Instructor Howard. Three visitors were walking down the beach toward them, including a tall red-haired woman, impeccably dressed in a gray business suit.

"How are the legs?" Meyers asked, kneeling and unlacing his own boots so he could adjust his socks.

Walker knelt to do the same. "Hurts like a big dog."

"You gonna make it?"

"Is the pope Catholic?"

"Try and stretch the Achilles tendon more and it'll give you some relief at least."

Walker nodded at Meyers, who was a Navy corpsman by trade. If anyone knew how to get more from the body, it was him.

With his shoes retied, Walker stood and stretched, grabbing the bottoms of his boots with his hands and planting his face on his knees. While he was there, he took a moment to pray. He only had four more weeks. If they'd leave him alone, he could do them on his head.

If they left him alone, that is.

3

CORONADO ISLAND. MORNING.

Alexis Billings strode behind Navy Lieutenant Commander Scott and Marine Major Benitez. She'd been smart enough to wear closed-toe shoes; there was nothing worse than sand getting into the inside of Donna Karans. Still, she took high steps and placed her feet in the packed footprints of the two officers who'd been assigned as her escorts.

She spied the class and the instructors about a hundred meters farther down. They all wore the ultrashort UDT shorts, which looked like khaki versions of 1960s basketball shorts, and boots. The instructors wore black T-shirts and black baseball caps. The students wore OD green T-shirts and no caps.

This visit was pro forma, but it had to be done. Senator Withers had made it clear that he didn't want her or the Senate Select Committee on Intelligence (SSCI), more commonly known as the Sissy, to be a faceless government organization. He wanted the Sissy to have a face, and in her case, a pretty one, especially when it had to do what it was about to do.

That her attractiveness was one of the things that had gotten her this appointment irked her. A graduate of Bryn Mawr and Princeton, she'd entered the working world with brains and a cache of connections.

"Don't take it personally," her friend and former classmate at Princeton, Lauren Rhodes, had told her shortly after her appointment. "Not everyone can have beauty, brains, and the family connection like you do."

Who knew that her father had parlayed his success and social prominence at owning eleven car dealerships into a personal friendship with the senior senator from Pennsylvania? When his daughter told him she wanted to get into politics from the ground up, she was given an interview and an appointment as a permanent staffer for the Sissy, all at age twenty-seven. The Sissy commanded oversight of all intelligence and special-ops training and operations, from the CIA, the Department of Defense, and agencies in between. Not only were they charged with being good stewards of the American taxpayer's hard-earned dollars, but they were also concerned with ensuring that all operations were conducted with the proper scrutiny. That's where she came in. Her job had been to become the expert on all things special operations. If a vote was coming up on a new program or a budget cut, it was her job to advise the members of the Sissy regarding the efficacy, loss, and possible repercussions, if any, that might affect current and future special operations around the globe. She had a staff of six, consisting equally of Ivy League graduates and former special operators. Although she had been inexperienced when she took the job, hard work, an ability to remember facts and figures, her determination to get things done right the first time, and her constant respect for those she served had made her a known entity in the community, as well as someone to whom senior flag officers showed respect.

Then, of course, there was her role as the administrator. Very few knew of this position outside the Sissy and the cabinet. She'd held that position for two years now. She'd had to make this walk three times, and on each occasion it was because a member of her team had been killed.

When they neared the instructors, she allowed the officers to step forward and deliver the letter from Admiral Franklin, commander of Naval Special Warfare Command. She watched as the instructors turned and saluted the officers. She noticed their postures and how they changed when they exchanged greetings, when they learned that they were going to lose one of their candidates, and finally when they learned it was because of some uppity broad in a business suit.

It was at the point when they turned rigid with anger that she stepped forward and introduced herself.

"Master Chief Kenny, Senior Chief Howard, I'm Alexis Billings. The Sissy wants to thank you for your cooperation."

"Cooperation?" sputtered Howard. "The Sissy?"

"Master Chief Kenny, Captain Pastora of DEVGRU speaks highly of you. Likewise, Captain Vitale speaks highly of you as well, Senior Chief." She held out her hand. "It's a true privilege to meet both of you."

She counted on the professionalism of the instructors. It always worked. They each in turn accepted her handshake. They might not like what she was about to do, but they were not going to disobey the orders of the admiral. She also didn't have to shove it down their throats. At the very least, she could let them know that although she was a woman who was stepping into a man's world, she was doing it with the utmost respect for their mission, tradition, and way of life.

"I apologize for being the bearer of this request," she said, softening the verbiage in the letter, which was far from a request.

"We get it," Instructor Kenny muttered. "Enough with the reach-around."

She nodded and clasped her hands in front of her. "Then let's get to it, shall we?"

"One question, ma'am," Instructor Howard said. "Why Jack Walker? No offense to the boy, but he's not our best."

"He's also not our worst," Instructor Kenny interjected.

"No, he's not our worst," Instructor Howard agreed. "But if the Sissy wants a SEAL for a special mission, why not just go to the teams? We have plenty of qualified SEALs out there."

"We don't want to disturb the organization of the teams," she said, offering him a firm smile.

"Then why not one of the other candidates? What about Marshall? Or Rosen?"

She leaned forward slightly and gazed at the memo. "I believe you'll see that Admiral Franklin authorized the release of Petty Officer First Class Walker. I don't believe there are any other names on that list, but I will take your recommendations under advisement."

Instructor Kenny looked pointedly at Lieutenant Commander Scott. "Sir? Anything to say about this?"

The Phase Three instructor couldn't know, but she'd already had the same conversation with the lieutenant commander and the major. Neither had been happy with her responses.

Screening and Selection for SEALs was filled with both mental and physical rigor. The psychological interviews and screening process lasted several days, so it hadn't been hard to sprinkle in a few questions here and there to ascertain those who could best fit the needs of the Sissy. Of the candidates currently in phases, Jack Walker was the only one whose answers and background made him a fit. But Kenny and Howard didn't need to know that. All they needed to know was that a military officer senior to them had made the order to release this particular candidate.

Major Benitez's frown said it all. She had to give Lieutenant Commander Scott credit, however. He definitely had a sense of humor and treated the entire event as some Douglas

Adams training program. He kept looking at her as if to check and see when she was going to give them the punch line.

But there was no punch line to give.

SEAL Team 666 needed a replacement sniper and Jack Walker was that person.

"Aw hell," Instructor Kenny said. "Walker! Get your ass over here!"

4

CORONADO ISLAND. STILL MORNING.

Petty Officer First Class Jack Walker felt like the crap had just been kicked out of him . . . again. As his instructors explained that he had to leave training, all he could think about was the wasted time. He glanced pleadingly back and forth between his instructors and the woman.

"But I have four weeks left. Can't you all tell her to leave me alone?"

"It's not just about her, son. The admiral has made his decision."

The blue sky seemed to sway above him as the sand danced across his vision. Strong hands caught his shoulders.

"Steady there." Howard held him tightly.

Walker turned toward where the woman stood five yards away. "What does this all mean? I've made all the events. Are you kicking me out? Because I'm not going to ring the bell."

"I'm not going to kick you out," Howard said.

"He doesn't have to," the woman said, approaching. "You've

graduated early. Come with me, Petty Officer Walker. We have a lot to talk about."

Howard whispered in his ear. "Don't know what's going on, Jack, but do as she says. You want to come back here and finish, we'll roll you in the last four weeks, no problem."

"Really, Senior Chief?"

"Maybe give you some time to take care of those shins."

Walker stared at the aging instructor and let out a laugh. Well, of course he'd known about the injury. Trying to keep anything from the cadre seemed impossible.

Howard let go of him. "He's all yours, Miss Billings."

The woman, who turned out to be as tall as Walker, spun and headed back down the beach.

Walker took one last look back at his mates in Class 290, gave them a wave, then hurried after her.

After about a hundred meters, they stopped. She pulled a cell phone from her pocket and spoke into it for a few seconds before jamming it back into her jacket. The onshore wind had teased a few hairs free from the bun at the back of her head. She stared into the surf as if waiting for something.

"What is this all about?" he asked finally.

"We need you to be a part of a special team, Walker."

"I was going to be part of a special team. As far as I know, the most special team in the free world. The U.S. Navy SEALs."

"There's a team more special than that."

He'd believe that when he saw it. Ever since he'd grown up in Subic Bay as a Navy brat, he'd watched the SEALs come and go from mission to mission, untouched by the rigmarole of the rest of the Navy.

Suddenly the sound of a helicopter rang over the surf. He spied it about a kilometer out. It was a Blackhawk from the 160th. It came close and flared.

She put a hand on her hair and turned away from the landing.

When it hit the sand, she ran toward it, low, her eyes down, as if she'd done it a hundred times.

He followed and climbed into the seat beside her.

The helicopter rose and pitched to the right, as if heading for downtown San Diego.

After smoothing her hair and brushing the sand from her clothes, Billings reached into her bag and handed him an envelope.

"Here. Sorry there's no ceremony. We were going to wait until you finished but there's a mission that has to be conducted now."

He accepted the package. It was just a plain manila envelope. He slipped his finger under the flap and tore it open. Inside were four things. The first was a letter of commendation from the president of the United States, congratulating him for becoming a SEAL. The second was a graduation certificate from the Naval Special Warfare Command announcing that he was a graduate of BUD/S Class 290 and a U.S. Navy SEAL. The third was a SEAL trident pin, freshly minted and as shiny as he was dirty. The fourth and final object was three brass 9s clumped together.

He stared at these for a long minute. He even let his fingers rub the gold trident of the SEAL BUD/S logo. He'd wanted this more than anything. He'd bled for it. He'd cried for it. But somehow, now that he actually held one in his hands, it felt less than what it should have.

He glanced up at her. "I guess there's something to be said for a little ceremony, huh?"

She gave him a tight smile. "You're a SEAL inside. No ceremony will make it any different."

He was struck by the raw truth of what she said. It sounded like something Instructor Kenny or Instructor Howard would say. It was very odd to hear it from a person who wasn't a SEAL.

"And the three nines?" he asked.

"The what?" She turned knitted brows toward him.

He held up the badge. "This brass thing with the three nines."

She reached out and turned the object in his hand 180 degrees. "Those aren't three nines."

He looked at them in the new configuration. "Three sixes."

"Six Six Six," she said. "That's your new team."

SEAL Team 666? He'd never heard of such a thing. The U.S. government had played fast and loose with numbering over the years. They'd created SEAL Team 6 long before they had a Team 4 or Team 5, just to make the Soviet Union think they had more SEAL teams. Even now, SEAL Team 6 still existed, but under the name DEVGRU, which stood for United States Naval Special Warfare Development Group. Although the reality was supposed to be highly classified, the truth of the matter was plastered all over the Internet. If that couldn't be hidden, how could something with a name like SEAL Team 666 be kept a secret?

He couldn't help but laugh. "No really. What does it mean?"

She raised a single eyebrow, much as Leonard Nimoy famously did on the original *Star Trek* series whenever Captain Kirk said something funny.

"Seriously," Walker prodded. "What does it stand for?"

"Knowledge of SEAL Team 666 is governed by a special access program, or SAP. SEAL Team 666 is a highly classified special unit under the direct command of the Senate Select Committee on Intelligence, with direct oversight from the Office of the Vice President and the President. The classification of the group is compartmentalized Top Secret SAP."

"You're serious." He sat forward. "What's the mission?"

"You'll get a mission brief shortly," she said, pointing toward the airfield below. They hadn't gone all the way to San Diego, just to the other side of the island. "I had the liberty of having your things packed and sent over."

"Thanks, but most of them need a good cleaning. Maybe by next week I'll—"

"No. You don't understand. You're going to get a mission brief from the team leader. You leave in less than an hour."

Walker looked at his hands and legs. They were filthy from the surf and physical training. "Can't I just clean up?"

"Jesus, Walker. You're a SEAL, not a princess. Act like one."

He was so startled by her tone and delivery that he barely noticed they'd landed until she exited the helicopter, running low beneath the whirling blades. He ran to catch up.

5

NORTH ISLAND NAVAL COMPLEX AIRSTRIP. NOON.

The FNG walked up the ramp of the C-141 Starlifter as if he were late for the first day of elementary school. To Senior Chief Petty Officer Tim Laws, who'd lived and breathed the movie industry while growing up in Hollywood, the kid was one part young Steve McQueen and another part Ryan Phillippe. The FNG, perennial military term for the Fucking New Guy, wore a buzz cut of blond hair topping a face made of angles and deeply set blue eyes above a mouth whose usual form, Laws guessed, was a smile. Now it was doing everything but smiling. This was the sort of man who wore his heart on his lips.

"Stow your gear and get out of those UDTs. This isn't a swim meet. This is an op." Lieutenant Commander Sam Holmes gestured to an empty space of bench along one wall of the interior of the aircraft. A rucksack with weapons stacked on top of it. "That's your gear. No time to personalize it. You'll just have to make do."

Alexis Billing, the Sissy administrator, came next, a phone

plastered to the side of her face. She plopped down near Holmes, but made no notice of him.

Laws watched as the new guy dropped his seabag and shoved it under the bench, strapping it to the wall for flight. Good. At least he'd been aboard an operational aircraft before. Laws had been with SEAL Team 666 longer than anyone. He'd seen seven members come and go. Four had left under their own power; the others had left in body bags. He figured he'd do the same when the time came. There was no other place he'd rather be.

The boy sat down and stared at a manila envelope in his hands. He rubbed something through the paper, then folded the envelope roughly, bent over, and stuffed it into his seabag. When he straightened, he grabbed one of the weapons on top of his rucksack—a Stoner SR-25 sniper rifle. To the kid's credit, he broke it down, inspected the barrel and bolt assembly. After he snapped it back together, he checked the ammunition.

He was probably acutely aware that everyone's eyes were on him, even if like Fratolilio they pretended not to notice. But he didn't act as if he knew it. Instead, he acted the opposite, as if he didn't have a care in the world. He seemed to have recovered from his previous nervousness. Laws had to give the boy praise for having the chops to insert himself into such a close-knit group.

Like he had a choice.

When the administrator chose you, that was that. How and why a person was chosen was up for grabs. No one really knew. Sure, there was speculation. Every member knew that the rubric was based on some of the questions in screening and selection, but which ones? The two days were loaded with *what would you do if* scenarios that individually seemed fairly mundane. But perhaps together with other questions they served to form a more three-dimensional vision of a person.

Laws had long ago given up trying to figure out why the

people who'd been chosen had been chosen. In the end, they seemed like naturals.

Tony Fratolilio was your classic Brooklyn Italian. He had joined the Navy instead of jail and made himself into quite the computer specialist. His street savvy never really left and he found himself breaking into all sorts of sensitive networks if there was a payday involved. Of course he'd been caught, but the boy's charisma and natural affinity for animals had the administrator sending him through BUD/S training class 243 as her own personalized U.S. Navy SEAL.

Johnny Ruiz was another who didn't fit the mold. He was a Mexican from West Virginia and spoke English with such a cracker accent that it was suspected he was just trying to pull one over on everyone. Ruiz had come from SEAL Team 3 with deployments to Yemen and Somalia. A graduate of Underwater Demolition Training as well as BUD/S training class 237, he was the team's explosives expert. That he talked funny was just a bonus.

The team leader was Lieutenant Commander Sam Holmes. A graduate of the infamous BUD/S training class 201, he'd commanded SEALs in Teams 3 and 5 with deployments in Liberia, Somalia, Afghanistan, and Iraq. Although he'd had some dicey missions he didn't talk about, he was one of the best leaders Laws had ever had. That he was a big man always made it fun to go out to bars with him. He was a constant target for the drunk and insane, as if he were some sacred mountain that they had to try and climb.

Then, of course, there was Laws himself. He benefited from an audiographic memory. If he heard it, he remembered it. Period. This facility enabled him to learn several languages including Chinese, Japanese, Arabic, and the Romance languages. While others called it skill, he felt more like it was a quirk of genetics because it was so easy. But he had to admit that it came in plenty handy when he was working straight human-intelligence operations and conducting interrogations in support of SEAL Team 1 and First Special Forces Group in the Golden Triangle.

Laws's attention was drawn back to the new guy, and what he saw made him chuckle. The boy was told to change and changing he was. Even as the ramp closed in the back of the C-141 Starlifter and the engines spun up, the boy had undressed and stood naked in the middle of the plane.

Laws glanced at the administrator, who was pointedly ignoring the naked SEAL.

Rifling through the rucksack, the new guy found what he needed to suit up for the mission. He quickly put the uniform and vest on, and as the plane rose into the air, he laced up his boots.

Laws waited about half an hour to see if Holmes was going to introduce the new guy to the team. When it obviously wasn't going to happen, Laws crossed to the other side of the plane and sat down on the bench beside the FNG.

"Tim Laws," he said by way of introduction, holding out his hand. "Intelligence, deputy commander, and the team welcome wagon."

The new guy shook his hand. "Walker, Jack. Sniper."

"What class are you?"

Walker looked at him in such a way that Laws immediately knew the answer. "You didn't finish, did you? What phase were you in?"

"Three. We were about to go on Live Fire."

Laws leaned back and laughed. "Four weeks to go and you were yanked. That's got to suck big time. You must be something special."

Walker shrugged. "I don't know anything about . . . whatever this is."

"This, my new friend and teammate, is the finest and baddest supernatural unconventional-warfare special-mission unit in the United States government inventory."

"We're the only one, Laws," Fratolilio commented.

"Supernatural?" Walker grinned, then let his grin fall when it wasn't shared by the others.

"Absolutely. Why, I could tell you—"

"Wait until mission brief," Holmes ordered. He was leaning back against the fuselage and hadn't even opened his eyes.

"Then I'll wait until mission brief. Let me introduce you to the other members of the team."

As Laws went about introducing Walker, he noted that the boy had begun to feel more comfortable in his new skin, which was good. If they were about to go on a mission and would require his backup, they needed to make sure that his mind was in the right place.

Finally, half an hour later, Holmes opened his eyes, brought out a folder, and gave the mission brief.

6

30,000 FEET ABOVE CENTRAL CALIFORNIA.

According to the big blond guy who was apparently the leader, they were going to Chinatown, where an anomaly had been identified. An interagency intelligence unit composed of operatives from the Air Force Office of Special Investigations and the Defense Intelligence Agency had discovered what they felt was the nexus for organizing illegal tech transfer to China. Informants had infiltrated the area and come back with an entirely different story, one that included rumor of human sacrifice, mysticism, and some kind of cult.

"So we don't really know what we're dealing with here. It's mainly an intelligence-gathering mission. We engage hot only when we are engaged or if there's a justifiable threat." He nodded to the administrator. "Miss Billings doesn't want us making the national news. I don't even want you making the local news. You aren't supposed to be operating on U.S. soil, but you have to. It's not like we have a local supernatural SWAT unit standing by to handle these things."

"Maybe we should," Laws said.

"What do y'all want to do, run a mobile training team and teach them the best and most efficient ways to kill a demon or dismember a ghoul?" Ruiz asked.

Laws grinned. "Sounds like fun."

"Barring the Sissy authorizing that, we have to go in ourselves." Holmes pulled out a map. "Based on current mission parameters, there's no utility in deploying a sniper for overwatch, so Walker, you'll stack with us inside."

"Yes, sir."

The rest of the mission briefing came and went. Everyone was given their mission particulars, including the dog. Walker had noticed the Belgian Malinois when he'd boarded the plane and thought of it as a mascot. But it seemed as if it was going to join them for CQB. This was something entirely new.

They were issued the primary and secondary frequencies for the MBITRs. They checked ammunition and tied, buttoned, snapped, and twisted anything that needed to be secured. When they were suited up in their helmets and gear, Laws came over.

"Excited for your first mission?"

"I've had other missions."

"Not with SEALs, you haven't."

"No, but I spent the last five years with Kennedy Irregular Warfare Group," Jack said. It was always the same. Everyone wanted to know where you worked and what you'd done. It was how you were measured and he'd done it many times. "I joined eight years ago. My first tour out of A School was as an intelligence specialist on the destroyer USS *Forrest Sherman*. I spent three years aboard, then was assigned to KIWG in Maryland. That put me on repeated deployment rotations to Iraq, conducting riverine operations against suspected insurgents, interdicting weapons from Al Quds, and collecting intelligence on Iran. I did that for almost five years. So, yes, I've had other missions."

Laws grinned. "But those weren't SEAL missions. Let me ask you again—are you excited for your first mission?"

Walker grinned. "Yeah, a little." His heart was hammering in his chest.

"Sure beats doing push-ups and flutter kicks back in Coronado, doesn't it?"

"Four weeks," Walker said, holding out four fingers. "I only had four weeks left."

Laws remained silent for a few moments; then Walker asked a question that had been bothering him. "Why is the dog coming with us?"

"She's part of the team."

"But it's a dog."

Laws grinned as he reached over and scruffed Hoover's neck. "So what about it?"

"Shouldn't the dog be lying on some front porch, or maybe smelling pot at some border checkpoint?"

"Not too loud or Hoover will hear you."

"The team I saw on the USS *Ronald Reagan* had a Belgian Malinois, too. That dog looked like it could do some serious damage, but it was kept around to sniff out explosives."

"They *can* do serious damage. They can smell explosives, drugs. They can smell illegal aliens. Hoover can smell all that plus fear. She can also sometimes smell something unsmellable—the presence of the supernatural." Laws noticed that Hoover was staring at them, and reached down and petted her again. "Don't you make no mind of this rube. He doesn't know what he doesn't know." To Walker, he said, "This Malinois can also smell death before it comes. I won't try and explain it, but you'll see for yourself if you stay with the team for any period of time at all."

Walker digested what he heard. He could almost believe what was being told to him, except for the part about how the dog could smell death and the supernatural. That was a little too much.

"One last question," he said. "Why Hoover? You named a dog after a vacuum cleaner? There has to be a story behind that."

Laws laughed. "No story at all. And it's not the vacuum. It's the president. This team has been in play since before the formation of our country and with it, in each incarnation, there was a dog, most often a Belgian Malinois, named after a president."

"What about the first one?"

"What about it?"

"If the team was formed before the country was, then we didn't have a president."

"Give the boy points for paying attention. The first dog was named George."

"As in King George?"

"The boy knows his history."

"All right, girls," growled the hulking team leader. "If we're done with Dogs 101, it's time to cut the chatter and focus on the mission."

7

SAN FRANCISCO CHINATOWN. DUSK.

Everyone except Billings, who'd stayed put on the plane, was shuffled into a waiting cable-repair van when they landed. They were whisked from San Francisco International through rush-hour traffic and finally into Chinatown, where they now sat across the street from the target building.

Through the steel walls of the truck, Walker could hear multiple Asian dialects. A cracked window let in the signature aroma of Asian food. He knew that if he closed his eyes, he could almost imagine himself seven years old again and in the Philippines. His father had been in supply and had made and lost several fortunes selling U.S. government products on the black market. He had taken little Jack and his older brother, Brian, with him wherever he went. Not only had the boys been lookouts, they'd been his father's alibis.

It struck Jack that it was only a few years after that memory that his life had gone to hell. His father died, his brother left; it wasn't until his brother had joined the Navy that they got back in touch. By then, it was almost too late. His brother had become a SEAL while Jack had been assigned to the USS *Forrest Sherman*. He'd received notice while on maneuvers in the Mediterranean that his brother had been killed on mission in Afghanistan. Over the years he'd asked around, but the most he'd ever learned was that it was a death that never should have happened, which begged more questions than it answered.

Fratolilio had earphones attached to a small tablet computer. He'd been pressing haptic buttons as they appeared on the screen since the van stopped, and finally he seemed satisfied.

He glanced at Holmes. "I got a lock into the landlines and used the receivers and transmitters. I'm not getting any conversations or background noise. Either the place is empty, or they're waiting on us."

"What else do we know about this building?"

"Other than it was built in 1932 and it's registered to Yam Phat Distributors, nothing. I accessed the blueprints, even bounced them against the old Ma Bell trunk drawing, but there's nothing to show that this is any more than what it appears to be."

"What are you saying?" Holmes asked.

"I think this is a wild-goose chase," Fratty stated frankly.

Everyone stared at Holmes as if they were waiting for him to call the mission.

"Wouldn't be the first time the intel we got from AFOSI and DIA turned out to be squirrelly," Ruiz said.

"We could always lay low for a day or two and let FBI see what they can see. If there's a reason for us being here, then we'll be ready," Laws added.

"What you're all saying is true and it makes logical sense. This lead came as a result of an interrogation of a Chinese tech smuggler by the Feebs. He could have said anything to save his ass. But . . . ," Holmes said, letting the word draw out. "I have an itch."

"Oh hell, boss has an itch." Fratolilio shoved the tablet into a Kevlar sleeve and stowed his headphones.

Both Laws and Ruiz checked their magazines. Laws carried an MP5 and Ruiz carried a Super 90.

"What's that mean, he has an itch?" Walker asked.

"Boss has intuition like a fiend sometimes," Laws said. "He's from Vegas and there are some casinos he can't go into. He doesn't count cards, he doesn't cheat, he just has itches sometimes. And when he gets them, there's always a reason."

"An itch?" Walker asked, trying to make the word make more sense.

"An itch," Holmes repeated. He flashed Walker a grim smile, then turned to the others. "We leave in thirty seconds. Check the sidewalk for traffic."

Forty-seven seconds later, they flung open the door and entered the target section of the building through the front door. A narrow set of stairs ran to the second floor.

The stacking order was Holmes and Ruiz, then Laws and Fratolilio, then Walker. Hoover padded beside him. Walker glanced at the dog as it glanced at him. He couldn't help but smile at the grinning mug. The dog seemed as excited as he was.

Holmes and Ruiz took the stairs and cleared the landing above. The rest followed, checking their sixes as they traversed the stairs.

Once they reached the landing, there wasn't much choice about which way to go. The hall doglegged right, showing a single door on the wall and a window at the front. Holmes edged forward, careful of booby traps, looking for displaced dust, lines in the floorboards, and tripwire signs, but there was nothing. He made it to the window without harm. He stared at the buildings across the way for a full minute to ensure that he and his men weren't about to enter a killing hallway. When he was certain that it was safe, he waved the others over.

Ruiz stayed at the head of the stairs to ensure that no one snuck up behind them.

Laws checked the doorjamb and the lock.

Walker moved in a crouch near the window and took up

the vigil with the aid of the Stoner's scope. He fought the exhilaration and concentrated on his assignment.

Fratty pulled out his tablet and showed the others what he expected the room to look like. It was basically a large rectangle. It had another window like the one Walker was staring through, but other than that and the door, there were no avenues of egress.

Hoover padded over and gave the door a sniff. She seemed to be interested in something.

Everyone went silent as Holmes and Fratty checked out the schematics one more time. When he was finally ready, Holmes ordered Ruiz and Walker to stay put, then stacked the remaining three SEALs at the door. He held up a hand and silently counted down to five.

Ruiz fired his Super 90 into the lock, and then Holmes kicked it open. The three of them crashed into the room, weapons aimed left, right, and center.

"Clear."

"Clear."

"Clear."

"What the hell, Fratty?" came Laws's voice. "There's nothing here."

"Ruiz, deploy a wire and get in here. Walker, you follow."

Each of the men squelched the radio to let him know they heard.

Behind Walker, Ruiz deployed an electronic tripwire at the top of the stairs and tuned to the same frequency they were using for a command channel on their MBITRs. Consisting of an infrared actuator and a transmitter, it would tell them if anyone was moving in behind them.

Ruiz finished with his setup, signaled Walker, then moved into the room.

Walker took one last look through his scope; then he too followed.

The room was empty. Not even a piece of trash littered the

floor. The far wall and the outside wall were made of brick, while the back and side walls were made of wood. The floor was a sickly green linoleum, peeling in places.

Laws shook his head. "I'll say it again. What the hell, Fratty?"

"I don't know what to say. We're at the right address. We're in the right room. It has to be the intel."

"Won't be the first time intel didn't pan," Ruiz said.

Hoover got tired of standing in the middle of the room and began to sniff the baseboards.

Ruiz and Laws checked the brick wall.

Walker again posted near the window and scanned the buildings across the street. For a moment, he thought he saw someone looking at them, but it was just a guy in his underwear, leaning over his balcony railing smoking a cigarette. Soon, he went back inside.

Fratty and Holmes checked the wooden walls. When they got to the back wall, they began to tap lightly. Finally, Holmes called Hoover over.

Hoover suddenly became animated. She didn't bark and she didn't howl, but she began to breathe deeply and paw at the floor.

"Okay. We got something over here." Holmes knelt and faced the wall. "There's something I don't like about it."

Walker glanced outside and tracked back to where the man in the underwear had been standing. He was gone now.

"What is it? An itch?" Laws asked.

Holmes shook his head. "Not quite. Walker, get over here."

Walker backed across the room to where the others were kneeling. "Sir?"

"Apply the TWR."

Walker slung his Stoner across his back and pulled the paperback-sized through-wall radar from a cargo pocket. Looking at the wall, he was relieved it wasn't composed of brick. The radar was still a new technology and wasn't powerful enough to penetrate anything other than standard drywall or wood.

He switched it on, let it cycle through its start-up protocols, then pressed the ready button. He moved to the wall and held it against it. While he waited for it to read and translate the three-dimensional line drawing on the tablet-sized screen, he noticed a tingling sensation begin to course throughout his body. The tingling increased until it felt like an electrical current was running through him.

Then it all went crazy.

His vision went supernova, then suddenly cut to black, like a galaxy imploding on itself. Not merely the dark of night, but the dark of an absolute lack of light, life, and anything good. A feeling of doom slammed into him as he realized that there was something on the other side of the dark. Something that wanted him. Something that had been inside him before.

It came darkly through the gloom. At first, it was nothing more than a spot of blackness; a pinprick, really. But it was coming closer, and Walker realized that he didn't want to see it. He closed his eyes, but that didn't make a damn bit of difference. It came inexorably toward him. He knew it before he saw it. He'd known this shape his entire life. A monster from his childhood. In the red glowing eyes, the shock of white hair, and the cruel little mouth, Walker discovered to his horror that he'd found himself. That child he'd been at nine, not like any normal child, but one who harbored the soul of evil; a child who spent his days staring balefully at the world while an entity scratched tic-tac-toe on the inside of his skull.

Walker screamed as memories flooded through him of the black thing that had once lived inside him. It had whispered secrets and told him things that no child should ever know. It knew what evil others had done and had detailed them to nine-year-old Jack until his mind was on fire.

And now, as the vision of himself surfaced like a bloated corpse from the depths of his memory, he heard the voice of the beast in his mind once more, telling him things that no one should ever understand.

Images flashed through his mind of Holmes, Fratolilio, Laws, and Ruiz dead, bodies burst from the ravaging of maggots and red, hoary beetles. Billings naked and staked to a wall with machetes, her body already scored with the burns of cigarettes, eyes smoking holes, teeth jagged and broken. A child curled up in fetal position in the back of a closet, covered in his own feces, his cheek resting in a puddle of urine as he vibrated with the rage of the ancient thing trapped inside a mind that wanted nothing more than to build a castle in which to hide.

A jag of light fired through the images like an electric shot.

"Walker!"

The child, now standing naked, body bruised and bitten as if animals had been gnawing on him, looked at him. Smoke seeped from the corners of his red eyes. The smoke took form and became a single hand tipped with talons. The smoke billowed and the hand came closer.

Walker wanted to back away but there was nowhere to go in his mind. He was trapped there, just as he'd been in those dark days of his nine-year-old life, when the beast took him over and turned him inside out.

"Walker!"

He felt a blow to his face.

Another supernova evaporated his being, but on the other side of this one was light instead of darkness.

He saw the hand descending and managed to block it with his own. He was on his back on the floor. Holmes knelt over him. Fratty, Ruiz, and Laws stared at him with worry and just a little fear in their eyes.

"What . . ." A single flash of his own red nine-year-old eyes shot through him.

"Walker!" Holmes called to him, somewhere between a hiss and a shout. The word was amplified through the MBITR and echoed through the now empty space of his mind.

Then, suddenly, he knew.

"It's down there," he said, pointing toward the wall. "Something . . . *wrong* . . . is down there. Through the wall."

He started to get up. Holmes grabbed him and helped him to his feet.

"You okay, SEAL?"

"Yes, sir." Walker wiped sweat from his face.

"Billings said this might happen. Chalk one up to her and her people."

Walker stared at the SEAL team leader. The woman from the Senate had mentioned that this might happen? How could she have known? How could anyone have known? But there was no time to contemplate. Now that he was back on his feet, he was once again a gear in the SEAL machine. Laws ran the TWR, and though it didn't show any evidence of a staircase down, it did show a room that was roughly five feet square and empty on the other side of the wall.

Ruiz pulled a line of detonation cord that had been salted with Semtex from his satchel. He attached it to the wall, creating the outline of a four-foot-high doorway. The rest of the SEALs stacked against the same wall, but several feet away. Ruiz attached an electrical lead, backed up to where the other SEALs were waiting, then depressed the contact button. Halfway between a zipping sound and a muted explosion, the cord went off, explosively sawing through the wall, but not completely obliterating it.

The SEALs moved quickly to the spot.

Ruiz pushed against the wall and the new doorway fell free to the floor on the other side.

Hoover was through first, followed by Fratty, Holmes, Walker, Laws, and then Ruiz.

The room was little more than a large landing for the set of descending stairs. From below, an unbelievable stench was joined by the sounds of clicking like the claws of a thousand crabs and the susurrations of Chinese voices. But all eyes were on the set of shackles bolted to the middle of the floor on the landing. Illuminated by a single dangling bulb, blood and claw marks surrounded the shackles. A broken piece of fingernail lay absurdly next to the metal bolt.

The SEALs looked at each other. In their eyes was the recognition that they'd just entered the Land of Fucked-Up.

Holmes grabbed Laws and pointed down the stairs. "You first. Translate."

Laws moved down the stairs in a crouch. When he'd gotten halfway down, he paused and listened. After a moment, he said softly through his MBITR, "Mostly from Fujian Province from the sound of it. The noise is sewing machines, I think. Sweatshop."

"And this is the center of the illegal tech transfer?" Fratty asked.

"We'll see what we'll see." Holmes glanced at the dog. "Hoover?"

The dog looked up.

Fratty shrugged. "Dog doesn't care about the state of illegal shirtmaking."

"Laws, take a look."

Laws crept down several more stairs. He pulled a thin metal cable from his side pocket and snaked it around the corner.

Fratty dialed it in on his tablet and they all watched as a dark and cluttered space sprang into a fish-eye view. Women of all ages sat in front of aged machines, spindles of thread twisting in the art of creation. Here and there, flames from candles in the background lit the women in a strange orange light, casting shadows that moved along the walls.

"What's that?" Walker asked, pointing toward the screen.

Fratty and Holmes peered at it.

It was Holmes who spoke first. "Looks like a pentagram."

"Or it could be a pentacle," Laws offered.

"What's the difference?" Walker asked.

"One is used as a religious symbol and the other is used in magic rituals," Ruiz said from where he was guarding their six.

"Which one is that last one?" Walker asked.

"A pentacle."

"Then I don't want it to be a pentacle."

"Laws, sweep the fish-eye around," Holmes ordered softly.

They watched as the monocular vision of the room moved from left to right.

"Don't see any beegees," Fratty said, meaning *bad guys.*

"Me neither," said Holmes. "Let's move in, but stay danger close. Hoover, to me."

While Laws wrapped the sniffer back into his pocket, the others stacked down the stairs with Ruiz bringing up the rear. Since Walker was in the middle, he shouldered the Stoner across his back and pulled out his 9mm pistol. There wouldn't be room to fire the rifle.

It was a blind landing at the bottom of the stairs, requiring a ninety-degree turn to the right. The sniffer had told them that the room extended to both the left and the right, but they couldn't discern how far without actual eyes on.

Laws was the first down.

"Left dead-ends at an office about ten meters. Right extends beyond LOS," he said, meaning *line of sight.* "Room is about twenty meters wide. Uh . . ."

"What is it?" Holmes asked.

They were only a few meters from the bottom of the stairs, and if there was danger looming, they all needed to be able to prepare for it.

Laws's voice broke through the static of the headsets. "No beegees. Just strange is all. Like a satanic taxidermist lives here. The room is smoky from candles and something that smells like hell's own ass."

Walker and Fratty exchanged looks with Holmes in between them.

"So it's clear?" their leader asked.

Walker saw the knuckles of Holmes's left hand tightening on the grip of the MP5.

"Clear, boss," Laws said.

"Then move out. Danger close. Alternate."

They moved like a centipede, each SEAL a part of the whole. Each was close enough to touch the SEAL in front of him. Laws held his MP5 at shoulder level and crouched forward. Fratty came next with a Super 90, then Holmes with an MP5, then Walker with a 9mm, and then Ruiz with a Super 90 covering the team's six.

Walker felt a tingle, as if the room's energy were wired directly into his skin.

He searched for evidence of weapons on the women hunched over their machines. What was becoming increasingly strange was that not a single one of them looked up from their work. He and the other SEALs had to be registering in their peripheral vision, but not a single curious look made it their way, as if their glances couldn't be spared, or perhaps they'd been convinced that distractions weren't part of the program.

Each was manacled to her chair by thick bracelets connected by lengths of rusted chain. Several of the women were also chained by the neck, heavy links holding them inches from the dancing needles of their sewing machines. Most were nude below the waist. Some were completely naked, their bodies covered in filth and excrement.

Then Walker saw them even more clearly.

"Oh my God," he said. "Their lips are stitched shut!"

Their SEAL machine paused while everyone assessed the stitched-lip seamstresses. Then it was Holmes who, in a voice raw with emotion, whispered, "Keep moving."

They began edging forward again.

Pentacles with arcane symbols in English and Chinese adorned virtually every surface. Many of these had been applied with glow-in-the-dark paint and shone brilliantly in the gloom.

Here and there, rats, small dogs, and cats had been tacked to the walls. They'd all been cut from head to tail. Many had flesh peeled back and held in place by threads that crisscrossed the room, stretching from spindles atop machines to hooks on the ceiling, like a web or a net. If these interlocking threads had been any lower, it would have been impossible to cross the room. As it was, they intersected and ran about a head taller than Laws, the tallest of the SEALs.

"Watch your feet," Laws said.

Piles of excrement, half-eaten food, the intestines of small animals, and scraps of cloth had been pushed against the walls. Closer examination showed the marks where the floor was stained from the continual pushing and sweeping of the offal.

The ravaged animals, the taxidermy threads, the host of hunched, naked, and chained workers had sent Walker to the edge of what he could handle. He felt his eyeballs spasm as they tried to unfocus in order to relieve his mind of the horror of his vision.

Hoover growled about the same time Walker saw something sweep past. It was just a blur, but it seemed to have hands. The only problem was that it couldn't have been any larger than a doll, or maybe a Stretch Armstrong. Walker remembered fighting over the toy in the orphanage, he and little Henry Jimmison pulling at each arm. Any other doll would have burst in half with the efforts of the two kids, but not Stretch Armstrong. As good as its name, it had stretched and stretched and stretched, until the arms were twice the length of its body.

Yeah, that's what the thing had looked like.

Fratty groaned. "Homunculus. Damn, I hate those things."

"What did you say?" Walker's peripheral vision caught another movement, but try as he might, he couldn't get eyes on. "Hunkuless?"

"Homunculus," Laws repeated. "An artificially created life, usually through alchemy."

"Fucker won't stand still," Ruiz drawled, trying to aim toward it.

"Also from the Greek, anthroparianism," Laws continued. "The creation of a golem-like being with its own sense of will."

"What does that mean?" Walker asked.

Holmes said, "It means we have a small humanoid monster of immense power whose primary ability is to remain unnoticed."

Laws nodded. "That's what I said."

"Except the boss said it in English," Fratty noted.

The harder Walker tried to see the thing, the more impossible it became. It was moving so quickly that it didn't seem like it could be real.

It struck Ruiz first. He went down, cursing into his MBITR.

Walker spun in time to see Ruiz falling to the floor, his foot jerked out from under him by a creature that couldn't have been more than two feet high. It glared at Walker with baleful red eyes set deep in its flat face, then dashed around the corner of a table.

Walker brought his pistol up to fire, but there was nothing to shoot at. He locked eyes with the woman chained to the chair in front of the table the homunculus had disappeared under. She was so terrified that she quivered. She couldn't hold his gaze for long. She quickly returned to sewing with the clack-clack-clack of the needle.

He found himself entranced by the way the needle pierced the gray material. It was made from something thick and pliable. The way she held the edge with her other hand made it look stiff as well. Almost as if it were . . .

"Skin!" he muttered.

Ruiz got back to his feet a second before Fratty went down. His finger must have been on the trigger, because as his back hit the floor, he let loose a 12-gauge shotgun round that chewed an angry hole through the ceiling.

Everyone on the team automatically turned toward the shot, which meant that they weren't looking down.

Walker felt his feet ripped out from under him.

Holmes went down hard beside him; then the homunculus leaped atop him and hammered him three times to his face. The leader brought his MP5 around to brush the creature off, but it caught the weapon as it came around and stopped the movement of Holmes's arms.

Walker brought his 9mm around in a wild sweeping arc and caught the homunculus in the back of the head. It flew hard against the wall and sank into a pile of offal, its long arms trailing like the tails of a dying kite.

He and Holmes got to their feet the same time that Laws opened fire with his MP5. A pair of tight three-round bursts were followed by shots from a larger-caliber weapon, somewhere deeper in the room.

"Triad. Saw them for a second down a set of stairs at the end of the room firing upwards. We've got the higher ground and are in defilade but stay low."

Pistol fire returned. Nine-mil and .45 rounds struck the wall and ceiling above them. Walker kept his head down and helped Holmes to his feet. He glanced at the offal and realized that the homunculus had disappeared.

"*San hong ji,*" Laws said in Chinese. "Three Triad enforcers." He took a step forward, fired another short burst, then stepped back. This one was rewarded by a shout. "Down one flight. We're safe on defilade."

Fratty suddenly moaned and sank to his knees. A hand went to his crotch. "Uggh. I hate those things." Then he pitched forward onto his face. "Will someone"—his head slammed against the floor—"please kill"—his head slammed down again—"this thing!"

Walker finally saw the long orange arms of the homunculus as they held Fratty's MBITR with both hands, using it to slam the SEAL's head into the ground. Walker snapped his 9mm up and took a shot, catching the homunculus in the shoulder and sending it tumbling.

Hoover skidded over and tried to grab it, but just missed as the homunculus used its arm to pole-vault over the downed SEAL. It scurried beneath the chairs and tables in the sweatshop. Women whimpered as it passed, unable to scream through their stitched mouths.

Walker noted that these were the first sounds he'd heard them make and it made him realize how terrible their existence must truly be. Suddenly he felt anger pour through him. He'd felt helpless once and had vowed never to be in such a position ever again. An orphan at nine, he'd been placed in a series of orphanages, starting with St. Francis's School for Boys in Manila. They tried to insist he speak Tagalog, withholding anything other than old rice and water for weeks until he was able to learn enough rudimentary words to please the Filipino monks who ran the place. He could still picture himself hammering his little fists against the stout wooden door of his closet-sized room, begging for food, milk, his brother, television, comic books . . . anything to sustain him and keep him from facing the reality that his parents were dead and his life was irrevocably changed.

Yeah, he hated helplessness and he hated whoever it was that had chained these women to their machines.

Hoover upended a woman in her chair as she scrambled to follow the two-foot-tall orange humanoid. The homunculus was fast like a cat on speed, where the Malinois was the canine equivalent of a linebacker.

Gunfire continued from forward of their position, both from the Triad members and Laws.

The homunculus launched itself into the air and began to transit the threads that crisscrossed near the ceiling. Like an Escher tightrope maze, as the creature pulled one thread, another tightened. Along the walls, the chests and stomachs of the eviscerated animals opened and closed with each tug and pull, making it seem as if they were coming to life.

Walker had been tracking the creature with his 9mm and

got a clear shot. He fired and struck the thing through its leg. The momentum of the bullet sheared the limb free from the homunculus. As the leg went flying, the creature fell heavily to the floor.

But it wouldn't be stopped.

Like a punch-drunk fighter, it pulled itself to one foot and locked its gaze on Walker. A tiny mouth with dozens of piranha-like teeth hissed at him. It staggered forward with outstretched arms, recognizing Walker as its tormentor. Then Hoover came flying through the air, grabbing it by the back of its neck. The dog shook the homunculus until it stopped moving.

Meanwhile, Holmes edged forward and joined Laws. They stacked on either side of a doorway, descending to what had to be a basement. Ruiz helped Fratty to his feet, while Walker crept forward.

Holmes fired.

Another cry went up from one of the Triad members.

Walker charged down the stairs. One large Triad member stood, reloading his 9mm. He looked up at the same time Walker put two in his chest and one in his head.

Walker paused at the bottom of the stairs and glanced left and right. A single room with a couch, a table and some chairs, several cots with wadded blankets, and a television with slippery vertical hold. Three cigarettes still burned in an ashtray. Beside these sat Styrofoam cups filled with warm tea. Box lunches lay decimated at one end of the table.

If this was a place for the enforcers to wait, then there had to be two more things that he wasn't seeing. One was a bathroom, and the other was a method of communicating with the outside. There could also be another exit. He took a step forward, then was roughly grabbed from behind.

"What the hell are you doing, SEAL?" Holmes wasn't asking a question. "You wanna be a cowboy, go buy a horse. You wanna be a SEAL, follow my lead."

Walker jerked his arm free. "He was reloading. I saw it and made my move."

"You don't have the right to make a move. We operate as a team. No individuals here." Holmes glanced around. "Stay right here. Ruiz, you got our six?"

"Got it. Hoover took a bite out of the homunculus. I set wires across the stairs."

"Good. Keep the dog away from the creature, please. Last time she ate one, she shit orange for a week."

"Skipper? What about the women?" Fratty asked.

"What about them?"

Laws bent down to check the two Triad enforcers without holes in their heads. "We got a live one."

"Fratty, leave the women for now. We'll make sure a cleanup team comes and takes care of them."

8

CHINESE SWEATSHOP.

Walker stayed where he was told, but he was fuming over Holmes's treatment. He could feel the tickling of his cheeks as they burned red with embarrassment. But now he heard something that took his mind off of his own plight. What was it they were going to do with the women? *Take care of them?* What did that mean?

Before he had a chance to get an answer to his question, Laws had the live Triad enforcer by the back of the neck. He tossed the man into one of the chairs. Yanking his arms behind his back, Laws took flex-cuffs from his utility pocket and ratcheted the man's hands together.

The Triad enforcer's hair was cut short on top and had been shaved on the sides, like a Ranger high-and-tight. Air and water dragon tattoos climbed from under his shirt up the sides of his neck.

Deep red blood soaked his white collared shirt where he bled from a shoulder wound. Laws prodded at it until the man screamed for him to stop. He tried to stand, but Laws shoved him back down.

"Bu zuo!"

The man's eyes shot to Laws. Walker watched as understanding dawned on the Triad enforcer that this white guy could speak his language.

Laws grabbed one of the cigarettes still burning in the ashtray. He held it to the guy's mouth and let him inhale. When he was done, he smiled amiably as he allowed the red-hot tip to hover teasingly next to the man's wound before he replaced the cigarette in the ashtray.

"Ni jiao shemme mingzi?" Laws asked.

Fratty came in and joined them. He took another seat and snatched one of the cigarettes out of the ashtray. He took a puff, then coughed, tossing the cigarette to the floor. He pulled his pistol and shot the cigarette. "Shit tastes like ass."

"Ni jiao shemme mingzi?" Laws asked again.

"Hong," the man said.

"Says his name is Hong," Laws said in a monotone. "But he's lying. It could be a nickname, but that's about it. Means 'red.' Like calling your kid 'yellow' or 'green.' "

Holmes wore a deep frown. "Just find out what's going on here."

"Any more parts of the homunculus?" Laws asked.

"Saved the best for stew," Fratty said.

Laws grinned. "Let me have it."

"Serious?"

"Serious."

Fratty moved to get up, but Walker stopped him. "I'll get it."

But before he could move, Holmes said, "Stay where you are, SEAL."

"Sam," Laws began, using the leader's first name. "Maybe the kid could—"

"Stay out of it, Laws. He needs to learn not to act impulsive.

Impulsive gets you killed and I'm tired of losing impulsive people."

Walker ached to say something, but gritted his teeth instead. His hands hurt from where he was gripping his pistol. He decided to holster it and wait out the team leader. It was clear that they were going to have a conversation about this later, and he was more than ready for it.

Fratty sighed dramatically. "I guess I'll get it then." He climbed to his feet. He was gone for a few moments. When he returned, he had most of the homunculus in his hand, minus an arm and a leg. Hoover followed him with a hungry look.

The Triad enforcer immediately stiffened. His eyes darted back and forth from the dog to the creature and back. He seemed to be afraid of both of them.

"Maybe Hoover wants to sit on his lap," Fratty suggested, chuckling.

Walker had been watching the Chinaman's eyes. They kept drifting to a door in the corner of the room beside the cot. Walker stared at the spot for a long moment, then made a decision. He pulled his 9mm from his holster, loaded a fresh mag, and cocked the trigger back.

"What are you doing, SEAL?" Holmes asked.

"Going to check out the room we never checked."

Fratty shot to his feet. Holmes stared toward the corner.

"What is it?" Laws asked.

"Has to be a bathroom or an exit or both," Walker said. "If we hadn't been playing freeze tag I might have checked it sooner. Will you unfreeze me?" he asked Holmes.

Instead of answering, Holmes moved past Walker without a glance. He silently commanded Fratty to set up with his Super 90. Holmes posted himself beside what everyone could now see was an almost invisible line in the drywall. On the silent count of three, he shoved it open.

A fourth Triad enforcer stood with a pistol aimed toward where the door had just been.

Fratty opened fire, smacking the man with two 12-gauge rounds that threw him against the sink, shattering the mirror behind it. He fell to the ground amid broken glass, blood, and bits of pulverized bone.

"Clear," Fratty said.

Holmes spun into the room. "Clear." He checked the pulse of the enforcer, then walked back into the room. As he passed Walker he said, "Freeze tag." Then he chuckled. "That's funny."

For the next thirty-five minutes, Laws interrogated the enforcer. He didn't water board. He didn't cause any pain. Several times he led the man to believe that he might get hurt. In fact, Laws kept two narratives running—one in English to explain to his team what was going on, the other in Chinese as he applied his techniques.

He'd wanted to use Hate of Comrades approach. "It's best used when several people are captured together because you can play them off each other, but since Fratty made sure that absolutely no one survived, that option is not on the table."

Fratty blew a kiss in response.

"But in the case of 'Hong,' here, I can talk about how incompetent he was and how his inadequacies caused him to get caught and the rest of the team to get killed. This we call Pride and Ego Down. If done right, it creates in our prisoner the need to defend his choices, behavior, and actions."

It took a while for Laws to get the technique working. At first, the enforcer was pointedly trying not to pay attention. But soon, after considerable badgering and Laws openly laughing at him, the enforcer started to become angry. Eventually he began defending himself. Rather than ask him questions, Laws laughed at him. He told the team to laugh with him and they did, everyone laughing at the enforcer.

Walker had been so entranced with Laws's dualspeak that

he'd forgotten how angry he was with Holmes. But when they were all laughing, he'd glanced around at Fratty, Laws, and then Holmes, and the sight of the leader reminded him. He laughed, too, but it was hollow.

Then Laws performed a switch. He told the guy he wasn't going to ask him anything else. After all, someone so incompetent couldn't know anything important enough to interest a team of U.S. Navy SEALs.

But as he began to back away, Holmes jumped in as if it were choreographed. They argued for a few moments, with Holmes poking Laws in the chest. Finally it was Laws who returned to the enforcer.

He pulled up a chair and sat on it like a cowboy as he began to explain what he was about to do. But he kept his voice low, as if he was explaining something so miserable he didn't even want to say it out loud.

"Now watch him," Laws said. "Look how he's going to begin shifting nervously, then he's going to get visibly upset. It's at that point, based on what I've been able to establish according to his baseline, that I expect him to tell me what he knows."

Then Laws began speaking in Chinese. Low at first, it was as though he and the enforcer were old friends and he was forced to explain something he didn't want to.

Walker watched with fascination as the enforcer displayed the exact behavior Laws had predicted. Then he glanced sharply at Holmes.

"I just told him what you said. Make sure you get this right, boss."

Holmes rushed to Laws and grabbed him by the arm, lifting him out of the chair.

"You will fucking take him out into the busiest street in Chinatown and put a billboard over his head. I want the billboard to talk about how incompetent he is. I want it to tell everyone that he was so fucked up that he's the reason everyone else got killed. Then I want it to say that the U.S. government thinks that he's a hero because of all the help he provided."

"But he didn't provide any help."

"Of course he didn't, but only we know that." He pushed Laws back toward the enforcer. "Now get back there and tell him what we're going to do to thank him for being the only surviving member of his gang."

Laws dramatically shook his head and sat roughly down. As he began to explain to the enforcer what Holmes said, the Chinaman sat forward and tried to explain himself. But Laws laid his hand on the enforcer and shook his head, pointing back at Holmes with a thumb.

This went on for a few more minutes; then Laws reached the point he'd been waiting for. The enforcer sagged in his char. Laws gave him a cigarette. As the enforcer puffed angrily, he told what he knew in order to prove he wasn't as incompetent as Holmes thought he was. The last thing he wanted was to be a billboard dummy.

When he was done, Laws turned around. "Okay, here it is. The boy spilled his guts. There's a limit to what he knows. He's low-level. He's not even an enforcer. He's a soldier—a forty-niner—for Temple of Heaven Importers. Triad. So he only knows what he overheard."

Holmes nodded. "Give."

"I got some information about this place as well as something about a ship."

"Where's the threat?" Holmes asked.

"The ship, I think. This is nothing more than some hocus-pocus sweatshop, where they make special suits for Shan Zhu, or the Mountain Lord—Triadspeak for head of the gang. The women were brought over by the Shi Tou, Snakeheads, and were guarded by these men. Most likely the women were destined to be some random food server at one of the billion Chinese restaurants, but ended up here. Hoover's little orange buddy here worked cleanup. The homunculus kind of freaked the men out, which is why they kept to themselves down here."

"What's up with the suits they're making?"

"These are tattoos from dead folks. He says they get them from all over, but he doesn't know what they're used for. All he knows is that they are sewn onto silk, packed away, and shipped out."

"Where?"

"He has no idea."

"And they're for the Mountain Lord?"

"Head honcho, yeah. But I think he's just attributing it to the Shan Zhu. I don't really think he knows. Kind of like us saying that we do it because the president wants us to."

"But in our case that's true," Fratty pointed out.

Laws flashed a grin. "Still, he doesn't know. I can tell."

"Okay," Holmes said, staring thoughtfully at the prisoner. "What about the ship?"

"All he knows is it's something big. There's been a buzz about it for months. Some guy reached out and offered them a shit-ton of money for one of these suits."

"He said 'shit-ton'?"

"In his own way. This mystery guy gave a demonstration to the head honcho, which impressed the hell out of him."

"What was the demonstration?"

"No idea."

"Where's the ship?"

"Macau."

"Any other information about this ship?"

"None."

Holmes glanced around the room and nodded slowly. Finally he said, "Okay, SEALs. Let's pack it up. Ruiz? Call in the cleanup."

9

KADWAN. FOUR MONTHS EARLIER.

He was a god. He'd spent the last few months being the hands of an unseen architect whose knowledge of the universe was unfathomable and perfect. He'd been told where to dig. He'd been told what to build. They'd explained the process of accumulating power. More importantly, they'd detailed the procedure for the creation of a special kind of chimera. There were steps he still couldn't take until he had his protection, but that had been arranged. Once he had it, he'd be warded against immolation. He'd already seen how his partner had been burned from the inside out when he'd channeled the spirit from the other side. The power of the other had been so great and pure and blinding that it had consumed the pathetic structure that composed the human body. Served him right for trying to steal what wasn't rightfully his. No, he'd wait until the shipment arrived before he moved on to the next step. Until then, he'd continue the act of creation and preparation with the knowledge that the world was so close to being his. After all, it wasn't a matter of whether or not it would happen.

It was only a matter of when.

10

C-141 STARLIFTER. NIGHT.

Holmes had treated him like a little kid and had made him stand in the proverbial corner. In Manila, they'd done the same thing to him, progressing past that to real corners, then real closets as he proved to be just short of incorrigible. He'd always preferred the term "unbroken," but the older he got, the more people mistook that attitude as arrogance.

How could he explain to them that there were times when he just knew what to do and his body took over?

Like Holmes's itch.

The team sat on benches on either side of the aircraft. Walker tried not to glower. He'd thought it was probably obvious to everyone that it was because of his attention to detail that they hadn't been shot by the enforcer. Laws sat next to him, busily cleaning the barrel with a rod tipped with gauze.

Fratty and Ruiz sat opposite them, their heads leaned back to catch some sleep.

Hoover was sprawled in the middle of the floor.

Holmes and Billings had their heads together. Holmes seemed

to be providing a laydown of the mission and his thoughts, while Billings relayed information via a video feed to a room filled with analysts to provide direct support to the team.

"You know he's right, don't you?" Laws kept his voice low. He removed the rod from the barrel and took apart the trigger housing to wipe down each piece, then applied a thin coat of oil.

"Who? Him?" Walker pointed with his chin toward Holmes.

"We operate as a team. If you see something, you communicate that to us."

"I had a clear opening."

"You walked into my line of fire, FNG," Fratty said without opening his eyes. "You're lucky you aren't wearing twelve-gauge tattoos."

"My body armor would have stopped it."

Fratty opened his eyes and stared. "Fucking unbelievable."

"What?" Walker glanced at Laws, but he seemed to be engrossed in putting his MP5 back together.

"We either work together as a team or we don't work together at all," Ruiz said. He opened his eyes and began disassembling his Super 90 after laying a clean piece of cloth across his lap.

This drew Walker up short. He'd felt that this was a Him vs. Holmes situation, not a Him vs. the Entire Team situation. He glanced toward the front of the plane and found Holmes looking at him. The team leader stared for a long moment, then turned back to Billings.

"What about the guy in the bathroom?" Walker asked softly.

"You want a medal?" Laws asked. "I have plenty. I'll give you one."

"I don't want . . . Never mind." He closed his eyes for he didn't know how long. He wasn't stupid but he felt like it right now. He had to get his thoughts in order. He'd never wanted to be jerked out of training. He'd been so close to finishing he could almost taste it. All he'd wanted to do was become a SEAL, join a team, and live the life. And it was a glorious life to be lived. Whether he would be stationed in Guam, Virginia Beach, or Coronado, it would be a life of fresh air, exercise, shooting, and being part of a brotherhood. He'd be on call to do the bidding of the president. He'd be a real live action hero, whose life was one long video game. He'd be that guy everyone else pretended to be, sitting day after day in their easy chairs, doughnut boxes and beer cans stacked around them as they shot, fought, and killed, using a video version of himself.

This unit wasn't exactly what he'd thought of when he'd wanted a brotherhood, though. A regular SEAL Team consisted of six platoons and a headquarters element. Each platoon had thirteen enlisted men, led by a chief and an officer. There were also SEAL Delivery Vehicle Teams, Underwater Demolition Teams, and Naval Special Warfare Teams, each offering support in their own way.

Looking around at the five of them, seven if you counted Billings and the dog, their *team* was awful short of a regulation unit. There was supposedly analytical support, a group of top-secret nerds to parse their information and provide them with the next target, but he didn't know who or where they were.

Fratty leaned forward and petted Hoover behind the ear. "This isn't like any other team," he said, as if he could read Walker's thoughts. "We allow for a certain amount of individuality. But we need to get to know you first. We have to be able to trust you not to do something that's going to get us all killed."

"But I—"

"Don't need to comment on this anymore. It's over and behind us. Now our job is to rest, clean up, and be ready for the next mission."

Walker took the hint and disassembled his own weapon. He loved the Stoner. It was so much more portable than the Barrett 50 he'd used on the Somali pirate last year. As he broke the Stoner down, he removed the rotating bolt carrier group. It was virtually the same as the piece-of-shit M16, which fired 5.56mm, but the Stoner was bored for 7.62mm as opposed to the 12.7mm of the Barrett. And also like the M16 and the AR15, the Stoner used a gas-impingement system to automatically move the bolt back and forth, enabling semiautomatic fire down the twenty-inch barrel. Rather than the regular floating barrel, the Stoner was reworked to incorporate the URX II Picatiny-Weaver Rail System, allowing for better application of any mounted hardware such as laser sights, telescopic sights, reflexive sights, tactical lights, and forward grips. It was a sweet weapon for sure and one that Walker was happy to have. Too bad he'd never had a chance to fire it. Still, he wiped it down and re-oiled it, just as he would have had he used it, just as he'd been trained to do.

When the weapon was put back together and racked into the weapon carrier on the wall above him, Walker asked, "Is it always like that?"

Laws had pulled out a comic book and was lying on his back and reading it. "Do we always kill beegees?"

"No. I mean the . . . things."

"Like the homunculus? We get all sorts. About half the time it's nothing, something that any other team could have handled. But the other half is a challenge."

"So that's our specialty. When you said it before, I didn't really believe it. But now that I've seen it . . ."

"We've been down some gnarly rabbit holes," Laws told him. "We have a mission log back at the Pit. When you get there, you can read all you want, that is, if it won't scare you too bad. It's like if Stephen King wrote nonfiction."

Walker chuckled. "What's the Pit?"

"Home sweet home." Fratty grinned. "It's our office, team room, and hooch. It's where we live, work, and play when we're not off staking some otherworldly beegees."

Ruiz laughed and shook his head. "Y'all are so Hollywood. You make everything sound so grandiose. What he means is that Pit stands for the Mosh Pit. It's your new home."

The pilot announced that they were descending, then ran through a pastiche of a commercial flight mantra, to include recommending that tray tables be put away. The members of the team checked their weapons in the brackets, buckled in, and leaned back as they prepared for landing.

Hoover rolled over and scratched herself behind the ear.

"Been to sniper school?" Ruiz asked.

"Scout Sniper in Hawaii."

"Just checking to see if they pulled you out of that early, too," Ruiz cracked.

"Very funny," Walker said.

"Didn't you hear about the sniper took out the Somali pirates last year?" Laws asked. "This is that guy."

Walker felt a twinge of pride, which immediately turned into embarrassment as everyone's eyes suddenly turned toward him.

"The *Maersk Alabama*?" Fratty asked, his eyes narrowing. "I thought that was Chief Garton from the USS *Boxer*."

"It was. Twitchy here wasn't involved in the *Alabama*."

"Please don't call me Twitchy."

Laws ignored him. "Remember the CNN reporter the pirates nabbed last year?"

Ruiz and Fratty nodded.

Walker did, as well as he remembered the shot. He'd been on the mast of a submarine with his Barrett 50. There wasn't a SEAL within a hundred miles and he'd been ordered to take the shot if he had one. On six-foot seas with a twenty-kilometer crosswind, he'd watched through his scope as the pirates ripped off the shirt and pants of the CNN reporter the free world had seen reporting from any number of war zones, her pretty face delivering the tragedy of the human condition in a way that allowed Middle America to keep their evening meal down long enough that they could see commercials about bathroom tissue and cars with five-star safety ratings.

The pirates had popped up sixteen hundred meters off the

bow of the cargo ship she'd been reporting from. Then, on an international news feed, they'd stormed the ship, shot her cameraman, and proceeded to tell the world their terms. Three hours later, the USS *Tennessee*, an Ohio-class ballistic missile submarine, arrived on station. Walker, along with seven others from the Kennedy Irregular Warfare Group, had been aboard ship, on their way back from Iraq. When the submarine commander had asked him if he could take the shot, there was no question that he had to try.

The distance was just over a mile. He could swim it in twenty-three minutes. He could walk it in twenty. He could run it in six and a half. But the .50-caliber round would arrive there 2.2 seconds after he pulled the trigger. Taking into consideration the velocity of the round, the curvature of the earth, the rise and fall of the bow of the target ship as compared to the rise and fall of the submarine that was idling perpendicular to the target, and the crosswind, it was an impossible shot. It was one he never should have tried. He just as easily could have shot the woman as missed the entire boat.

But as he'd watched the rape progress through the Leupold 4.5–14×50mm Mark 4 scope, he couldn't help himself. His fingers automatically adjusted the parallax focus, windage, and elevation knobs on their own, receiving mental calculations of the geometry needed to take out the target. At that distance, he couldn't hear her scream, but as her back arched and her body went rigid, it was as if he was standing right there beside her.

He fired twice.

Three seconds later, each pirate lost his head in mists of bone and spray.

All caught on international television and replayed by everyone over and over for the next several weeks.

Laws had narrated his memory for the other two. As the wheels bit the tarmac, Walker noticed a newfound respect in their eyes. At least they knew that he could back them up if needed.

When the plane came to a halt, the others stood and gathered their things. He joined them as they waited for the ramp to descend.

Holmes came up behind him. "Want to talk to you when we get to the Pit."

11

CORONADO ISLAND. NIGHT.

They piled into a white twelve-passenger van with smoked windows and the letters CPC on either side. They ran through the naval complex, finally stopping at a hangar that had a sign out front declaring it to be CORONADO PEST CONTROL.

They ditched their equipment in the front room and entered a conference room, where Holmes went over the mission step by step, laying out lessons learned and establishing their methodology. He stood at the head of the table, a line drawing of the sweatshop basement projected on the wall.

"At this point, we have more questions than we had when we entered. We have a nebulous threat to the U.S. We have a sweatshop that was creating tattoo bodysuits, at least according to the cleanup crew." He turned to Walker and looked at him for the first time. "Just so you know, we have backup teams when needed. This one was filled with reserve intelligence officers using a hazardous-materials team as cover. They've assembled all the items in a warehouse we have near the Salton Sea so that they can be studied. Also recovered was almost ten meters of skin and several finished full bodysuits. The women were also removed and will be debriefed and treated by doctors at the same compound. Hopefully we'll get more intelligence we can act on. But that's for another mission." He turned back to the team. "Anything else?"

When no one said anything, he sat at the head of the table and folded his hands. He looked at them for a moment. They were big hands, tanned by years of outdoor exposure. "Before we go any further," he said, "let's talk about that thing that happened on the op."

Walker watched as the other SEALs all stared at him.

"Do you mean when I shot the beegee?" Fratty asked, trying to ameliorate the moment.

"Fuck that. I meant the other thing."

Walker stared at his own hands, unwilling to look up.

"He means when you did the kickin' chicken," Ruiz said.

"I know what he means," Walker said. He said the next words carefully. "I just don't know where it's any of your business."

Out of the corner of his eye, he saw Laws lean back and glance at the others for a reaction. There wasn't any. Just silence that dragged on for several minutes.

Finally Walker said, "Why do I have to tell you guys? This is private."

Fratty shook his head. "Nice try, but that doesn't fly. We're a team and don't have secrets if those secrets affect the mission."

"And yours affected the mission," Ruiz said. "Don't get me wrong, it was in a good way. But that was this time. What about next time?"

"No offense, Twitchy, but I don't want you on the Stoner doing overwatch and have you shake, rattle, and roll when I need fire." Laws frowned and clearly wasn't happy with having to say it out loud.

"There probably won't be a next time," Walker said softly. Then he added, "And don't call me Twitchy."

Walker waited for someone to speak, but they were all staring at him. Finally he acquiesced. "Fine. Okay. Here's what I know: Nothing. It never happened before. It was . . . fucking terrifying for a moment there. When I opened my eyes and saw you guys there, I was so damn happy."

"Billings believes that it's the proximity to supernatural or evil that causes it to happen," Holmes said. "What she was hoping for, what would be helpful, is if you can figure out a way to control it. It might happen again."

At *it might happen again,* Walker looked up. The very idea was a terrible one, not to mention it happening enough times that he'd actually learn to get used to it.

"Where'd it come from?" Ruiz asked.

"Ahh, that . . ." Walker rubbed his face, got up, and filled a glass with water. He drank it and refilled it again. This one he brought to the table and placed it in front of him. He stared at it as he told his story.

"My father sold Navy supplies on the black market when he was stationed at Subic Bay. He pissed someone off. That someone turned out to be some sort of witch doctor." He laughed hollowly. "Evidently the witch doctor was so pissed off at my father that he summoned a demon and sent it into me. Anyway, that's what they told me because a lot of it is a blank spot in my memory. I remember some of it, but a lot more came back to me on the op."

Walker held his breath as he waited for their laughter, but there was only silence.

Finally Holmes said, "Go on."

"Six months later, I woke up. I was told about some things. Memories pop up and I don't know if they're real or not. Most of the time they scare the shit out of me."

"You were possessed?" Ruiz asked.

"Like Linda Blair but without the split-pea soup."

Fratty nodded and grinned. "That's kind of cool."

Walker gave him an unbelieving look.

"Ever tried to use that as a pickup line?" Fratty asked.

Walker smiled weakly and shook his head. "Think it would work?"

"Most definitely." Fratty stood and mimicked picking up a girl, using Ruiz as the girl. "My name is Jack Walker. I'm a Virgo and a U.S. Navy SEAL. I like long walks on the beach, poetry by Keach, and, oh by the way, I was possessed when I was a kid."

"Can I have your baby?" Ruiz joked.

They all laughed, and as they did, Walker began to feel better about it all. He wasn't going to be called on the carpet for his actions, and it seemed he might even be accepted into the group.

"It's Keats, by the way," Laws pointed out.

"What?" Fratty didn't get it.

"Keach was the actor. Keats was the poet. 'Can death be sleep, when life is but a dream?' "

Walker stared in wonder. Was there anything that Laws didn't know? It seemed like he had an answer for everything.

Laws saw Walker's expression and waved it off. "I have an audiographic memory. Whatever I hear, I remember." He paused, then added, "It's a curse."

12

THE MOSH PIT. NIGHT.

Ruiz led Walker out of the conference room and into the hangar proper for a tour of the Coronado Pest Control facilities, or as the SEALs referred to it, the Mosh Pit. The cavernous interior of the metal building had fifty-foot ceilings and ran half a football field long and wide. Offices ran along the left side as well as the conference room. Five suites along the back wall were designated as living quarters for the members of SEAL Team 666. Each suite had a bedroom, a media/sitting room, a bathroom, and a kitchenette. To the right of the hangar's door were the armory and the equipment room. Entrance to the building was through a small foyer with a false wall and a reception area, just in case someone came in and actually wanted pest control.

The center of the room was filled with any number of plush leather chairs, leather sectionals, and stools. Tables were arrayed strategically around the room with academic books, supernatural tomes, and magazines of all shape and size including *Mother Jones, Jane's Defense Weekly, Smithsonian, National Geographic,* various comic books, *Jane's Intelligence Review*, *Esquire*, and *Soldier of Fortune*.

Walker noted the broad selection. *Mother Jones* was a magazine known for its stances on human rights, conservation, and culture, dominated by deep anti-military sentiment. That it was among the selections said a lot about the team.

Ruiz, who saw Walker pick up a copy of the magazine, said, "Holmes likes us to be well versed in everything that's going on. Sometimes I've found leads in there that helped me."

Walker put *Mother Jones* down and picked up a comic book with Wolverine on the cover. "And this one? Glean any secrets out of the pages of this stately tome?"

Ruiz chuckled. "No. But it helps pass the time between ops."

An immense climbing wall took up space near the back of the room. Thick-roped cargo nets could be raised and lowered from the ceiling, along with several rope lines that were most likely used to practice climbing and fast-roping. Windows were set in the eaves near the roof to let light in all the way around the building.

The rooms and the offices were enclosed with drywall and wood. But because they were only standard height, their roofs were repurposed. Above the suites was a full kitchen and a fully stocked bar. An assortment of chrome café tables and chairs were arrayed in front of this. The space above the offices held weight-training equipment, including free weights, treadmills, and StairMasters.

But as incredible as everything was, what amazed Walker the most were the pictures, paintings, and things adorning the walls.

The *things* were clearly trophies of past ops, including strange horns, clawed hands, one large immense tooth, jaws, the tail of something that had to have been a Buick-sized lizard, and the stuffed head of some kind of demonic creature that had wiry horns, a flat face, and wide-slanted eyes. This memorabilia covered two walls from floor to ceiling. It was as if a big-game hunter had stumbled into the world of the supernatural.

An eye-level platform extended from one of the walls by three feet. Affixed to this stood a taxidermically stuffed creature resembling a muscular Great Dane, albeit this creature had a twisted spine and legs, and twisting ram horns coming from its head. A plaque on the side of the platform read CHUPACABRA, MEXICO, 2004.

Twin clamps held a six-foot-long red worm. Hairs bristled its hard skin. A puckered indentation covered the lower end of the worm, while triple rows of razor-sharp teeth covered the upper end. A plaque read MONGOLIAN BLOOD WORM, 1964.

He could stay and stare at these for hours, but the pictures and paintings drew him to another wall.

Two separate walls had distinct groups of pictures. One wall held photos and paintings of men, and one woman, going back over two hundred years. Their uniforms changed with the times, going backwards from the present through Vietnam, Korea, the World Wars, the Civil War represented by both the Union blue and Confederate gray. Then the photos were replaced by pictures going all the way to a man in a white wig, who was clearly landed gentry from the time of George Washington. The newest one was a handsome Asian lieutenant, the date of his death reading May 2, 2011. Walker knew that date.

"That's the SEAL you replaced. He was a great man. You want to find out what happened in Abbattobad, check the mission logs. In fact, you'll find them more interesting than anything else you've ever read."

Walker had seen the glass-enclosed shelves containing the volumes. Where the newest ones had glistening black spines, the older ones were frayed, with pieces of fabric jutting free. He definitely wanted to read them and learn the history of his new unit.

It was funny. Before he'd felt gypped, thinking that he'd not be able to live the life of a SEAL the way he'd wanted. But the more he listened to the others and the more he looked at the sheer magnitude of their missions and history, the more he began to appreciate the fact that he'd been selected to be a member of the most elite organization in the history of the free world.

The other set of photographs were of dogs. The recent dogs were all Belgian Malinois, but there were also German shepherds, a few Great Danes, pit bulls, bulldogs, many unidentified mutts, and finally, the earliest dog on the wall, an oil painting of an English spaniel.

Holmes stuck his head out of the conference room and glanced around, then yelled at Ruiz. "You're not done yet? Get him his gear and tell the others. We got to prep. We leave in three hours. Special Projects Group got a lead on the ship in Macau. We're going to investigate."

Ruiz glanced longingly at the bar atop the living quarters. "Three hours? Hell, that's barely enough time to shit, shower, and shave. You sure SPG got it right?"

"Get your ass in gear, SEAL," Holmes growled. "You'll have a chance to unwind when the world is safe." He grinned momentarily. "Or at least when this is over. I could use some unwinding myself." Then he was all seriousness once again. "Now get the FNG his stuff and get ready." Then he went back into the conference room and shut the door.

Ruiz turned to Walker. "You heard the man. Let's get your things and I'll show you your digs. Then we gotta get ready."

13

SPG OFFICES. NIGHT.

Half an hour later, Walker drove one of the team jeeps across Coronado and pulled in front of a building with a sign out front that read SPECIAL PROJECTS GROUP. The lights were on inside and cars were still parked in the lot. That it was near midnight meant nothing to the mission. He parked, ran up the stairs, opened the door, waved a hand at the secretary, and was down the hall into an office.

A slim woman with red hair and a splash of freckles turned toward him when he entered. She didn't have time to say anything before she was swept into his arms. Walker kissed her deeply. At first she had her hands on his arms, trying to push him away, but soon she relaxed and hugged him tightly. She returned the kiss and they remained that way for a long passionate minute.

When they separated, her face was so flushed that her freckles were almost hidden. Her blue eyes were wide.

"I was wondering where you were," she said. "You landed hours ago."

His mouth opened. "How did you . . . ? I was coming to tell you about my assignment."

She pushed him away gently and walked to her office door and closed it. "Come on. Since when have I not known what's going on? SPG has supported SEAL Team 666 off and on for more than a decade."

"You knew about them, Jen?" But of course she knew about them.

"I know a hundred other secrets that you don't know, Jack. You know how it works. Need to know, and until today, you didn't need to know."

"But now—"

"Now you're the newest member of SEAL Team 666." Her smile fell as she got serious. "It's a dangerous assignment."

"Being a SEAL is dangerous."

"Not like this. This is more than just run-of-the-mill SEAL danger."

Walker grinned at the phrase—*run-of-the-mill SEAL danger.*

His girlfriend of the last twelve months punched him in the chest. "I'm serious, Jack."

He caught her hand before she could punch him again. "I know you are. I'll be prepared. That's what careful really is, right? Being ready for anything."

She cupped his face and seemed about to kiss him; then her phone rang. "Hold on." She went behind a desk that held two large-screen monitors and sat down. Three different telephones were arrayed side by side. They were differentiated by colored stickers. Green was for unclassified, red was for secret, and yellow was for top secret, which was the phone she was using now. A nameplate on the desk read JENNIFER COSTELLO, PROJECT CHIEF.

She didn't say much to the person on the other end, just occasionally acknowledged something that she heard. Once she flicked her gaze at Walker, but otherwise she kept looking at the desktop. After two minutes, she put down the phone.

"Wait here, will you?" She stood. "I have to go do something real quick."

She pecked him on the cheek, left the room, and closed the door behind her.

Walker decided to sit for a few minutes. He'd been going since first bell, at 5 A.M. Half an hour after a mad scramble to get dressed and in formation, he'd been running on the beach with Class 290, trying desperately to send his shin splints to a place beyond the finish line. The pain had been excruciating but he'd long ago learned to ignore it.

"Screams are just pain leaving the body," Instructor Reno loved to shout. "Scream all you want, just don't give in to the pain."

And Walker never did. He'd known pain before and wouldn't succumb. Holding out the palm of his left hand, he stared at the starlike scar in the middle of his palm. Like the Patpong hooker had told him as he plowed through a gallon of Mekong whiskey, "Looks like your life line exploded." That simple statement had meant more than she knew. He could almost remember the pencil that had plunged through his tiny hand, but he didn't remember how it had gotten there, although sometimes a flash after a night of drinking or in the early-morning hours would reveal that it had been his own demon-spawned inertia that had delivered the blow.

Even now, after more than twenty years, the pain still lingered. Yes, he knew pain. They'd been traveling companions for a long time.

He felt his lids growing heavy as this and a hundred more thoughts tumbled off cliffs in his mind. By his mark, it had been sixteen hours since he'd slept. Three for training, four to travel to San Francisco, four to conduct the operation, four to return to base, two to brief and be introduced to the Mosh Pit, and a half hour to change, shower, and get over here. Now, nearing eleven, he was sitting in his girlfriend's office while she was out working. . . .

His eyes slammed closed as his body shut down. His dreams immediately took on an underwater quality. He smelled the sweatshop. Sweat, not only from labor but the vinegar-tinged sweat of fear. A vile stench insinuated itself into everything. Coffee burned somewhere on the bottom of a pot. The scents of Chinese food, old and rotting from the kitchen next door.

Images of women with lips sewn together swam through his mind, merging with his boat crew from Class 290 and the beaching drills.

The orange-skinned homunculus ran roughshod through his childhood, jerking memories of both good and bad into a twisted braid of his life with its long orange arms.

Then suddenly his mind was a flat plane covered with television sets. Not the new flatscreens, but the old boxes, flipping vertically, blizzards of interference making the scenes almost unintelligible. One by one they snapped into focus, revealing a scene of a little boy, dancing like a maniac, barefooted atop a Manila trash dump. Every television displayed the same image. Then somewhere a radio crackled, Culture Club's "Karma Chameleon" sung by a Filipino with a tenor voice, stumbling over the words, barely intelligible if Walker hadn't heard it in a hundred thousand other dreams.

He awoke with a start and almost leaped out of his chair.

But he was held in place by Jen's strong arms. She'd been smiling, but when she saw the fear on his face she quickly grew concerned.

"Another one?"

Walker sat back. He breathed heavily and wiped sweat from his forehead. "Yeah."

"Didn't you talk to someone about them?"

"I was too busy, Jen. They don't care about your bad dreams and bogeymen in SEAL training."

She removed her hands and stood up straight. She waited a moment for him to say something. When he didn't, she crossed her arms.

Walker knew he'd been short with her. He couldn't help it. That fucking dream of the dump, or a version of it, came far too often.

She turned and walked behind the desk, putting the two and a half feet of pressed wood between them. He could reach across and grab her, but each second that passed sent her a mile farther away.

He jerked through the last tendrils of his nightmare and slid quickly around the desk and grabbed her. Her arms were still crossed and she had a frown on her lips, but he could tell it wasn't full on.

"Sorry," he whispered, offering her a smile. "It was the trash pile again."

Her blue eyes dilated. "Where they found you?"

He nodded. "Tommy told me it means I need closure."

She rolled her eyes. "Tommy? You're going to listen to your old Navy buddy? The one who has three Filipino wives in three different ports?"

Walker grinned. He knew her feelings for Tommy. He'd never said such a thing, but anytime he invoked Tommy's name she became so exasperated she forgot what she was really mad about.

"He doesn't have three wives. He has four now. He married a delightful young Thai girl he found wandering around the streets of Patpong."

Her eyes widened, then narrowed, and then she punched him in the chest. "Now you're messing with me."

He stole a kiss, silencing her.

"Forgiven?"

"For being an ass? Yes."

He kissed her again.

"Who do you think I am, sailor?" she asked slyly.

"I think you're my girl and it's been a long time."

"And what do you propose?" She glanced at her desk and laughed. "Here?"

Walker raised his eyebrows suggestively and grinned like a kid about to open his Christmas presents.

But just as she opened her mouth to say something, another phone rang. He didn't recognize the ring. Hell, he didn't even have a phone, but he was pretty sure it was coming from his jacket pocket. He reluctantly let her go, reached in, and found a cell phone. He flipped it open and put it to his ear. "Uh, hello?"

"Walker, where the hell are you?" came Holmes's voice.

"I'm—"

"Never mind. Just get your ass back. We're wheels up in sixty mikes." Then the connection went dead.

Walker closed the phone slowly.

"I was going to tell you," Jen said, putting her arms around his neck. "We're the ones who found your ship."

He stared at her. "How?"

"I told you that we support you guys. Billings requested immediate analytical and a targeting package. We're normally here for NAVSPECWARCOM emergencies. When there's no time to go through official Special Operations Command channels, we're your support."

"That's where you were when you left?"

"Yeah, took us about an hour."

"How long was I out?"

"About an hour." She grinned.

Walker shook his head and laughed sourly.

"What?"

"Damn Holmes. Even my girl is jumping to his commands."

"Hey! That's not fair."

"Nah, it's okay. We got some kind of threat and need to find out what it is." He spared a longing glance at the desk. "Next time for sure."

She kissed him deeply and let him go.

14

SOMEWHERE OVER THE SOUTH CHINA SEA.

Macau was plus fifteen hours from Coronado's Pacific time. By the time they reached their target, it'd be 0100 hours the following day, local time.

Macau was an Asian anachronism, originally developed by the Portuguese as a foothold on Asian trading in 1635. The first treaty allowed the Portuguese sole right to anchor ships and conduct trade, but it didn't allow them the rights to stay onshore. The Dutch East India Company, who saw themselves as the emperors of sea and trade, already had rights to the Cape of Good Hope, the Strait of Magellan, and the Strait of Malacca, and had repeatedly tried to wrest this important foothold from the Portuguese; they failed in all attempts. Macau became the premier place for the transport of Chinese slaves to Portugal and the locus for what would eventually start the Opium Wars. In the Treaty of Amity and Commerce, signed in 1887, the Qing Dynasty ceded to Portugal perpetual rights to occupy and govern Macau in exchange for Portuguese cooperation with Hong Kong to smuggle and tax Indian opium for increased profits all around. The island nation survived World War II and Japanese occupation, but it couldn't survive Portugal's own internal political machinations. So when local Portuguese rule was overthrown in 1974, Portugal decided it was time to relinquish all overseas holdings, thus putting in motion the end of a nearly five-hundred-year relationship with Macau. In 1999, formal sovereignty switched to Mainland China, but Macau's identity as the Las Vegas of Asia continued with the construction of more casinos.

The island, which had subsequently been connected to the mainland by a silt-laden sandbar and landfills, was located sixty kilometers southwest of Hong Kong. Its flat terrain was broken only by a series of central hills, the tallest rising to six hundred feet. Their target ship was moored on an older section of the outer harbor along the newly reinvented Macau Fisherman's Wharf. Built as a theme park, it included a forty-meter-tall erupting volcano, a replica of a Middle Eastern fort, a Roman-themed shopping center, an outdoor coliseum, Vasco de Gama Waterworld, and associated shops, restaurants, casinos, and offices.

The wharf where the target ship was moored rested on the other side of replica of a Tang Dynasty fortress, which was still under construction. The hundred-foot battlements hid the area from any possible tourist observation and kept the place as private and secluded as anything could possibly be on the jam-packed island of Macau. The seclusion was an unasked-for yet appreciated windfall to the SEAL team members, who now didn't have to contend with the possibility of tourists interrupting their operations. They were lucky. Even at 0100 hours, the area on the other side of the fortress construction site would be filled with people eager to spend their money and see for themselves what made Macau such a lusted-for pearl of the Orient.

After the mission brief, which took up the first thirty minutes of the flight, everyone sacked out for five hours. This time

Walker didn't dream. Exhaustion took hold and smashed him down until he was shaken awake by Ruiz.

"Where are we?" Walker asked groggily.

"We passed over Guam an hour ago."

Walker pulled himself to his feet. The plan's transponder identified it as a commercial cargo plane, and this C-141 had been painted the colors of a well-known package-delivery carrier. The ruse would grant them access to the airspace and allow overflight of their target. In addition to their battle rattle, each of them had been assigned High Altitude/High Opening (HAHO) tanks and masks. Normally they'd get a chill suit to defray the extreme cold of the upper atmosphere, but they were going directly into combat and they didn't want to change clothes in the middle of a firefight. Although Walker had never participated in an actual HAHO, he'd practiced them at KIWG.

"Holmes wants to see you," Ruiz said. He stood next to his gear and ran through it item by item to ensure it was in perfect working order.

Walker glanced at his own pile of gear. Pack. Gator case for carrying his Stoner during the jump. Ammunition box. Body armor. MBITR. Vest. NVGs. Various other pieces of equipment he hadn't yet inventoried, all of it looking as if it had just come off the shelf of the Super SEAL Team Wal-Mart. Yeah, he knew what Holmes wanted. He'd stared daggers as he'd given the mission brief. Walker had known full well that when he'd chosen to steal a few moments with Jen, he'd have to pay the price. It looked like it was time to pay. Picturing Jen, though, it was hard to argue that it hadn't been worth it.

"Yes, boss," Walker said. He stood at parade rest with his hands folded into each other behind him.

"'Sir' will do," Holmes said, not looking up from the imagery he was studying on his tablet. "Ruiz says boss. He's from the South so I excuse it."

"Yes, sir." Walker fought the urge to roll his eyes. Whatever old-school textbook Holmes had used to learn how to be a leader, he must have excelled on the chapter about *how to be aloof but tough*. Walker much preferred the in-your-face style of Instructor Reno or any number of Navy chiefs he'd had the displeasure of getting crossways with.

Finally Holmes set his tablet on the bench beside him. Walker watched him, knowing that the man had two choices. He could either stand up and get in Walker's face, or he could sit back and relax, demonstrating that he didn't have to work in order to get his point across. Walker had seen both worked to perfection and knew how to deal with each.

"SEALs need to be ready at all times. I spoke with Instructor Reno a little while ago and he said that he was disappointed that your equipment wasn't prepared."

Ouch! Holmes knew that there were few men on the planet that Walker respected more than Reno. Walker stood straighter and squared his shoulders. "You spoke to him?"

"I did. He told me that you were one of his better SEAL trainees. Not the best, mind you, but among the better. He asked why you'd been chosen, but I explained that it couldn't be disclosed at this time. Did you ever let *him* down?"

"No, sir."

"And why is that?"

Walker noted the effectiveness of Holmes's ability to deal with the situation. He looked too calm, too cool, sitting back with his arm resting along the backrest of the bench seat.

"I respect Instructor Reno, sir. I—"

"But you don't respect me?" Holmes shook his head.

"No, sir. It's just that I've spent the last eleven weeks with Instructor Reno and I know him better."

"Ahh. So you have to know someone to respect them."

"No, sir. I respect those appointed as superior over me."

"And what did I tell you?"

"To get my gear ready, sir."

"And did you?"

"No, sir."

"You're full of 'no sirs' tonight, aren't you, son?"

"No, sir." But then as Holmes raised an eyebrow, Walker said, "Yes, sir."

Holmes leaned forward, draping his elbows over his knees. He rubbed the Annapolis ring that was in place of a wedding band. "When you fail to live up to the standards set by Instructor Reno, you have to do more physical training. When you fail to live up to the standards of SEAL Team 666, you let down yourself, the other team members, and me, and you put all of our lives at risk."

Walker felt the air leave him as disappointment at his own failings filled his chest.

"More important than our lives, you put America at risk, Walker. The president and the Sissy expect us to perform a mission, one in which the sovereignty and safety of the United States of America is paramount. To ignore orders that support this mission is akin to loading rounds into the weapon that kills Uncle Sam. Is that clear?"

Walker gulped. "S-sorry, sir," he stammered.

"Don't be sorry, SEAL, just stop acting like an FNG."

"Yes, sir." Walker stood for a few seconds before he realized that he was released. He turned to go, but evidently Holmes wasn't quite done.

"Make sure you zero that Stoner. Get Ruiz to help you. I don't want you winging me in the head when you're shooting a hundred and eighty degrees the other way."

"Yes, sir."

Walker moved back toward the others near the rear of the plane feeling like he'd just been punched in the gut, chest, and head.

Laws spoke first. "Did he give you the Ring Speech?"

Walker looked at Laws through hollow eyes.

"Was he rubbing his ring while he talked to you?" Laws

asked. "Did he use the word 'paramount'? We call that the Ring Speech."

Fratty snickered. "That's a good speech. Left me feeling like a deckhand on the *Titanic*."

"I wanted to crawl under a rock," Ruiz admitted with a sad smile.

Walker suddenly felt a little better. Being singled out was the absolute worst. But the shared-misery philosophy was a foundational belief in the military and was the cement that kept men together even during the toughest times.

Walker set about unpacking his gear and laying it out on the decking of the C-141 Starlifter. Soon Ruiz was next to him, helping him organize and unwrap the new items. Fratty joined a few minutes later, then finally Laws.

"Was she worth it?" Fratty asked.

A smile crept across Walker's face as Jen's freckles appeared before him. "Yeah."

Over the next hour, they readied his gear and repacked it for the mission. Since he'd lugged his entire issue, he had a lot of redundant items that he wouldn't need. These were in a separate pile.

As they worked, Walker found the other SEALs opening up to him a bit more.

Fratolilio was an anachronism. His was a join-the-Navy-or-go-to-jail scenario, but instead of boosting cars or stealing hub-caps, he had been a hacker who'd been caught changing the grades for all the seniors in his high school. For the first time in the history of Clara Barton High School, everyone graduated—one hundred percent, including the three unwed mothers taking the year off to have babies and the young man doing time for selling X during the homecoming dance.

Johnny Ruiz was another anachronism. To close your eyes and listen to him, you'd imagine a white West Virginia cracker. To look at him, with his swarthy skin and coal-black hair, you'd wonder if he was in America illegally. His southern drawl delivered from a Mexican-American mouth was sometimes too odd to witness. Ruiz was another join-the-Navy-or-go-to-jail recruit. He was caught purchasing marijuana in a drug bust for his mother's habit. Ruiz's expertise had always been explosives. His father, uncles, and brothers had stayed behind to work the West Virginia mines, something they'd done for generations. Ruiz learned at an early age the correct amounts of explosive to blow things sky-high, whether it was something as small as a tin can or as large as a bulldozer. Walker would bet that in Wheeling, West Virginia, Ruiz was a big man on campus and wasn't self-conscious at all. But on SEAL Team 666, he was the quietest among them and always seemed concerned about how people saw him.

Timothy Laws was just plain weird. Unlike the other two, he hadn't been forced to join the Navy. His father had been a set designer for MGM and Universal Studios in Hollywood and Timmy had grown up meeting the famous and infamous, befriending stuntmen, and helping with set designs since he was ten. School was easy for him—too easy. It wasn't until he was in junior high that he realized his ability to memorize everything he heard wasn't something everyone could do. When he joined the Navy, his language testing was off the charts and he was soon learning the first of eventually four dialects of Chinese.

Walker opened up to them as well. He told them about his experience with the Somali pirates and a little about growing up in an orphanage in Manila. For a few moments during the preparations, they felt like a small brotherhood. Walker liked that feeling. This was what it was all about. Being part of something.

The last thing they did was zero the sniper rifle. The best way to accomplish this would be on a rifle range with a spotter, but they'd have to make do with the space they had inside the fuselage of the Starlifter. Walker set up near the front bulkhead and lay prone, the Stoner aimed toward the rear of the plane. In actuality, he wasn't actually zeroing the rifle, but the Leupold 4.5–14×50mm Mark 4 scope. He attached it to the Picatinny-Weaver rail mount system on top of the weapon and set it to factory standard. Then he grabbed a laser sight with a universal mount from the case and attached it to the front of the barrel. It made the weapon heavy, but he attached the bipod, which alleviated the weight and would keep the rifle still. Using a digital leveler, he aligned the laser with the barrel, then turned it on. A beam of light shot from the device down the length of the plane. He aligned it so that it hit the center of the target, then concentrated on the scope. It took a few moments of adjusting the knobs to get the illuminated mil dot within the crosshairs aligned. Then he tightened the knobs in place.

Next he got with the rest of the team and conducted prebreathing, which consisted of intaking one hundred percent oxygen to flush the nitrogen from their bloodstreams. They'd be jumping from higher than twenty-five thousand feet, and the lack of pressure could lead to hypoxia or decompression sickness if all the nitrogen wasn't flushed. So for thirty minutes they sat side by side, using the Starlifter's oxygen supply and going over the mission in their minds, preparing for what would be an intense physical challenge in less than an hour.

Finally it was time to load up.

Over Walker's body armor went the MC-4 free-fall parachute system, comprising the chute, an altimeter with a compass, an automatic parachute activation device, and a bail-out small oxygen tank, the latter which he'd eject once he was below seven thousand feet. The bulky reserve chute went in front. As always, he found himself resting his arms on it.

His Stoner was in an M1950 weapons case that was attached to the chute on a D ring to a lowering line, used just before impact to lessen possible damage to the weapon. Lastly, he put on his Protec skate helmet modified for MBITR.

After a commo check, they were ready to go. All the remaining gear had been tied down. They now stood at the edge of the closed ramp. The red light above it switched to yellow. The ramp began to open.

Fratolilio was scheduled to be the center man in the formation. Hoover was attached to the front of his parachute by her own harness, replacing the reserve. In addition to the harness, the dog had a muzzle protector, bubble glasses to protect her eyes, and a warming cloak worn beneath the harness. Hoover acted as if this was nothing special.

The team's only odd uniform concession had been to wear ballistic masks that covered their faces but left holes for the eyes, mouth, and nose. Though they were concerned about video surveillance, there was nothing they could do about their mission possibly being recorded and reviewed by the People's Liberation Army at a later date. But they could mitigate the PLA's ability to record their identities for possible future use.

Holmes's mask was black with a white slash across it.

Ruiz's mask was a deep blood red.

Fratty wore a solid white mask.

Laws wore a mask with a green camouflage pattern.

And Walker, probably thanks to the tried-and-true tradition of fucking with the new guy, wore a mask so pink that it was fuchsia.

The Starlifter's crew chief was attached to a monkey harness. When the ramp opened fully, he walked to the edge and glanced out at the darkness. The rush of cold air and the wave of sound hit the team like the slap of a giant hand, but they held their ground.

"Five minutes," came the chief's voice through their headsets. "We're at twenty-seven thousand feet and forty miles southeast of the target."

All five SEALs checked their altimeters and GPS to confirm.

At the one-minute mark, they conducted a final radio check, then prepared to embrace the dark.

The chief counted down from thirty. When he hit zero, they ran off the edge of the ramp like a gang attacking the night. As they hit the air, they were torn backwards in the jet wash. Last in line, Walker kept his weapon case gripped in his hands just below the reserve chute. It was an awkward position, akin to falling face-first into the water with your hands at your side.

The air temperature was thirty degrees below zero. There was a danger of frostbite if they remained at altitude for any period of time. Thankfully they were falling fast and had already reached terminal velocity of 110 miles per hour, or 56 meters per second. Walker always loved the idea of hurling his body through the air faster than he'd ever driven a car . . . with the exception of Jen's Corvette, which he'd gotten to 140 once on an empty stretch of Interstate 8. Of course, there was always the danger of crashing in the 'Vette, but here in the wide black night, there was nothing to crash into except another SEAL.

"Prepare to deploy." Holmes's tight voice broke through the rush of air.

Walker angled his left wrist so he could see the altimeter. The digital numbers flew by as they fell lower and lower in the earth's atmosphere. They were almost to fifteen thousand feet. Below, Walker could see the twinkle of lights and a larger glow from what could only be Macau. The air temperature had warmed to zero degrees. He felt great. No sign of hypoxia or anything else.

They'd flattened out so that they were no longer falling on top of each other, but side by side. Holmes counted down to zero and as a unit they deployed their chutes, each jerking upward as their velocity went to almost nothing. Walker managed to retain his grip on his weapon. He lowered it on the line, then reached up and adjusted his risers until he was following the others, five SEALs moving silently through the Chinese night sky toward their target, nineteen miles away.

15

MACAU. THE WITCHING HOUR.

They'd soared to within a hundred yards of a cruise ship glittering beneath them, laughter and music drifting from it at 0130 hours. The passengers would be witness to the events that were about to unfold if they were sober enough to grab a telescope or high-powered binoculars.

The approach was the trickiest part of the operation. They weren't prepared for a water landing. A two-hundred-meter length of the second wharf had been designated as their landing zone. A building and rack of storage containers would screen them from the target if they played it right.

Overhead imagery had identified six roving guards and several static cameras, all easily overcome or ignored.

They landed one after the other, coming in low and flaring at the last moment, their black chutes and body armor blending in with the sky, then the close shadows of the night-drenched wharf.

Holmes took out a guard who was lighting a cigarette as they landed. With sound suppressors affixed to all the weapons, his two shots to the man's chest sounded like loud coughs.

The team wrapped their chutes, harnesses, and oxygen tanks, then dropped them over the edge of the wharf into the South China Sea. After a weapons and commo check, they began to move.

The cargo ship was docked at the end of the wharf. A single guard stood beneath a light at the gangway. Like the other one, he wore the green uniform of the Chinese army. A billed Mao hat rested on his head. He carried an AK-47 at his shoulder. The thing about guards was that they spent their entire lives preparing for a single moment when they had to be ready. It was a minuscule number of guards who didn't eventually succumb to the boredom inherent in such a task. This man was no exception. He'd found a place to lean, and by the rocking of his head, he was back and forth between the waking world and his place on Mao's Long March.

Walker had the Stoner out of its case, the optics installed and ready. He helped the guard along his way with a 7.62mm nudge through the head. The guard's hat popped off as his torso rocked back; then he slumped to the ground.

Another guard ran down the gangway. He'd been obscured by the railing. He was fumbling with a walkie-talkie on his hip when the Stoner coughed again. The QD sound suppressor was about a foot long and extended the barrel length of the Stoner by about six inches. The extra weight was a surprise to negotiate, Walker realized. The first round took the guard in the hip, shattering it and spinning him around. The second round took him in the upper back, exploding a fist-sized hole out of his chest.

That left three more guards somewhere aboard the ship.

Holmes ordered Walker to find a high point, then took the other SEALs and quickly made their way along the dock to the gangway.

Walker already knew where he was going to go. He'd spied a place atop one of the cargo containers that was hidden from view on both sides. Hoover had been ordered to stay with him, so the dog could watch his six.

It was a quick climb to the top and Walker lay prone as he aimed through his sight. If anyone showed up, it would be like shooting fish in a barrel.

16

MACAU WHARF.

Fratty loved his Super 90 more than he'd loved any other weapon. He slept with it. He'd filed down the trigger to make it as sweet, quick, and easy as gunfighter's pistol. He'd never even fired a shotgun until he'd joined the SEALs. He'd concentrated on firing different automatic rifles and pistols, mesmerized by the ability to fire more and more and more rounds one right after the other. But once he'd felt the sheer power of the Super 90, it was love at first shot.

Holmes had him moving first in the formation. He swept left and right as he ran at a crouch. He knew the others were behind him. He didn't need to look back. He trusted his fellow SEALs implicitly.

They arrived at the gangway unnoticed—Fratty, Laws, Holmes, and Ruiz. Both MP5s were deployed inside the line of SEALs, bookended by the Super 90s. The only sounds in the night were the waves lapping at the dock and the grand tinkle of laughter from the cruise ship just off the coast. On the ground lay both guards with gazes staring off to the sky.

Laws reached down and grabbed one of the walkie-talkies and shoved it into his cargo pocket.

Then they moved onto the ship. It wasn't large by any stretch of the imagination, but it was big enough to be seaworthy and to have a central hold. The access hatch was open and a dull light emanated from within. Lights were also on in the wheelhouse, but as far as Fratty could tell, there was no one in there. He reminded himself that he could still be on camera, so they had to move quickly and quietly.

Holmes and Ruiz remained back, while Laws and Fratty moved to the ship's stern. Fratty took lead, with Laws moving left, right, and also rear, using the barrel of his MP5 to sweep through the possible dangers that might come into his field of fire. That way he wouldn't have to re-aim—he'd already have barrel on target. They soon cleared the main deck, checking behind containers and over the edges of the rails in the event someone was hammocked on the other side.

The wheelhouse was two stories tall, common in pre-eighties ships. Many of those that were still seaworthy kept to the coastlines, but ships this size had crossed both major oceans since before the founding of America, bringing wheat, gold, weapons, and slaves to and from brave new worlds. This ship didn't have any of those things in the hold. If they were to believe the Triad enforcer, it was something much worse. Fratty couldn't wait to find out what.

Laws flex-cuffed the doors to the crew compartment and the engine room, both located at the base of the wheelhouse. The Teflon cuffs wouldn't stop anyone from getting out but would sure slow them down. He stepped quickly up the stairs and shoved the barrel of the Super 90 against the window, only to find an empty control room. He opened the door and stepped inside, wary of tripwires and booby traps. They found the lights and equipment turned on. A cold cup of tea sat on a counter beside a crumpled package of Chinese cigarettes and a glass ashtray holding a mound of butts and ash.

Fratty paused to check the computer equipment on the bridge. He also checked to see what operating systems they were using. Overly simple. If he decided they needed to use the ship for something—like a battering ram or a diversion—he'd be ready. He reported this to Holmes through the MBITR. Holmes told him to stand fast for a moment while he reconned the hold.

Fratty stared out the window and tried to make out the FNG across the way. He was green and he still thought with his pecker, but he'd make it. That is, if he kept his head down and away from Holmes. There was some history there, even if the boy didn't know it.

Try as he might, he couldn't locate Walker. The boy had made himself invisible. That was a good thing. Fratty glanced around the control room. It was like pretty much every other modern ship. There was no steering wheel like the ones ships had in the old movies, but a host of digital readouts and analog switches instead. By the model numbers, Fratty could tell that the ship's electronics had been updated sometime in the late 1990s.

His gaze fell on a calendar. Not a Chinese calendar, but a Dallas Cowboys Cheerleaders calendar. The Cowboys might be America's team, but those cheerleaders were the world's darlings. Fratty had seen their posters and pictures in more Third World shitholes and Arab palaces than he cared to count.

"Clear. To me," Holmes said.

Fratty and Laws grinned. Now to see what was in the hold.

17

MACAU. CARGO SHIP'S HOLD.

The entrance to the hold reminded Ruiz of the West Virginia mines his family called home. *Black to go in and black to come out,* his father would say to his son when asked about the black coal dust that coated his every pore and crevice. He never really did come clean. The closest he'd ever come was one Christmas when the mine had shut down for two weeks. His father's skin had taken on a burnished tan those fourteen days, the only reminder of his work in the mines the deep creases in his knuckles, which wouldn't let go of their deep veins of black.

With a flick of a switch, the hold went from nightmare to green. Ruiz descended carefully down the steel-cored stairs. First into the hold, he stared eagerly through the green-tinged darkness, examining each shadow for movement or an untrue color, like a deeper green or a deeper black.

The hold ran the better part of the length of the ship—probably sixty meters. All of that space was filled with row upon row of wooden boxes. Each about six by six by six, they were packed so closely together that there was little room between the topmost crates and the deck above. Nor was there any room between the crates. That also meant there was no air circulation. Only here and there was there more than an inch or two, usually because of an odd-shaped crate. The Ruiz clan knew volumes about this subject, having been on one side or another of a cave-in where miners drank air like it was made from Dom Pérignon.

"Report, Ruiz."

He described what he was seeing, standing on the second-from-the-bottom stair, waiting, watching, ever-careful, his Super 90 moving along his line of sight, an extension of himself.

A large area, probably a dozen feet across, was open at the bottom of the stairs. A single crate rested against a floor-to-ceiling wall made of more crates.

"Frat, get the rear. Laws, move next."

Laws descended and swung the barrel of his MP5 around in a tight arc. Holmes came next, followed by Fratty.

18

MACAU. CARGO SHIP'S DECK.

Walker watched as all four of his teammates descended into the hold. Now they had no cover. Walker lifted his eye from the optic and looked around. He lowered his NVGs over his eyes and ran them through the spectrum, checking infrared and starlight. There was no one and nothing at his twelve, three, six, or nine o'clock, which meant that he wasn't doing anyone any good.

Fuck it.

He folded the bipod and hooked it to his leg. He began to back down from his perch.

Hoover growled.

Walker spun around, searching, then realized that the dog was growling at him. He switched off his MBITR. "What is it, girl?" He moved to lower himself.

Hoover growled again.

"You think I should stay? Is that it?"

The dog sat on her haunches and cocked her head. The result was a perfect *What the fuck do you think you're doing?* look.

Walker grinned and hopped down. "Easy there, Wonder Dog. I know what I'm doing. I lost line of sight and need to get a better position is all."

He began to walk away, but Hoover remained. Walker went another five feet, then turned around. "Well? Are you staying there or coming with?"

Hoover looked from the top of the cargo container where Walker was supposed to be and then back to Walker. Finally she made up her mind and padded toward Walker.

"There you go," Walker said. "Good girl." He reached down to pat the dog's head, but the dog dodged away from him and took the lead. All Walker could do was follow. He kept his NVGs in place as he wondered who was in charge, him or the dog.

19

MACAU. CARGO SHIP'S HOLD.

Laws found a light switch on a pole that was part of the structural support for the stairs. He let Holmes know, and after a moment's hesitation, Holmes told him to flip the switch.

The danger, of course, was that the light might be noticed by someone. But this wasn't their usual mission. If this were a hunter-killer mission, they'd be in and out after taking down or capturing their target. But in this case, they were gathering intelligence. Had they been able to communicate to the Sissy, they'd be relaying the mission narrative as analysts viewed their real-time footage. But with the threat of Chinese signal interception, they were running old school and off the grid. All they had for backup was the new guy. At least he had the dog to supervise him.

Laws lifted the NVGs so that they rested on the top of his helmet. He closed his eyes as he flipped the switch, then cracked them open, letting light in a little at a time. Now that there was light, he could see more details of the boxes. He'd expected

Chinese writing, but instead found himself reading English beneath a logo that displayed a pink and blue big top and an elephant: *SUWARNABHUMI CIRCUS*.

"Do you think there are clowns inside?" Fratty asked. Like Laws and the rest of the SEALs, he'd racked his NVGs onto his helmet as well. Even when he was whispering, his smartassedness came through.

"Shut it," Holmes commanded. "Walker. Come in."

After a moment, "Walker."

"You still in position."

"Roger. NTR," came the boy's voice, saying *Nothing to report*.

"We're inside so if there's any movement, anything, report."

"Wilco," Walker said.

Maybe the boy was going to work out after all. He was headstrong, but then most SEALs were the same way. As long as he could work within the team, he'd be all right.

"We need to crack one of these open," Holmes said. "Ruiz and Fra—"

Suddenly a Chinese man rolled free from a space near the ceiling made from a stack of smaller crates. He fell hard to the floor and lay there for a long moment, long enough for Laws to think that he was dead.

The SEALs had reacted, aiming weapons in every direction except toward the man, but there didn't seem to be anyone else. Then their weapons swung toward him.

The man popped to his feet. His arms shot in the air as if he were a doll on wires. No taller than five feet, he wore stained white underwear and an equally stained white tank top. Red and orange gore stained his chest. His hair was cut in a buzz. He had three-days' growth on his face. He wore plastic-framed glasses, taped at the corners and the crosspiece. One piece of glass was covered with tape.

"What the hell?" Ruiz backed away as the man began to dance in a circle.

Holmes moved to his left and put his back against a wall of

crates. Seeing him do it, Laws mimicked the move on the other side. They both trained their MP5s on the man.

"Nimen dou si le . . . Nimen dou si le . . . Nimen dou si le . . . ," he sang, repeating the words over and over in a singsong, off-key version of a nursery rhyme.

"What's he saying, Laws?" Holmes asked.

"He's saying we're all dead, sir. It's Mandarin. Beijing dialect."

The man still danced as if he was being controlled by someone, but it was ridiculous really. There were no strings attached to him, nor was there anyone else nearby.

"Nimen dou si le . . . Nimen dou si le . . . Nimen dou si le . . ."

"What do we do?" Ruiz asked, his eyes narrowing. He glanced toward the shadows at the tops of the rows.

"We don't do anything." Holmes adjusted the grip on the MP5. "Laws, why is he saying that?"

"Don't know, sir. Want me to ask him?"

"Why don't you do that?"

"Weishenme ni shuo women dou sile?" Laws asked.

"Nimen dou si le . . . Nimen dou si le . . . Nimen dou si le . . ."

"Zhu shuo! Zhu shuo!"

Suddenly the old man did stop. He lowered his arms and crouched like a monkey. His head reared back and he gave a high-pitched scream that made the SEALs wince.

"What the fuck is he doing?" Fratty demanded.

"Take it easy, SEALs." Holmes had pressed himself against the crates and now moved forward a few grudging inches.

"Everyone okay?" came Walker's voice, slightly out of breath over the MBITR.

"You wouldn't believe it," Fratty said.

"After the Stretch Armstrong, I'd believe anything."

"Walker, stay put." Holmes's eyes narrowed. "And why are you out of breath?"

Before Walker could answer, the Chinese man leaped into the air and landed atop the lone crate. He ripped off his shirt, revealing a bandage wrapped around his torso. He reached behind his back and pulled out a knife.

"Knife!" Fratty yelled.

The appearance of the weapon sent everyone into a crouch, fingers itching to pull their triggers.

20

MACAU WHARF.

Hoover sniffed at the body next to the gangway and gave Walker a look. For a dog, she had a pretty remarkable ability to render readable expressions.

Walker shouldered his Stoner and, working with Hoover, pulled both bodies to the edge of the wharf and shoved them over. After they hit the South China Sea with a satisfactory splash, he turned, got the Stoner back in hand, and followed the dog up the gangplank.

He'd been listening to the operation in the hold over the MBITR. He wondered what the man looked like. By the comments from his teammates, things had entered crazy town on a freight train. He remembered listening to some of the tales of ship boardings the SEALs had conducted in the Red Sea against Somali pirates. His father had talked about when he was a kid and how he'd sneak the radio to bed at night and listen to faraway broadcasts of *Mystery Theater* and *Science Fiction Theater*, the words painting pictures as big and bold as any multiplex screen. That was how the tactical radio broadcasts were to

Walker. He could imagine, based on his training, where the SEALs stood in relation to the crazy man.

A square of light from the hatch punched away the darkness in front of him. It was the hold, and the closer he got, the more electric his body began to feel. He shook it off as pins and needles from lying in a prone position too long.

He found what he'd spied from his previous position—an air vent. The cowling was about two meters off the ground and a perfect place for him to keep overwatch and see through the hatch into the hold. It was positioned in such a manner that the communications mast next to it would block him from surveillance from anyone other than the partygoers on the cruise ship far out to sea.

As he climbed into place, he heard all hell break loose as the man drew a knife. He got into place just in time to see him raise it over his head.

21

MACAU. CARGO SHIP'S HOLD.

Fratty gritted his teeth so hard his jaw ached. The crazy fuck had the knife over his head and was screaming something in Chinese. One pull of the trigger would end it all, a 12-gauge slug ripping his screaming head free and leaving a wet spot on the wood behind. All he had to do was give just a little more pressure to the trigger and—

"Easy," came Holmes's calm voice. "Easy, SEALs."

That the man was freaking Fratty out was an understatement. The man standing atop the circus box with the knife over his head and his tiny Asian pecker sticking out from the side of his stained underwear was an image that would take a case of beer and a thousand ice picks to dislodge.

Suddenly the man stopped screaming. The silence that rushed into the space was stark. Then he looked at Fratty and began to whisper in a rough, low voice, "Fratty, Fratty, Fratty, Fratty," over and over.

"Boss? How the hell does this freak know my name?"

"Dunno. Just be easy until we find out what he's—"

Holmes never finished his sentence. The man brought the knife down in a vicious arc into his own abdomen. He grunted as it bit through, but he didn't stop there. He jerked upward, then across. Then control left him. The knife fell to the crate a moment before his intestines roped out in a gush of blood that emptied his gut. He fell face-first atop the crate, his eyes staring directly at Fratty.

Then silence.

"What the hell just happened?" Ruiz said.

"I think he just killed himself," Laws answered.

"No shit." Fratty poked the dead man with the toe of his right boot. "What gave you that idea?"

"Easy boys," Holmes said, lowering the tip of his MP5 and looking around. "Be ready."

"Loo-look at the bl-blood," Ruiz stammered.

Fratty saw it move across the flat wooden surface as if it was all part of the same gigantic amoeba, some edges moving faster than others. The blood took on an oblong shape as it slid into several of the circular holes that had been cut in the top of the crate. He hadn't notice them before, but the holes had been the least of his worries. Right now, he was more concerned with how the blood was moving of its own accord and why.

"That is not right," Laws murmured.

Fratty couldn't get past the fact that the man's blood seemed to be alive.

"Fratty, check the body," Holmes commanded.

A cold sweat broke out beneath Fratty's shirt. "But it said my name!"

"I don't care if it sang 'The Star-Spangled Banner.' Check the corpse," Holmes commanded in an even yet firm voice.

They all heard Hoover bark at the same time. It wasn't over the MBITR. It was close. Too close.

They all turned toward the stairs and stared out the hatch in time to see Walker, who wasn't supposed to be anywhere near there, spin to face someone.

22

MACAU. CARGO DECK.

Hoover saved his ass. Walker spun toward the movement behind him. Three Chinese soldiers had managed to sneak up on him. Two wore the green uniforms of regular forces, while the third was dressed in slick blue camouflage. Walker wasn't up on his foreign uniform recognition, but it was probably Chinese navy or marines. They'd had to have come out of the crew compartment at the base of the wheelhouse—must have broken through the flexi-cuffs. Walker knew that if he'd been in his original position, he would have seen them and been able to remove them before they became a threat.

All this went through Walker's mind in an instant; then he was engaged with the first soldier, who grabbed for his collar. Walker was forced to drop his Stoner, which clattered roughly down the stairs and into the hold. He let his opponent pull him from his perch on the air vent, then became a dead weight and fell into him. His opponent took several steps back as he tried to find his balance, during which Walker reached into the holster at the man's waist, pulled out the Chinese Type 59 pistol, and shoved it over his opponent's heart. Walker put four rounds into him.

Out of the corner of his eye, he saw Hoover mangling the other soldier's hand, teeth on pressure points, shaking it like a rabbit that needed to be dead. The only problem was that the hand was still attached to the man's arm and the guy was now screaming. The man tried to punch at the dog with his free hand, but Hoover kept pulling and twisting to avoid it.

Which left the blue-cammied man.

As his opponent fell, Walker brought the pistol up, but the other man was too fast. He whipped around and cracked it out of Walker's hand with a reverse hook kick. Walker's hand went numb as the pistol flew into the sea.

Then they were up close and personal.

The man's long, thin face bore a three-inch scar that went from the corner of his left eye to the corner of his mouth. His eyes didn't show fear, but projected the concentration one would expect from an expert fighter. He punched Walker twice in the chest, backing him up against the air-vent cowling, then front-kicked.

The first punch tore the wind from Walker, but he rolled with the second. He saw the kick coming and dodged it so that it intersected the cowling. Then he turned and dropped an elbow on the knee. He tried to sweep his opponent's base leg out from under him, but the man limped free.

They each took a moment to appraise the other. This man wasn't a simple People's Liberation Army soldier. He had to be something more, one of their Special Forces or quick-reaction forces.

Walker took the initiative. He fired two punches at the man's left shoulder, knowing that they'd be blocked, then slammed the elbow of the hand that had worked its way into his opponent's guard into his chin.

The man reached out to grab his arm, but Walker was ready for that. His feet moved to enable his hips to pivot into a coiled spring. Walker leaned and turned, allowing the man to come even closer. Then he whipped his body around thanks to his savage pivot and caught the man in the jaw with his other elbow.

The man stumbled backwards, but Walker wouldn't let him recover. He stayed in close so he could reach down to his left thigh. He pulled his knife free from its sheath and slashed it across his opponent's throat, so deeply that he could hear the man's last breath sluicing through the slit.

Walker put a hand on the man's forehead and pushed him over.

He fell, his fingers probing pathetically at the wound.

Walker glanced over and saw that Hoover had subdued his man, now on his knees, his head down. The dog had the soldier's hand in his mouth, teeth clamped down hard. Every time the man twitched or moved, Hoover would bite harder and pull back. She'd probably broken all twenty-seven bones in the man's hand and was scraping them together.

Moving quickly, Walker slit the man's throat; then he stood and wiped the blade on the man's uniform.

As he was resheathing his knife, Holmes rounded the air vent. "What the hell are you doing out of place?" Holmes barely glanced at the dead men.

Walker realized his mistake. If it was up to him he'd never do it again. Still, he hated being called out a second time. "I wanted to get a better view."

"This isn't television. You don't get a better view."

"But I—"

"Shut the fuck up. We'll talk about this later. Thanks to those gunshots, we'll probably have the entire People's Liberation Army on our ass in no time and we haven't even found out what's so special about this tug."

"Boss?" Fratty said, over the MBITR. "There's something down here."

Holmes's eyes flared. "Hoover, come. Walker, come." Then he turned on his heel.

Walker followed, just like the dog.

The hold was pretty much as he'd expected. The only difference was the body atop the crate. It was hard to believe that just moments before, the man had been alive. His entire being had been drained of blood.

Ruiz and Laws stood to one side. Fratty was closest to the box, but his stance made it obvious that he wanted to get away from it.

"What's going on?" Holmes asked.

"Inside the box," Ruiz said, failing to suppress a shudder.

"In that one?" Holmes looked back and forth at his men. "Fratty, I thought I told you to search that fuckwad."

Fratty gave the box a long look, then asked, "Can I shoot it first?"

"What? The box?"

"Yeah."

Then they heard the scratching, like from the claws of a large animal. The box shuddered. Once. Twice.

"Yeah. Go ahead and shoot the box," Holmes said, narrowing his eyes and frowning.

Fratty raised his Super 90 at about the same time the crate's side exploded in a hail of splintered wood. A monster now crouched in the opening.

The size of a pony, the beast had six legs, a thick, muscular body, and the head of a prehistoric saber-toothed cat. Spikes jutted from its body and head as if it were a dinosaur. Except it wasn't a dinosaur, it was something that should never have existed.

The creature didn't pause to be admired. It reached out with a talon-tipped paw and swiped at the nearest moving object—Fratty. The swipe took off the left side of his face, sending ribbons of blood arcing across the hold. The SEAL fell on top of his weapon, blood pulsing out of his ruined face.

Laws opened fire first. Nine-millimeter rounds slammed into the creature with little effect.

Holmes joined in, as did Ruiz and Walker, all firing virtually point-blank at the fell beast. Its body shuddered with the impacts of the rounds, but otherwise it ignored them. It turned baleful eyes at them and swiped again.

The SEALs kept out of the way.

Laws's magazine emptied first. He ejected it and slid another in place without breaking rhythm.

Holmes did the same.

The noise inside the hold was deafening. Cordite and dust filled the air. At first, the rounds didn't seem to have any effect, but bits and pieces of the creature began to fly off with the multiple impacts.

When Ruiz ran out of ammo for the 12-gauge, he dropped it, pulled out his SIG Sauer P226, and fired at the beast's head.

Walker, Laws, and Holmes reloaded and continued firing. Damage to the beast was evidenced by larger and larger pieces of it falling away.

Finally the beast fell to its knees, snarling. It tried to get its legs back under it, but it couldn't seem to manage.

Everyone took a step forward.

Laws was the first to run out of ammunition. He dropped his weapon and let it hang. He snatched up a length of wood and began to beat the creature on the back.

Walker ran out next, but managed to pull Fratty's weapon free from beneath him. He fired as he drew it level, then kept firing.

Finally Holmes inched up to it, shoved the barrel of the MP5 into the beast's mouth, and let loose his last magazine, screaming at the top of his lungs as he did it.

The beast lurched to the ground, held up only by the spikes jutting from its side and head.

The silence was shocking after the violent assault.

The thing lay still. Whatever it was, it was no longer a threat.

Holmes ran and knelt beside the downed SEAL and turned him over. Fratty's face looked like raw meat. His eyes were fixed.

"Ah, hell! Ruiz, give me a hand. You two, Laws and Walker, get this ship under way. All this shooting couldn't have gone unnoticed. We still need to do a search and the army's going to be down on us any fucking second. Got it?"

Both men nodded numbly.

"Wait? Where's Hoover?" Holmes asked.

They spied her under the stairs, tail between her legs, terror in her eyes as she stared at the dead beast.

They coaxed the dog out and let her smell the corpse. When Laws and Walker left the hold, Hoover gladly followed them.

23

SOUTH CHINA SEA.

It took both of them a good ten minutes to remove the anchor lines. On the bridge, Laws was only able to start one engine. He got the ship moving away from the dock just in time. They could see police cars speeding in their direction, lights flashing. Laws pulled a walkie-talkie out of his cargo pocket, but it was silent. Whatever frequency the police were using, it wasn't the same one the guards had tuned in to.

After checking to ensure there were no recording devices, they removed their masks, slipping them around so they rested on the backs of their heads.

"We got about twenty minutes before they get their shit together and get a boat in the water or a bird in the air to come after us. We need to do forensics on the computer," Laws said, "but Fratty isn't going to be able to help us any time soon."

"He's not going to be able to help us at all," Holmes said, coming onto the bridge with the dead SEAL hanging over a shoulder. He laid Fratty down gently, then removed his own mask.

Hoover went to Fratty and whined. She lay down and rested her head on his chest.

Ruiz came in behind him. He took off his mask, revealing a dour expression. "I checked another crate. It had another of those creatures but it was made of stone."

"Chinese tomb guardian. I recognized it from a description in the mission log," Laws said.

"Why'd it look like that . . . all pieced together from other animals," Walker asked.

"It's a chimera. They're not natural. Like a golem, they're the creation of magic."

"Enough of the zoology lesson," Holmes said to Laws. "How far are we away from getting off ship?" Turning to Ruiz, he asked, "Are the charges set?"

Ruiz nodded. "Just waiting for input."

"It was the blood that brought it to life," Laws murmured. He walked over to Fratty and knelt down. "Damn it. He was a good SEAL and friend."

"Had to be the blood," Ruiz said. "That thing down there drank it or something."

"More like a sacrifice," Laws pointed out. "I think it was more than the blood. It was probably the spirit too."

"How can you be so sure?" Walker asked.

"I can't. It just makes sense to me."

Walker stared at the body. He'd barely known Fratty, Anthony Fratolilio, and now he never would.

Holmes pointed at a workstation. "There. Walker, turn that on."

Walker did as he was told. It was a regular desktop computer from a popular brand. But when it booted up, it was all Chinese. "Uh, Laws?"

Laws came over and went through the boot-up. "This is just a cargo ship. It's not a military or an intelligence vessel, so I'm not anticipating any serious software. How goes it outside, Ruiz?"

Ruiz had moved to the window. "Right now, a bunch of police are standing on the wharf scratching their heads. You dispose of the bodies, Walker?"

"Yes."

Holmes shook his head. "At least you did something right."

Before Walker could respond, Laws interrupted. "Damn. Some sort of firewall. I can't do anything else. I speak Chinese, not computer."

Holmes checked Fratty's side pocket and came out with a box that had several cables connected to it. "If he were alive, he'd be using this right now."

"What is it?" Walker asked.

"It allows someone to break into a system by establishing an uplink to NSA. They have several geeks on standby who know exactly what to do."

"Can't we do it?" Walker asked. "I mean, if it's that easy, we could hook it up, right?"

Holmes held the device in the air. Eight different wires hung from it. It had several buttons and one knob. Might as well have been a warp drive for a starship. "Let me see if I can get help." As mission commander, Holmes carried the satellite uplink. They hadn't wanted to use it, but now it seemed like they'd have to if they wanted any chance of success . . . any chance to give meaning to Fratty's death. After a good minute, Holmes connected to an NSA switch, but couldn't get any further. Although the others heard the exchange over their own headsets, Holmes told them, "NSA is currently supporting operations in Afghanistan. There's a big push for HVTs right now," he said, meaning *high-value targets.* "I'm told they're unavailable."

"They wouldn't be able to make any push if we hadn't got Geronimo. Can't they show us any love?"

"Wait a minute," Walker said, his eyes opening in wonder. "You got Geronimo. I thought—"

Holmes waved off the question. "All of their ears are on the mountains in South Waziristan. They don't have the ability to spare anyone. So they say."

"So they say," repeated Ruiz.

"Sounds like they lack the will." Laws shook his head in frustration. "Is this how we end the mission? Did Fratty die for nothing?"

Walker angled his head. He had an idea. "What if we get some help from someone else?"

"Like 1-800-Free-Hacker?" Laws muttered.

"No. More like CIA SPG."

"SPG is a good choice." Holmes nodded. "Go ahead and call your girl. I'll report to Billings while you see if you can get hold of SPG. Ruiz?"

"Sir."

"See if you can contact our recovery vehicle. We might need it in a hurry."

"Wilco."

Everyone switched their MBITRs to private mode, so they could each establish private networks. Remembering his classes at the beginning of Phase III training, Walker went through the protocols, finally connecting to the Joint Special Operations Command (JSOC) operations center. He'd actually been to the command at Fort Bragg on one of their field trips and had met several of the operations officers, so when he heard the voice on the other end, he knew exactly who it was.

"JSOC C and C."

"This is . . ." He covered his mouthpiece. "Who are we?" he asked the room.

Laws raised an eyebrow. "We're Ghost. You're Ghost Four."

"This is Ghost Four, requesting connect to SPG Coronado."

There was a pause. Then, "Ghost Four, we don't have you on mission. What's your five?"

Laws, who'd tuned in to the conversation on his own MBITR, shook his head.

"We're on mission. No location. I need the connect ASAP."

Another pause. "C and C requires your five for plotting."

Laws was about to jump in but Walker held up his hand. "Burt, how many energy drinks have you had today?"

"Ghost Four, do I know you?"

"Two words. Pure Titanium."

This pause was much shorter than the others. "Connecting SPG, out."

Since SPG didn't have a secure communications system tied into JSOC, Walker was routed to a landline. As it rang, he saw Laws mouth the words *Pure Titanium*?

"It's a strip club on Bragg Boulevard."

"I know what it is. What's it have to do with old Burt and the energy drinks?"

"Burt had so many energy drinks, he couldn't get his pecker to wake up. He had three free lap dances and an invitation to a private room for his birthday and all it did was sleep. The girls started calling him Floppy."

"Ahh. That would do it."

A tinny voice answered on the other end. Walker asked for Jennifer Costello. After another wait, he heard her voice.

"This is Jen."

"Hi Jen, this is Ghost Four."

"Jack? Wait—where are you calling from?"

"No names," Laws interrupted. "This is Ghost on mission, we need SPG assist. Can you go secure on your end?"

"Give me a moment," Jen said, efficient and official. A high-pitched whine shot across the miles, then dissipated. When she came back on the line she asked, "Is everyone safe?"

"I'm safe," Walker said. "Jen, we need an assist." He looked meaningfully at Laws.

"This is Ghost Two. We're a man down and need to get access to a local computer. Can you help?"

There was silence for a moment before she answered. "Glad you're okay, Ghost Two. Good question. What do you have in the way of equipment?"

Walker held up the device that Fratty had been carrying. There were no labels or markings. "A rectangular box with different cables connected to it. Our man would have used it, but . . ."

There was a moment of silence. "So sorry, Ghost Team. Listen, is there a USB and a coaxial cable?" she asked.

Following her instructions, it wasn't long before they had a connection established through the satellite uplink.

"I'm running this through an isolated server just in case there's a failsafe." Two minutes later they were past the log-in screen.

Laws began to read the characters on the screen.

Holmes came over. "What's your status?"

"Looks like there's a captain's log as well as a link to the navigation system." Laws began clicking the mouse and bringing up different screens. He turned in his seat and looked around. "See a printer in here?"

Ruiz found himself standing next to a printer, an ancient dot matrix. He said as much, then turned it on.

It was soon printing one line at a time, making a sound like the world was ripping apart.

"Recovery vehicle says we have to get moving. They have aircraft inbound in ten mikes."

"I could write faster than this printer," Walker said, tearing off one page.

"Can we upload to your server?" Laws asked.

"We're not set up for that," Jen said, "But let me check."

Holmes went into action. "Ruiz. Set the charges for seven minutes, then meet us at the bow. Laws, you've got exactly two minutes to get what you need out of that computer."

Laws glared at Holmes, then shrugged. "Tell your girl thanks," he said, standing up. He jerked out the power cord to the computer, then pulled his knife from its sheath. He jammed it into the back of the computer and pried off the side panel. After a moment of sawing and breaking, he came out with the hard drive. "Possible capture by the People's Liberation Army is the mother of invention."

"Save it for the inspirational poster. You all ready?"

Laws and Walker nodded.

"Do you need me anymore?" Jen asked from across the world.

The sound of her voice made Walker long for home. Given a proper evac and recovery, he'd be there soon enough. "Leave the light on," he said.

"Wilco," she replied. Then, "And be careful, honey." Then she disconnected.

Laws broke into a grin from ear to ear.

"Don't say it," Walker growled.

"I wouldn't dream of it . . . *honey*."

Walker rolled his eyes, but couldn't help smiling. But that evaporated as he noticed Holmes standing over Fratty's body. "I'll carry him," Walker said, hurrying over. He flexi-cuffed Fratty's hands and ankles together the way he'd been taught, which would make him easier to carry both in and out of the water. Then he lifted the body and arranged the weight on his left shoulder.

Holmes watched him through the whole process. Then he went to the controls and checked the speed and direction. "Okay, let's go. Masks on."

They donned their masks, and then the three of them moved down the stairs together, Holmes in front and Laws in back, Walker in the middle with Fratty's limp arm around his neck. The ship was about a mile out and they could still see the lights of the police cars on the wharf. There were more than a dozen of them now. The cruise ship was off the port side of the ship and less than a thousand meters away. Drunken revelers on the deck waved and shouted to them. They were close enough to be seen and maybe even recorded. But Twitter and Facebook, in addition to all the other social networks, would be scoured by the Ladies in Blue Shoes—a name for a special unit consisting of wives of SEALs past and present, who used state-of-the-art software to wipe evidence from public Internet spaces. They loved their jobs and treated each mission as if they were storming the beach themselves.

When they reached the bow, Holmes secured a rope and dropped it over the edge. Ruiz came running over a moment later.

"Three minutes," he said.

Holmes, who'd removed the canine harness from Fratty earlier, secured Hoover in the harness, then went over the edge. The dog had been thoroughly trained in water operations and accepted the treatment like a professional.

When they were all safely in the water, they formed a square with Fratty floating in the middle. They kick-paddled away from the boat. They weren't frantic, but they were efficient, each knowing that if the ship went up, they needed to be a safe distance away.

Walker began to feel a strange current beneath them, as if something large, some leviathan from the deep, had come up to glimpse the night air. He could almost feel its weight as the water was relocated beneath him. And when it touched his foot, he was ready for the submarine to take them home.

24

SUBIC BAY. TWENTY-SIX YEARS EARLIER.

They said it was a Hantu Kabor—a grave demon. Sometimes he could still feel its oily fingers slithering through his thoughts. The feeling was so acute, it felt as if it had never left. And in those panicked moments, he experienced the return of the helplessness that had so consumed his life in the months it had owned him.

He'd been walking home from school when it had entered him. He remembered the day perfectly. School had let out. He'd ended up leaving late because of detention. The streets were empty except for the occasional passing car, and even then, the windows were so heavily tinted that he couldn't see the people inside. The feeling of being alone crept up on him, until finally it was the echo of his own footsteps against the brick-walled buildings that brought his fear alive.

The sky hung heavy with the threat of rain, lugubrious gray clouds ready to let go. The crisp air swirled with a cold wind that carried trash down the street in blustery gusts. Jack remembered the feeling of being watched. He'd turn around to check, but there was no one else there. Where the feel of invisible eyes touched him, it left spots that glowed with cold.

Then came the whispers. At first they were unintelligible. Multilingual, he could catch snippets of Tagalog, English, what sounded like German and Chinese, plus thousands of other words. Always on the edge of comprehending, he found himself trying desperately to understand as the whispers chased him down.

The first time he tripped, he blamed it on the uneven sidewalk. He fell hard to his knees, skinning both of them so that blood seeped from the dirt-encrusted wounds. He climbed back to his feet and began to run. The whispers grew louder. He thought he heard a single word—*Jackie*. Then he fell a second time, the pressure of an invisible hand between his shoulder blades propelling him forward.

He got up slowly as the wind increased and the voices grew louder. Now and then he could pick out a word he recognized, but he couldn't string enough together to figure out the meaning. He'd begun to cry, although he wasn't sure when. His knees and hands burned with fresh wounds.

He'd dropped his books somewhere behind him and now he staggered toward his home. His hands were out in front of him and dripping blood; he had only two more blocks to go when the whispers and the wind stopped so completely it was as if the world had just been paused.

Jack stopped himself and turned. He saw only buildings with gaping empty windows, the forlorn street, piles of trash and leaves as still as if the world had become a snapshot. He was entirely alone.

Alone.

Except for the breathing.

Imperceptible at first, the sound grew in strength. Low huffs from a beast, the sounds emanated from right behind him. Afraid of what he might see, he still couldn't help turning around, trying with increasing desperation to see what wasn't there.

Then he felt the *other,* as if a greasy hand was laid on the back of his neck. He screamed and tried to shake it off, but it increased in weight and ferocity. Suddenly it shoved him to his knees. His head slammed against the ground. His back arched and the greasy hand slid inside the back of his head with an explosion of pain so great his jaws couldn't make any sound.

Then his universe exploded like a sheet of black glass and fell away.

At that moment he could understand the voices. They'd been telling him to run. They'd been telling him to get far away. Most were sorry that he'd joined their ranks. But there were some who were happy to have his company. Locked inside the limitless mind of the grave demon, they were eager to live again. Jack represented a newness they could eat and consume, and they would take his memories and make them their own until there was nothing left of little Jackie Walker or until eternity burned away.

25

STARLIFTER. OVER THE PACIFIC OCEAN.

The peregrination back home had been one of tired solemnity. Fratolilio was laid in state in the middle of the Starlifter that had picked them up from Guam. It had taken six hours for the submarine that had recovered them to rendezvous with the aircraft carrier USS *George Washington*. Both the sub commander and the carrier-group commander had wanted to relieve them of the body, but Holmes and the other SEALs vigorously ignored the attempts to get them to relinquish their teammate. They'd never left a SEAL behind and they wouldn't start now. The mission started at Coronado and it would end at Coronado. For Fratty it would end there forever.

Signal officers aboard the *George Washington* took possession of the hard drive from the target ship. Their job wasn't to decode or decrypt any of the data, but to transfer it to SPG so that it could be worked on while the team was in transit back to base. Once extracted by SPG, the raw data would be analyzed for future target allocation, if possible. Reports from the submarine's sonar crew, as well as local reports from Macau fire and rescue, told a tale of the ship aflame and sinking in the harbor.

Only the team and a few drunken revelers from the cruise ship knew the truth. One report of masked hockey players with a dog attacking the ship made it through the Internet lockdown, but that would likely die the death of a thousand spams as soon as the world read it, then dismissed it as a mad tweet from a drunken cruise passenger.

No one was in much of a mood to talk. The mission had left them numb. The constant adrenaline surge required to stay alive would send any normal person into a coma-like recuperative state. Even the SEALs with their hypermetabolisms found themselves leaden and exhausted, unwilling and partially unable to relive and recount the events that had just transpired. The electrolytes and intravenous nutrition provided on both the submarine and the carrier helped greatly, but no man-made drugs could ever repair the hole in their hearts and their idea of self, represented succinctly by the man lying in the middle of the aircraft.

Still, Walker had a lot of thoughts working in his mind, not the least of which was the reality that there were creatures and forces out there that had an intent to harm his great Red, White, and Blue, if not the world. He'd been preparing to fight other men only to discover that he was now fighting creatures whose existence could only be foretold in myth and legend.

He felt a hand on his shoulder. It was Laws. "How you doing, FNG?"

"I'm not an FNG anymore," Walker said softly.

"Why is that?"

"My first mission is behind me."

Laws nodded. "Normally that would be the case. But you see, you're the FNG until someone new comes to replace Fratty. Whether it's a day, month, or year . . . until that happens, you're the FNG."

"Who made up those rules?" Walker asked.

"The great god of FNGs." Laws leaned back and closed his eyes. "Now get some shut-eye. No telling what's going to happen when we land."

Walker remained silent for a long while. His head rested on a pile of cargo netting. Finally he prodded Laws in the shoulder. "Is it always like this?"

Laws opened one eye. "What do you mean?"

"Going out and fighting creatures that aren't supposed to exist. All in a day's work, right?"

"We don't always fight creatures. Sometimes it's the usual type of monster . . . the human kind."

"But fighting the creatures . . . the monsters are a pretty common trend with Triple Six, right?"

"Sure." Laws yawned. "Now get some sleep."

But Walker was too wired to sleep. "I'm so damn juiced, I feel like Superman. I feel like I could fly if given the chance."

Laws opened both eyes and propped himself up on an elbow. "Batman. Not Superman. You want to feel like someone, feel like Batman."

"What?"

"Superman is bullshit."

"What?" Walker asked, drawing out the word. "Superman is bullshit? What the hell does that mean? He's the most powerful superhero ever created."

Laws shook his head. "Nah, I call bullshit on the Man of Steel. Look . . . he's so powerful because of Earth's yellow sun, right? He doesn't even have to try, as soon as he landed here, he was all-powerful."

"And Batman has no powers. He had to do everything himself. Okay. I see."

"Do you? Because the folks at DC went miles trying to hide the obvious."

"Okay, now you lost me. What is this *conspiracy* involving Superman?"

"Hey, don't roll your eyes at me. You're the one who couldn't sleep and had to keep talking." Laws paused, flashing a menacing grin. "And yes, 'conspiracy' is a good word. It's simple. The fact is that Superman should be *fat*. He should he a lard-assed superhero with flabby arms, a beer gut, and soft muscles."

Walker laughed softly as he imagined that version of Superman. "Okay, man. You gotta explain that one. I have no idea what you're talking about."

"Okay. Look at Batman. He's buff, right?"

Walker nodded.

"And why is that?"

"Like I said, because he works out."

"Like U.S. Navy SEALs, right?"

"Right."

"Great. But when Superman bench-presses a Cadillac, he doesn't even break a sweat. It's like picking up a bag of feathers. Would Batman be buff if he bench-pressed feathers? Because that's essentially what Superman does every day."

Walker thought about it. The stronger you were, the more you had to do to keep that strength. SEALs weren't muscle mammoths, but they were in elite shape, much like Batman. They went for strength rather than size. He did know that if he didn't keep up the exercise, he'd lose it faster than it took to gain.

Walker thought on this for a moment. "Holy shit, you're totally right. Why doesn't anyone ever talk about this?"

"Conspiracy," Laws whispered. "Now sleep."

Walker laughed, then turned over and forced himself to close his eyes. Soon he was dreaming of Batman as a U.S. Navy SEAL, embracing old Stumpy with the rest of them.

26

SPECIAL OPERATIONS HANGAR. CORONADO.

They landed at 1 P.M., taxiing down the runway beneath an overcast sky. The Starlifter rolled to a stop at the restricted end of the base, where a formation of SEALs stood waiting. No sooner was the ramp lowered than six of the SEALs peeled away and came aboard with a wooden stretcher. They carefully slid it beneath Fratty, lifted him, and carried him out the ramp. Hoover kept close, sniffing the high-held body. The surviving SEALs followed, tiredly carrying their gear with them.

Billings met them on the tarmac. She wore a smart black business suit with a Wounded Warrior Project pin prominently on her lapel beside the U.S. Senate pin. Her eyes and nose were red, the only concession to her sorrow. She put a hand on Holmes's forearm, stopping him and the other SEALs. She didn't say anything. She didn't have to. Everyone nodded to her, acknowledging their shared loss; then she lifted her arm and the procession continued.

A hangar had been prepared. The only piece of furniture in it was a long table with a white sheet draped over it. At the head of the table was a helmet with an M4 rifle in a stand. Fratty's dog tags hung from the front sights. Unlike most other service members, SEALs weren't allowed to take them on operations. A tan U.S. Navy Chief Petty Officer cap with a glistening black bill and gold anchor rested atop the barrel.

Once Fratty was laid on the table, his wound covered by a piece of linen, a door opened at the far end of the hangar.

Walker knew what to expect. He'd made the same walk during his training. All SEALs, those in training and those who'd already graduated, including those who'd retired and were close enough to the base to make it, would walk past their departed brother. Those who'd served with the departed were asked to leave something that could be shared with the family. A picture. A memory. Anything. Those who'd never met the SEAL filed by silently.

As it began, music started on the hangar's speaker system. Every SEAL chose the song they wanted to have played. It took Walker a few moments to recognize the old Aldo Nova song. When the sounds of the helicopters kicked in, the song suddenly seemed perfect. "Fantasy" was the name of the song and the electronic music filled the hangar to the rafters, the whining guitar like an anthem for the living.

The team stood solemnly at the foot of the table during the entire viewing. They never put down their gear. They remained covered in mission grime that even the ocean hadn't washed away. Part of Walker felt devastated that he'd let Fratty down. That was a part of this, to vow never to let it happen again. But another part was to acknowledge the mission, the sacrifice, and the men who'd brought back their team member.

Walker recognized the members of his class when they came, led by Instructor Reno. His classmates looked questioningly at him, but he couldn't answer. All he could do was nod and watch as they passed. Reno paused beside the body and looked hard at every one of them. Unlike the others, he had something to say to Holmes.

"I get them ready. You take them out. You bring them back. Just tell me, SEAL, is it mission complete?"

Holmes swallowed hard as he nodded. "They all came home," he said, voice cracking.

"Good. Then I'll keep sending you more." Then Reno left, only pausing to touch each and every member of the team on the arm. It was a small touch, but it weighed heavily enough.

As Reno departed, Walker couldn't help wonder what would have happened if Holmes had answered differently. No SEAL had been trained in recent memory without Reno. One had to wonder if a SEAL could even *be* trained without him. Walker watched him leave, feelings of fear, admiration, love, respect, and the desire to grow up and be just like him swirling in the midst of his abject thoughts.

The song replayed seven times before the viewing was over. Finally they were left alone with their friend.

Each teammate, beginning with Holmes, took a private moment with the man, and Walker was left for last. He approached the smartassed SEAL, wishing his ruined face would crack a smile and he'd tell them one last joke. Eventually, Fratty's body was taken away. He no longer belonged to just the SEALs. They'd return him to the world he'd died saving. He'd be cleaned up and sent to his family with the thanks of a grateful nation.

The surviving members of SEAL Team 666 were taken to the Pit. They put their gear away. They cleaned themselves up. Then for a time they just sat around the conference table and stared at each other. It was a long while before someone finally spoke, and when it happened, it was Holmes, beginning the after-action report.

Everyone knew that it had to be done. But not a single one liked it.

27

IMPERIAL BEACH. MORNING.

After the mission brief, they all turned in. The following evening there'd be a wake for Fratty, but for today, it was all about recovery. Walker was past tired. Toward the end of the briefing, he'd felt loopy, severe enough that he didn't trust himself to speak. So when Holmes highlighted the fact that he'd disobeyed an order—which had almost compromised their mission—Walker had remained silent. It would be a conversation for another day. Sure, he'd disobeyed an order, but at the time it had been based on a sound decision. His view of the crew door had been partially blocked by the same air-vent cowling to which he'd repositioned. Rethinking the situation, he couldn't be sure that from his initial position he would have seen the three men before they were close enough to fire at the SEALs in the hold.

He went to bed angry and exhausted. The battle aboard the ship replayed in his dreams that night. But as dreams are wont to do, they twisted reality, changing the Chinese soldiers into demons and the creature in the hold into a dragon. They fought a long hard battle, expending every last piece of ammunition. Just as they thought they'd won, a klaxon sounded from somewhere and a tide of orange-skinned homunculi erupted from the hold. They crashed into the SEAL team, their sheer numbers smothering the team's members. Walker felt a hundred tiny hands pressing him to the deck, while a dozen more wrapped around his neck and tried to squeeze the life out of him. As his eyes bulged, he recognized the thing inside of them by the way it glowed from their eyes. He knew it as well as he knew himself . . . after all, it *was* himself for a time.

He awoke gasping and covered in sweat. For a moment he didn't know where he was. Then he remembered he'd been installed in his new bedroom suite at SEAL Team 666 HQ. He rolled out of bed and headed to the bathroom. He lowered his head into the sink and let the cool water run over his head. Then he turned so he could drink straight from the faucet. After several deep gulps, he stood and stared at himself in the mirror.

He'd slept ten hours. That was more uninterrupted sleep than he'd had in the last six months. It was actually too much. He felt groggy.

He threw on a shirt and some shorts and went into the main room in search of coffee. Ruiz was already there and offered him a mug. They sat on a leather sofa, staring at the ceiling and letting the caffeine attack the exhaustion that lingered in their systems.

"I was thinking last night about the mission," Ruiz said after a good ten minutes. He was wearing shorts and a T-shirt that read *WEST VIRGINIA MOUNTAINEERS*, along with the school logo of Davy Crockett.

"Me, too," Walker said.

"I know. We can't help it, can we? Anyway, you're the team sniper, which puts you at a great distance from the action."

Walker thought it was stating the obvious. He didn't know where the conversation was going. "So?" he said, letting the word draw long.

"So we all have a reason we were selected for the team. Most of the time we aren't sure whether it was the way we answered a question, something in our past, or something else we aren't even aware of. The psychs sure aren't forthcoming."

"What are you getting at?"

"It seems pretty clear to me why you were chosen. I mean, you're good, bro, but there are a lot of good SEALs out there. But as far as I know, none of them do what you do when they get near something supernatural."

Suddenly Walker knew where the conversation was turning.

"I can't help but wonder that if you'd been *with* the team instead of standing off to watch our backs . . . if you would have felt that thing in the crate before the shit hit the fan. If you'd been there, then—"

"Then Fratty might still be alive," Walker said, finishing the statement.

"Exactly. We wouldn't have to attend another fucking wake for a dead friend."

Walker inhaled during the silence that followed. Was this the life he'd subscribed to? "How many wakes have you attended, Ruiz?"

"Total? Thirty-two. For my own team members from all my team assignments? Six. For SEAL Team 666? Two. You can see them on the wall. They're the best America has ever made. Their only faults were to be at the wrong place at the wrong time, and to not know how, or why, or fucking *when* a creature that the rest of the world doesn't even know exists was going to reach out and snuff the life from them."

Laws entered the room and grabbed a cup of coffee of his own. "Easy, Ruiz."

"Fuck easy! This shit *sucks*."

Walker nodded. It was the only thing he could do. As bad as he felt now having lost one team member, he couldn't imagine losing six.

But Laws laughed, drawing angry glares from both Ruiz and Walker. " 'This shit sucks,' " Laws repeated. "It could be a T-shirt. It could be a slogan. Or maybe, 'Don't Die and Make It Suck.' "

Walker chuckled in spite of himself in recognition of Laws's gallows humor.

Ruiz grimaced and turned away, but Laws wouldn't let him get away so easily. "Come on, man. I know this shit sucks, but you can't let it get to you."

Ruiz turned farther away.

"Hey," Laws pressed. "What is it you rednecks do in West Virginia when you're mourning? Look at goat porn?"

Ruiz turned halfway back, seemed to think about it for a moment, then turned the rest of the way. He stared at Laws. "We blow shit up."

Laws laughed out loud. "Hear that, Walker? Ruiz says he blows shit up when he's sad. Fuck it. Let's go blow something up."

Ruiz's face actually brightened. "Seriously?"

"Absolutely. Grab some clothes and some Semtex and we'll go out and do it."

Ruiz looked back and forth between Walker and Laws, waiting to see if it was a joke. After a minute, he took off.

After he'd gone, Walker asked, "Are we really going to blow something up?"

Laws nodded.

But Walker couldn't make sense of Laws's reaction. While everyone else was in a state of mourning, Laws seemed to be as nonchalant as if it were any other day.

Laws pointed a finger at Walker. "Don't confuse my ability to compartmentalize with lack of caring. I deal with this in my own way." He removed his shirt, revealing dozens of words written on his torso. At first they seemed to be in a strange language; then Walker realized that they were printed in reverse. They were names, indelibly etched into his skin with tattoo ink. Laws pointed to them. "These are—*were*—my teammates and classmates. Everyone I've served with since I've been into the teams. Your name's going to go up here as soon as I can break away."

Walker noticed that about a third of the names had lines through them. "And the lines through them?"

"Are the friends I've lost." He pointed to the name Anthony Fratolilio. "This is for Fratty. I'll cross him out after the wake. But crossed out or not, he'll always be a part of me. I can see him and he can see me."

"Why is it in reverse?"

"Most people wear tattoos as a statement to the world. Something they want someone else to notice. I don't give a shit about that. These are for me. They're for me to look at and remember." Laws lowered his voice. "They're so I won't forget. Ever."

Half an hour later they were in Ruiz's red two-and-a-half-ton pickup and heading into what constituted the town of Coronado. They pulled an old wooden skiff they'd appropriated from BUD/S school. They stopped for a six-pack of Longboard and headed for Imperial Beach.

Imperial Beach was down the isthmus from Coronado. The southerly drive down the highway was bounded by state beaches and the Pacific Ocean on the right and military housing on the left. That soon gave way to marinas and then the low-slung buildings of Imperial City. Originally constructed as a place for farmworkers to go, its proximity to Tijuana made it a place where most San Diegans feared to tread. So other than the families and descendants of farmworkers from the Greater Imperial Valley, most of the population was composed of military members who'd lived and retired there.

A bronze statue of a surfer had been placed on the boardwalk and was a frequent target for graffiti artists and vandals. It was currently wearing a white and black polka-dotted housedress with a purple plastic lei. That a police car was parked nearby and the officers had made no effort to remove the clothes was a testament to what the city thought of the statue.

Laws, Ruiz, and Walker found the city boat ramp and lowered the skiff into the water. Ruiz paddled it out, while Laws and Walker parked the truck, then found a spot on the beach to observe the events that were about to transpire. Although it was nine in the morning, the beach was filled with tourists and families. Several pods of surfers gathered together where the waves hit the best, taking turns, and sometimes fighting over the waves as they tumbled in.

The beer was cold and hoppy. Walker drank half of his, then leaned back on an elbow and watched the women in their bathing suits. From young to old, they were all beautiful. He was reminded of Jen. He hadn't been with her for almost three months. Something was always getting in their way. He needed to find the time to be alone with her, some time when he wouldn't be called to mission, or she wouldn't be called away to work. It occurred to him that now would probably be a perfect time. It was a Saturday morning, and although her schedule was a lot like his, chances were that she was off work.

But here he was on the beach, supporting the mourning rites of a teammate.

Just then, Ruiz waved to them. He was about fifty yards out. He'd dropped anchor and dove into the water. He didn't surface until he was more than halfway back to shore, assisted in the distance by his flippers. By then he was in a crowd of people wading in the surf. He leisurely paddled the rest of the way in. Soon, he was plopping down beside them, grabbing a beer and drinking deeply.

They each finished a beer, then opened another. Ruiz pulled a small electrical device from his beach bag, which Laws had brought from the truck.

"For Fratty," he said, the held out his bottle with the other hand.

Walker and Laws clinked bottles and repeated the toast.

Then Ruiz depressed the single red button set in the black plastic.

The boat went up in a ball of heat and red fire. The explosion stopped everyone in midplay. Tourists stood agog at the event, but the locals, those who knew that this was a place for SEALs and other Navy personnel to blow off steam, took it in stride.

The only ones who seemed to be concerned were the police, who began conferring with the lifeguard. It looked as if he was about to point them out, when a scream went up from the other side of the lifeguard station. The lifeguard leaped from his platform, grabbed his orange buoy, and ran toward the water, where a woman was holding a little boy's limp body. As it turned out, it was a false alarm. Her son was just playing dead and ended up with a good scolding by the lifeguard. In the meantime, the three SEALs took advantage of the distraction and returned to the truck. Laws unhitched the trailer and left it in the parking lot.

28

THE MOSH PIT. AFTERNOON.

When they returned, Walker had planned on calling Jen, but a Navy seaman was waiting for him near the front door. He held a stack of papers. When he saw Walker, he impatiently beckoned him over. Ruiz and Laws continued inside, while Walker sidetracked into an office. Bureaucracy had caught up with him. After being chastised for going on mission before he filled out his paperwork, he was provided with a stack of forms to complete. He spent the next two hours filling out everything from emergency notification forms to hazardous duty pay allotments. He transferred his jump log and dive log, updated his EPSQ clearance forms, and filled out enough paperwork to eventually satisfy the gods of *administrivia*. Even the clerk seemed satisfied, but there was one form left. It was a simple piece of paper that asked a single question, and it had a space for the answer and a line on which to sign. What song did he want them to play at his viewing? He took the paper in hand and sat back roughly in the chair.

He stared at the words, remembering Fratty's viewing the

day before. He supposed that he'd have his own one day. They were told not to worry about it, not to anticipate it. Theirs was the most dangerous job on the planet and the odds were against them surviving for very long. It was only because of the training and instructors like Reno that they were able to stay alive for as long as they did. And now they were asking for the song he wanted them to play in the event of his death.

"Can I have some time to think about this?" he asked.

The clerk shook his head. "I need to have it now. If you can't decide, I'll put down my favorite song."

"What's that?" Walker asked, hoping for some inspiration.

"Madonna's 'Material Girl,'" the seaman said with a straight face.

Walker definitely didn't want that to be played at his viewing. It had never occurred to Walker when he was listening to Aldo Nova yesterday that he'd have to come up with one of his own. He found himself staring at the sheet. Minutes ticked by as he went through his mental catalogue of songs.

"Can we get this done?" the clerk said. "I have a date tonight."

Walker looked at him. Yeah, he needed to hurry. He wouldn't want the choice for his death song to get in the way of the young seaman's sex life. He grabbed a pen, jotted down the title and the band, then signed the form. "Here you go. Are we done now?"

The clerk read the choice aloud: "'Wheel in the Sky,' by Journey." He shook his head. "What is it with 1980s hair bands?" But he didn't wait for an answer. He stacked the papers together and placed them in a classified carrier. Then he stuck out his hand. "Good luck, SEAL."

Walker accepted the handshake. "Uh, sure. Thanks."

The clerk walked out.

Walker got up and went into the main room of the Pit. Billings was there, as was someone new. As he came into the room, they all turned.

"Walker, this is your new team member. Chief Petty Officer Ali Jabouri, meet Petty Officer First Class Jack Walker."

They shook hands. The new guy was of Arab descent. Although he wore a grim face, he had smiling eyes. He was shorter than the rest of them but didn't act like it bothered him.

"Call me Yaya," he said, with an accent that sounded more like Philly than Saudi Arabia.

"We've had Chief Jabouri's file for some time now. While myself and the members of the Sissy share our most sincere condolences for Chief Fratolilio, I'm hoping that you'll welcome Chief Jabouri."

Walker caught her looking at him appraisingly as she said it. He also saw the other team members offering their own tight smiles to her statement. Her subtext was clear. They were gears in a supernatural defense machine. One gear broke and here's another. Plug it in and get instant continuity of operations.

"Now that we've had introductions, I've got to be on my way." She pointed at Holmes. "Can I see you for a moment?"

Holmes nodded but spoke to the team first. "No one goes into Fratty's room until I get a chance to clear it."

Everyone stared back at him. The thought had never crossed their minds. Until Fratty's belongings were cleared, the room was essentially the man's shrine. Not a single one dared to enter, much less remove anything.

Holmes turned to follow Billings into the conference room and closed the door behind him.

Everyone stared at each other for a few moments.

Yaya looked at Walker. "Is it always like this?"

Walker shrugged. "Don't ask me. I've only been here for two days."

"Three," Laws corrected, holding up three fingers. "Or it could be four," he said, examining his own fingers with critical eyes. "Going back and forth across the dateline confuses me."

"And you've already had one mission," Yaya noted.

"Two," Laws corrected again, holding up two fingers this time.

"Yeah. Two missions. I just now signed all my admin forms."

Yaya raised his eyebrows. "I filled mine out . . ." He let it fade, then said in a much lower voice, "Last night." He shook his head. "Listen guys. I'm sorry. I just don't know what to say."

Ruiz went to the bar and grabbed beers. When he returned he passed them around. He opened his and held it up. "To the FNG."

They all opened their beers and drank slowly and deeply.

Laws held up his left hand and spread his fingers Spock style. "Live long and prosper."

Ruiz snorted in his beer and Walker couldn't help but laugh. They'd turned a somber moment on its head and were soon lounging around the leather couches in the middle of the Pit, exchanging résumés. Common in every military unit since Hannibal's poop scoopers had crossed the Alps behind the elephants, military members had shorthand for telling where they'd come from, where'd they'd been, the sorts of missions they'd done, and what their skills were.

Yaya had been born and raised in Philadelphia. He was a red, white, and blue American who'd joined the Navy right after 9/11. A modestly devout Muslim, the behavior of the few who'd flown jets into the buildings and a Pennsylvania pasture had so incensed and insulted him that he wanted to demonstrate that theirs was the exception rather than the rule. As it turned out, a belief in the spiritual is at the root of Islam and it was known that certain caliphs and mullahs were deeply involved with the supernatural. In fact, Yaya had let this be known during his screening interview, which he believed was one of the reasons that he was selected for Triple Six.

He'd been a member of SEAL Team 4 since Class 258. As an East Coast SEAL out of Little Creek, Virginia, he didn't know many SEALs from the West Coast. But he'd heard of Holmes.

Although Team 4's mission was focused on Central and South America, Yaya had spent the last four years on repeated deployments to the Middle East. His most recent mission was as part of a task force to take down an old oil platform off the coast of Yemen that had become home to a force of AQAP (Al Qaida on the Arab Peninsula) pirates threatening ships entering the Gulf of Aden.

Then the others introduced themselves to him. When they got to Walker, his story was much shorter. He told the story about how he was jerked out of training, which earned him a look from Yaya that was both shocked and impressed.

"I'm definitely not all that," Walker said. "Right now I'm specializing in not doing what I'm told."

Ruiz nodded. "You're good at doing what you're not told to do."

"Ain't no one does the kickin' chicken better," Laws laughed.

Ruiz held out his fist and kissed knuckles with Laws. "Amen to that."

When Yaya gave a blank look, both Ruiz and Laws glanced at Walker for permission.

Walker shrugged. If they wanted to talk about it, then more power to them. He wouldn't do it, though. It just felt too weird.

Ruiz and Laws jumped right in. They sat on the edge of their respective couches talking animatedly with their hands, diagramming the mission to Chinatown. When they got to the part where Walker fell to the ground and started thrashing, Ruiz demonstrated on the couch, by rolling on his back and shaking his arms and legs spastically. Soon, they were all laughing uproariously, even Walker, who found it funny in a self-conscious he-couldn't-believe-it-happened-to-him sort of way.

Their laughter stopped when the door to the conference room opened and Holmes stepped out. He called Laws over and they spoke for a moment. While they conversed, Billings left with her briefcase in hand. Soon Laws returned to them. Holmes walked past, hardly acknowledging them. He went into Fratty's suite and slammed the door.

"What was that all about?" Ruiz asked.

Laws frowned and shook his head. "Okay, here's the scoop. SPG pulled some data off the hard drive. We have a mission brief tomorrow morning at 0900. Tonight's the wake for Fratty at McP's. We all need to go there. Until then you're on your own."

He turned to go, then paused. "Oh yeah. I'm in charge for the immediate future. Skipper has to stand before a board. Once he's cleared, he'll be back in command." Then he headed to his own suite.

Walker sat back. "That was an 'oh yeah' comment?"

"He didn't want to put any weight on it," Ruiz said. "Happens every time. The brass conducts a board to ascertain the events surrounding a death of a SEAL. But in this case, it's two within one month. First Lieutenant Chong, who Walker replaced, then Fratty."

"They call it due diligence," Yaya added.

"They going to ask us questions?" Walker asked.

"Probably." Ruiz shrugged. "Just answer truthfully. We all saw what happened."

"What did happen?" Yaya asked after a few moments of silence.

Walker got up to leave. With all the time he had, he could give Jen a call and see if she was available before he was due at the wake. He left Ruiz talking about the HAHO jump into the mission and the beast aboard the ship.

29

CORONADO ISLAND. MIDNIGHT.

Although buzzed from Fratty's wake, they weren't ready to call it quits. Walker and Laws liberated a cooler from a passed-out fisherman and headed down the beach. The lights of San Diego glowed in the distance like an earthbound galaxy. A barge bleeped its horn as it cruised forlornly down the middle of the empty harbor. They found a place to park, grabbed beers, and went down to the water.

McP's had been closed for the wake and filled with SEALs old and new. Pictures and plaques adorned the walls. Team names and patches were everywhere. This was as much a museum to what it was to be part of a team as it was a bar. They drank beers and sang songs. They shared what stories they could about Fratty.

Then after a time, Holmes got serious. He pulled Walker aside, grabbed two beers, and took him down the beach a ways. They found a spot where only the surf and the stars could overhear. After Holmes opened the beers and passed one to Walker, he began.

"You might as well know that I knew your brother, Brian."

Walker stopped drinking and started to ask a question, but then paused, seeing the serious look in Holmes's eyes.

"In fact, not only did I know him, but I led the mission where he was killed."

Walker lowered his beer slowly. "Like Fratty? And Chong?"

Holmes shook his head. "Not like them at all. They died performing their mission."

The waves at night were a dark gray against an abysmal blue sky. Way out to sea, lights blinked from passing ships. The world seemed so large at moments like this, so improbably large. "So then how'd my brother die?"

"By disobeying orders."

Walker glared at Holmes. The beer had become acid in his stomach. "So it was his fault? That's convenient."

Holmes took a slug of his beer and stared out to sea. "Your brother made a choice, much like you did on the boat. I told him to stay put, but he didn't do it."

"What happened?"

"We were on the road, chasing down a Taliban operative, and your brother set off an IED."

"So where does the disobeying orders come in?"

"A group of kids was playing in the middle of the road. He was worried about them. We were in a natural ambush site. First he called to them, but they wouldn't come, so he went to them." Holmes took a final slug of his beer. "That's when the IED went off."

"Did he feel anything?"

"I doubt it. It was a very big bomb."

Walker didn't know what to say. He imagined his brother first trying to help the kids, then getting blown to bits. He took a slow sip of the acid in the bottle. Finally he asked, "Why didn't you tell me sooner?"

"It wasn't the right time."

"How come I feel like this is a lesson?"

Holmes turned to him. "Because everyone's death should mean something. I've seen too many SEALs die, too many of our soldiers and sailors, too many bad guys. I've breathed death for so long I don't know what life tastes like." He stared hard at Walker for a moment, then turned and strode away. Walker stood there for a good ten minutes not knowing what to think or say.

Laws arrived bringing several beers, clinking together in his hands. He placed them in the sand, then retrieved one, opened it, and slung it back. "So he finally told you."

Walker nodded. "You knew?"

"Yeah, I knew."

"You didn't say anything."

"It was his to tell you." He took another drink. "I would have told you eventually if he hadn't gotten around to it."

"I used to think my brother's death meant something," Walker said.

"Sometimes the death doesn't mean anything except in context for the living. I think your brother's death can help you understand the man. I didn't know him, but I know people who did and they all say he was a great SEAL and a terrific guy. He was a shepherd without a flock. I think he punished himself for not being able to take care of you and sought out avenues to take care of others."

"So you think he felt bad about leaving me behind?"

"Of course he did. Anyone would. But it sounds like he made the right decision. He would have been a terrible father figure when he was younger."

"According to Holmes, my brother died saving children."

Laws grinned as he drained another beer. He went over to the cooler, grabbed two more, brought them back, and passed one to Walker. "Listen, I've been around. I've seen death on four continents. There are three kinds of death in this world: those that we see coming and gladly embrace if it promotes the mission and/or saves lives; those we don't see coming but know that our actions are inventing the possibility; and finally, those that are an absolute surprise. The measure of a man is in how he travels the path towards the inevitability of any one of those deaths. Because death *is* certain. By the very nature of our mission, we place ourselves in the second category. Your brother did just that. Sure, he disobeyed an order, but most of us would have done the same. Children of any race, creed, or religion are the progeny of us all."

"Do you think that a part of him felt like he was doing something for me? Not for the *me I am now,* but for the *me I was when I went into the orphanage*?"

"Absolutely. He saw you in those kids. But that doesn't make it your fault. You can't control how someone else will act or deal with their own internal demons."

"I know. It's just that—"

"What?"

"I wish that I'd been able to tell him that I was never angry at him. That I loved him . . . that in my eyes, he was a great brother."

Laws shook his head. "Shit, man. Don't you think he knew it?"

"No. How could he?"

"Then all you can do is honor his actions and his name. Pay it back. Pay it forward. Remember that he saved those children and someday do the same."

"That's all I can do, isn't it?"

"That's all you can do."

Then they proceeded to get totally shitfaced.

30

SUBIC BAY. 1985.

The first time his father knew something was wrong was when he found Jackie in the closet covered in the entrails of a roadkill pig. Walker had only remembered the scene recently. It played across his mind like something he'd seen, not something he'd done. But the memory of the smell of the rotting entrails, blood, and offal, the stench of the puddle of vomit and urine that little Jackie lay within—it was so powerful it had to come from his own memories, however imperfectly they were set within his mind.

At first his father had stood there, one hand on the door, the other at his mouth. What he was seeing wasn't understandable, it wasn't explainable. There were no words that could have been used to describe the feelings of helplessness, outrage, and fear that played a devil's jig on his psyche as his youngest boy giggled with the voice of an old man.

"Halikan mo nga ako, Tay," it said. *Give us a kiss, Daddy.*

His father had slammed the door shut immediately, leaving

him in the darkness with his own insane giggles as he let the voices in his head take turns using his mouth.

"Why'd he do that?"

"You're an ass licker."

"Tatay?" Daddy.

"Fuck a duck."

"Ibalik mo sya." Make him come back.

"Suckie suckie on the rubber dubber duckie."

"Tay, parang awa mo na." Daddy please.

The door opened slowly, almost of its own will. Jackie's father was already backing away from the sight of his child, the lascivious look of hunger curving his little lips into something inhuman.

"Fuck a duck, Daddy. Fuck a duck."

It would take three months for the father to find a way to get his son back, and in saving him, he'd find his own demise.

31

KADWAN. TWO MONTHS EARLIER.

The shipment from Temple of Heaven Importers had arrived. He'd had a dozen men bring the thin, man-sized box into the room he'd spent the last six months preparing. The walls, ceiling, and floor bore the results of his creation. A single brazier mounted in each corner of the room provided a dull glow.

While he sat languidly in lotus position, becoming one with the room, the men placed the box in front of him and hurried out, their eyes flashing their naive fear. He waited for the scurry of their steps to diminish, then resumed listening to the screams that were just on the edge of hearing. The power and energy of the women's pain mixed inextricably with the swaths of their blood that he'd finger-painted upon the cold stone walls. He'd added the crushed petals of flowers to the mix, creating alternate pigments that breathed life into his work. So instead of a mere abattoir, he now had six planes of hand-painted hell, created through the agony of one hundred and fourteen women, three boys, seventeen men, and an elephant. What had once been a universal red had been transformed into an elegant multicolored creation of geometric slashes and curls, as if his artistic command of their lives had caused the blood to reshape into its own outraged intelligent designs.

With the mad screams of the dead loud in his ears, he opened the box before him. It took a while. The Chinese loved their knots and used them to keep both good and evil at bay. Finally he lifted the lid and stared at the thing that lay within the luxurious gold satin interior.

It glistened below him, telling the story of so many people who'd allowed their bodies to be colored. A tattoo of a snake here, a dragon there, a garish anchor with a naked Western woman next to the letters of someone's long-forgotten lover, and a hundred more, all stitched together with thread stolen from the mandala rugs of Tibetan monasteries.

Touching it with a trembling finger, he felt its paper-thin fragility. Yet no matter how fragile it seemed to him, to the other it would be like a suit of titanium Kevlar. The men and women who'd gone into the creation of this wonder would keep the creature from latching onto his soul. It would allow him to survive the channeling and give him power over the one who'd been speaking with him all these months.

Trust me, it had said.

But he knew better. The suit of tattooed skin would be his commentary on the being's desire to be trusted.

He unfolded his legs and stood tall. His angular shoulders and hips pressed against his rib-thin, naked brown body. His skin was a road map of self-discovery, crisscrossed with charts from thirty years of self-mutilation.

As he stepped into the suit of other people's skin, he was delighted to hear the screams grow louder.

32

GOLDEN BUDDHA. IMPERIAL BEACH. LUNCH.

Walker and Ruiz sat in the ratty vinyl booth comparing birth dates on the Chinese zodiac. They were dressed in loose-fitting cargo pants, Hi-Tec boots, T-shirts, and hoodies. The hoodies hid the 9mms in quick-draw shoulder holsters. Their cargo pockets were filled with magazines. Each also had an MK3 knife strapped to his left calf. Walker's T-shirt was from a restaurant in Salt Lake City called Steaks and Bitches, and had a prominent picture of a cowgirl with a steak on the end of a long fork. Ruiz wore an Old Navy shirt.

"You're a cock," Ruiz said.

"And you're a goat."

"But you're a cock." This time his smirk was in full force.

Walker shook his head. "It's a rooster."

"They're the same thing. 'Cockerel' is the term for a young male fowl. We call them cocks for short. 'Rooster' is the slang term for a mature male. They made you a cock. Not me. Anyway, don't blame me, blame the Chinese zodiac."

Walker stared at Ruiz as though he'd just answered a Double Jeopardy question as the young Chinese waitress delivered their hot tea and bowls of steaming hot and sour soup. Ruiz dug in right away. Walker waited until the waitress left, then reaffirmed, "I'm a rooster."

"Cock," Ruiz said in between slurping his soup.

Walker ate a few spoonfuls. The taste was heavy with mushrooms, the way he liked it, and only had a bit of bite. He usually evaluated a Chinese restaurant by their ability to make hot and sour soup. This one was pretty terrific. It was going to be sad at the end of the day when they were no longer able to make the soup. But that's what they deserved for housing a Snakehead sweatshop and way station in their basement, or so said the intelligence gleaned from the ship's hard drive. At first, SPG wasn't sure if it had any relevant information, but then one of the analysts began tracking the ship's route of travel based on navigational buoy beacon responses along the coast and discovered that the ship had been anchored off the coast within ten nautical miles of the restaurant. What turned out to be a gold mine was a deeply hidden file with latitudinals and longitudinal, each with notations using the word "Pifu," which translated roughly to "skin suit."

When they finished, the waitress brought two heaping serving dishes of twice-cooked pork and Mongolian beef, along with a large bowl of steaming white rice. As he had with the soup, Ruiz dug in right away.

"You're actually going to eat?" Walker asked.

"Sure, why not?"

Why not? Walker checked his watch. They were six minutes from making their move, that's why. He looked around the restaurant. Five other tables were occupied. Three of those were regular customers. One table held a heavyset, mean-as-a-Rottweiler NCIS agent named Alice Surrey, and at the other sat Laws and Yaya. Holmes was still waiting for the board. He was forced to stay back and keep Hoover company. While Laws was yammering away at one thing or another, Yaya looked miserable. Or at least his eyes did, because that's the only part of him that wasn't covered in black fabric. Being the newest member of the team and conveniently Middle Eastern, he was chosen to wear the burka. Not only did it lend some authenticity, but it allowed for a lot of fabric with which to hide the weapons he had secreted beneath.

"Y'all might as well eat," Ruiz said, barely intelligible around a bite of food.

"How can you eat at a time like this?"

"The food is good. Eat."

"You're a goat, all right."

"Just being practical. You're going to need the energy." Ruiz glanced around without moving his head. "Plus, you need to look like you're eating rather than sitting round scoping the place."

Walker picked at the pork with his chopsticks. He slid one piece into his mouth, aware that they only had three minutes. His increasingly heightened tension made it taste like clay, but to keep up appearances he chewed the piece of meat until it was macerated into a paste.

Finally it was time.

Yaya, dressed as a woman, got up at the same time as Surrey. They both made a beeline for the bathroom. Surrey was there first, but Yaya pushed her out of the way, entered the bathroom, and slammed the door behind him.

Surrey tried to open the door, but it was locked. She began to bang heartily on the hollow wooden door. "It was my turn!" She began shouting at the top of her lungs, "Get out!" Each protest was accompanied by a thump on the door.

The entire Chinese waitstaff came running, shocked and dismayed by the ugly American antics. One of them, a petite waitress, put her hand on Surrey's arm and was shoved away for her efforts. Meanwhile, Surrey had added *bitch* to her shouted mantra *Get out!*

By now, everyone was on their feet. One of the tables of real customers, a father, a mother, and two daughters couldn't take it anymore. They left, but not before the father threw a scalding look at the interior of the restaurant as he dropped a pile of bills to pay for their meal.

Laws acted the part of the confused husband as he approached the door. But instead of speaking English, he spoke Arabic, which confused the waitstaff and seemed to enrage Surrey.

Surrey whirled on Laws and threw a punch toward him. The waitstaff shrieked at this. Laws ducked aside, backing away with his hands out.

"You better run, Arab lover," Surrey growled.

The remaining customers took off without paying.

Ruiz and Walker approached the group surrounding the door. "Can I help?" Walker asked, turning on his boy-next-door charm for the Chinese to see.

Surrey gave him a smoldering look. "Sure, if you can get the towelhead out of the bathroom so I can cop a squat."

Those Chinese who spoke enough English to understand the vulgarity whispered harshly to the others. Two male cooks who'd been standing at the door came into the front room. One held a cleaver that looked as if it had been used in the Boxer Rebellion to decapitate British soldiers.

It was time. If the ICE and FBI agents reacted according to plan, the restaurant staff had been segregated from the Triad members in the subbasement. Communications had already been cut. A cell-phone jammer was positioned outside, as was an FBI QRF, in the event the cavalry needed to be called in. Walker hoped it didn't come to that. If it did, it meant that their mission had failed and one or all of them were dead.

The door to the bathroom opened wide. But instead of the burka-wearing Middle Eastern woman, Yaya stood there in full combat gear. He swept a Super 90 toward the waitstaff. MP5s and other gear hung from his shoulders and neck. Surrey pulled a Walther from her purse and pointed it at the waitstaff.

"Everyone outside," Laws said in both English and Chinese.

The waitstaff's eyes had gotten as large as soup bowls. They complied meekly, moving as a single multi-limbed mob out the front door.

The cook with the cleaver bolted. He only got as far as Ruiz, who caught him by the neck. He disarmed him and soon had him in a choke hold.

The other cook held up his hands, ducked, and hurried toward the front door.

Yaya passed MP5s to Laws and Surrey. Ruiz, having deposited the unconscious cook into one of the booths, grabbed his Super 90. From a bag, he passed around enough NVGs and MBITRs for the team and Surrey.

Walker had his 9mm in hand and was poised at the door to the kitchen.

Laws made a commo check. Everyone acknowledged, including the two ICE agents who were undercover delivering food and the FBI agent who'd been busily pretending to be a health inspector. What had begun as a hastily designed, multiagency mission the previous evening appeared to be coming off without a hitch. It had taken some doing for the FBI to relinquish operational control, which they'd initially insisted upon because of the presence of the threat on American soil. But a phone call from Senator Withers of the Sissy to the director of the FBI had ensured that cooperation would be forthcoming. All they asked was to be allowed to participate.

With the restaurant staff safely outside, Laws, Yaya, Walker, Ruiz, and Surrey moved into the kitchen.

Laws reached into the fortune-cookie box, broke one open, and read it over the MBITR. " 'You will soon be surrounded by good friends and laughter.' "

"In bed," Ruiz added.

"What's that?" Surrey asked.

"One of our departed brothers used to say that at the end of every fortune in a Chinese cookie you could add the words 'in bed' and they'd make perfect sense," Laws explained.

"Then it sounds like we have an auspicious beginning," Surrey said. "Can't wait until I'm surrounded by good friends and laughter."

"In bed," Ruiz added.

"In bed," Surrey corrected herself.

FBI agent Stephens waited in the basement along with the ICE agents. They wore black ballistic jackets with their agency affiliation in big white letters. Each of them held a 9mm. Although they had MBITRs, they weren't assigned NVGs. They seemed eager to get to the subbasement, but they weren't eager to walk into the mouth of a dragon, even if it was sleeping. That was something better done by SEAL Team 666.

It was believed that the subbasement had only one avenue of ingress and egress, the stairs down from the actual basement where the restaurant kept its stock of supplies. Under cover of the preceding night, a Special Warfare support team had used ground-penetrating radar, originally designed for demining operations, to try and detect any tunnels. They'd found none.

One of the strategies they'd discussed was to flood the subbasement with gas. Without knowing what sort of ventilation they had and without knowing who they had down there, the fear of accidentally asphyxiating innocents like the sweatshop seamstresses convinced everyone that this strategy wasn't the right one.

In the end, they decided to conduct a frontal assault. The power would be cut and they'd move in quick. They synced watches, then donned the NVGs. Ten seconds later, the power was out and SEAL Team 666 and Surrey spun up the green universe. They had about fifteen seconds before the backup generator kicked in.

Yaya was the first one down the stairs, with the rest of the team stacked behind him. The stairway opened directly into a large rectangular room filled with furniture and people. As soon as his aiming laser touched a Triad member, he let free two-round bursts. *PopPop! PopPop! PopPop! PopPop!* Four men went down hard.

Now in the room, the rest of the team fanned out behind him.

Laws's MP5 snapped, the sound like rapid-fire dog barks.

Walker tracked the action, but held fire, just as Surrey did.

Ruiz's Super 90 roared once.

When the lights snapped back on, they pushed the NVGs back on their heads.

One Triad enforcer was trying to get to his feet. Surrey shot him in the leg. Walker shot him in the head. When she looked questioningly at him, he said, "We're not here to arrest anyone."

She turned back toward the room, her face even more serious than it was before.

Eight enforcers lay dead on the floor. Several sets of tables took up the middle of the room. Couches hugged the walls, where posters of fancy cars were taped. Toward the rear of the room was a kitchenette with a microwave and a full-sized refrigerator. A steel door was in the back wall.

"Damn," Yaya said, straightening up. "I guess there goes the element of surprise."

Agent Stephens came down the stairs wearing his FBI jacket, three-hundred-dollar loafers, and wool pants. He had the clean features of a football player, a frat boy, or a serial killer. He wore yellow ballistic glasses. Behind him came the ICE agents in their own jackets. They went straight to the bodies and began checking for pulses.

Laws merely glanced at him before asking Ruiz, "Got something for that door?" He snapped a new clip into his submachine gun.

Ruiz cocked his head. "Not for the door—too thick—but look at what it's set in."

"That can't be drywall. Are they that stupid?"

"I've seen it before."

"Could be reinforced with MDF. They would almost have to in order to hold the weight of the steel."

"So can we go through the wall?"

"I can do that," Ruiz said.

Agent Stephens looked from one SEAL to the other. "Any word on how many we're facing?"

Laws shook his head. "Nada."

Agent Stephens shifted his expensive loafers. "I'm used to having more information."

"I feel your pain," Laws said. "This is more of a military op, but *posse comitatus* says you get to be here and supervise."

"Is that what you call my participation?" Agent Stephens laughed. "I just don't want to get in your way."

"Me neither," Laws admitted matter-of-factly. "Just follow our lead. We're going to do this the right way and take our time. We've already lost the element of surprise, so it's not like they don't know we're here."

Agent Stephens checked the chamber of his pistol and nodded.

"Right now, our Snakehead friends and their associates from the Temple of Heaven Importers don't know what they don't know. They don't know what happened to these guys. They just heard some gunshots. Even though they know someone is here, they don't know who, so we still hold an element of surprise."

"Are we sure anyone else is behind that door?" Agent Stephens asked.

"This is a Snakehead safe house. They're the preeminent human smugglers on the planet and have been doing it longer than America's been a country. You can tell by looking at it. Triad soldiers guarding it, here to protect the interests of whoever set this up. Behind that door is the rest of the safe house, which should be filled with either illegals or people they're moving into the U.S."

The ICE agents joined their group.

"Find any pocket trash?" Laws asked.

"Nothing specific. They were pretty sterile," said one.

"They were from Chinatown. San Francisco," the other ICE agent said. "Tattoos identified them as Temple of Heaven forty-niners. We're definitely on the right track."

Laws nodded toward the door. "Ruiz, you good?"

Ruiz had been busy attaching det cord in an upside-down L shape. What looked like a cooking timer was affixed to the wall beside it.

"How far below the surface are we?" Walker asked.

"About fifteen feet," Yaya answered.

"See how the floor slopes towards the door?" he said, pointing out a pool of blood that seemed to be sliding away from one of the bodies.

"What about it?"

"I'm wondering how deep this might go. I doubt the GPR can see more than ten or fifteen feet into the ground. They might have a way out."

Walker glanced at the blood and watched as it slid with gravity. "Good catch. Be ready then."

"This could be an old pirate hideout," Surrey said, walking up to them as she adjusted her body armor. It was more than snug around her waist and bosom and seemed to be cutting off circulation.

"As in sunken treasure?" Ruiz asked.

"As in sunken treasure," she repeated. "They've found hideouts like this from back in the eighteen hundreds."

Laws eyed the explosives that were ready to blow. "What does it mean if this is an old pirate hideout—what should we expect?"

"None of this," she said, waving her hand toward the walls

and the ceilings. "Although they could have improved upon it, I doubt they would. I'd expect a cave, with maybe a concrete or wooden floor. They've probably since blocked out the ocean, but if I was them I'd have left some method to get in and out secretly. That would allow someone to anchor a boat offshore and come inside without ever having to surface."

"A drug runner's dream," the FBI agent said.

"Or a human smuggler's dream," added one of the ICE agents.

"Okay then. So expect an unconventional space on the other side of that door," Laws said. He pointed to the older of the two ICE agents. "You stay here and guard our six. The rest of you follow behind. We're going to go in hot. There are probably innocents down with the beegees, so show some fire discipline." He went to turn, then thought of one more thing. "And don't any of you get so excited you shoot one of us in the back."

Yaya and Walker stood next to each other, ten feet from the steel door. Ruiz leaned his back against it. Laws stood off at an angle to the det cord that would allow him to immediately see inside the room. When everyone appeared ready, he nodded to Ruiz.

Five seconds later an explosion halfway between a rip and a bang peeled back the wall from beside the door. A dull red light emanated from the other side, but no one had a chance to check it out because they came under immediate fire.

Bullets bit into the table and counter in the kitchenette, sending chunks of Formica and pressboard popping into the air. The ICE agents and Agent Stephens ducked, but Surrey and the SEALs let the bullets fly. Finally the barrage subsided.

Walker started to approach the opening and felt the now-familiar buzz of electricity. With each step, it got stronger and stronger. By the time he was halfway to the hole, he was completely frozen. His legs quivered, but wouldn't move. He held the 9mm at the end of paralyzed arms. Even his teeth vibrated. Had this been in the middle of a firefight, he'd have been full of holes.

"You okay?" Laws asked, heading to the same destination. But when he saw the fear in Walker's eyes, he stopped and turned back. "Walker?"

It was as if the electric hum had invaded his bones.

Laws grabbed him by the shoulders and shook him hard. "Is it the feeling? Is there something in the room?"

Walker tried to answer, but he lacked the capacity to move his mouth.

Laws smacked him across the face.

Walker felt some of the buzz decrease. "More," he managed to say through clenched teeth.

"What the hell is going on?" Agent Stephens asked. "Is the boy scared?"

Laws shot a heated look at the agent, and the man shut up. Then Laws turned his attention back to Walker. "Here goes. Sorry, bud," he said, then he hit Walker four times in a row with the flat of his hand.

On the fourth blow, it was as if he'd been released. Walker sagged, almost falling to his knees.

Laws helped him so that the metal door was between them and the other side.

"Jesus hell!" Walker finally managed.

"Looks like his spooky meter is turned all the way up," Ruiz said.

"Walker? You okay?" Laws asked.

Walker really didn't know. Was he? He didn't feel anything now. He nodded and rubbed the side of his face. "Yeah. I'm good now."

Walker slid to the right of the door. He spooled a cable from his cargo pocket, screwed it into a transmitter, and slid it around the corner. He held it in place with his left hand, pulled out a tablet, and turned it on. It took about thirty seconds, during which time Walker stuck his pistol around the corner and fired several times. It felt good to do something, especially since there was a moment there when he was afraid he wasn't going to be able to do anything . . . ever again.

When the tablet was finally synced with the sniffer, Walker and Laws took in the fish-eye image of the other room. Walker was taken aback. At first it looked as if the ceiling was dripping blood. But the resolution and the focus came and went as the sniffer tried to adjust the picture for the low red light. What looked like blood on closer inspection appeared to be long red ChemLights, dangling from the rough-hewn ceiling of the room. He'd used ChemLights since he'd been in the Navy but he'd never seen them used by anyone outside the service, except maybe at raves. To see the cylindrical plastic tubes that when broken emit a colored light here in a pirates' cave infested with Triad enforcers made the event seem surreal. Then, when he saw the skittering of a small orange figure, it went from surreal to grotesque.

"Homunculus," he said.

"I figured one would be here," Laws said.

Walker saw several more orange blurs. "I'd say there's more than one. We might be in trouble." The image of a gang of demonic Stretch Armstrongs slinging themselves from the top rope of his imagination like whacked-out serial-killer midget professional wrestlers wrenched his vision back to his compatriots. He knew this wasn't going to end well.

33

IMPERIAL BEACH. PIRATES' CAVE.

A heavy stench of unwashed bodies and saltwater rot filled the air. The room was more or less what Surrey had prepared them for. It had been water-carved from the rock, which even now wept moisture. The ground was concrete, but had been covered with so much dirt and detritus that it was a mottling of grunge atop the concrete gray. There'd been rows of cots along one wall that had been hastily shoved to the back of the room. The strangest thing about their view into the room was that they didn't see anyone. Walker couldn't even make out the homunculus that he'd spotted just a few seconds ago, which meant that there must be more to the room than they were seeing.

Laws saw it first. "Look. See the darkness there . . . and there."

Walker discerned it the moment Laws pointed it out. Twin ovals of darkness in the far wall that could be cave openings, large recesses, or deeper caverns. But seeing into either of them was impossible. Then he had an idea.

"Wait for me," he whispered. Then he stood, grabbed a broken chair leg, and began to hammer at the overhead lights. The ICE agents, Agent Stephens, and Surrey covered their heads and moved out of the way.

Soon they were in darkness, the only light leaking from the door at the top of the stairs and the red ChemLights dangling in the other room. It would have to do.

"Laws, ever play video games?" Walker asked. The view of the room and the cave openings was considerably lighter, but he still couldn't make out any figures.

"Uh, yeah. Does Super Mario Brothers count?"

"Dude. My mother plays that," Yaya said.

"Do you listen to Tears for Fears too?" Ruiz stage-whispered.

"Does Spandau Ballet count?"

"For God's sake," Walker laughed softly. "Then you get to take the MP5. Activate your laser targeter; I got an idea."

Laws handed the tablet to Walker, who immediately switched it to infrared. On the tablet screen, the walls of the room turned purple. The edges of the cave openings turned yellow, sliding through the spectrum toward a dark green, then went to black. Shapes appeared as mottled orange and red. Where there were none before, Walker now counted six. They seemed to be huddled behind darker objects, which by their shapes could have been boxes, televisions, or engine blocks . . . anything as long as it was square.

"Laws, see if you can aim the MP5 into the room."

"I can't see what I'm aiming at."

"But I can. Just aim and I'll adjust your fire. You're my joystick."

Ruiz snickered over the MBITR.

Laws did as he was told, angling the weapon awkwardly so that he couldn't see where he was aiming. Suddenly a line of raw red laser energy pierced the infrared darkness, spearing a dark wall toward the rear of the room.

"Shift aim left, slowly track until I say stop."

Walker watched the screen as the line of light shifted from the wall toward one of the openings containing several orange-hued figures.

"Down a little. There. Continue left. And . . . there! Stop. Two rounds."

Laws double-tapped.

A figure on the screen went flying backwards and disappeared from view.

"Left again. Stop. Fire."

Another dropped from view.

He spied a head poking around a corner, the red and orange orb obvious against the cold rock.

"Up. Left. Up. No down. Left a hair more. Nice. Fire."

The head evaporated in a spray of red and orange.

Suddenly the people in the other cavity opened fire, the flashes momentarily blinding both the sensors and Walker.

Laws pulled back just in the nick of time as the remainder of the counter evaporated in a hungry hail of bullets.

Walker switched back to real vision just in time to see gunfire emanating from behind the stack of cots. There was probably a third opening behind that one, from which more Triad enforcers were firing.

The firing subsided. Walker was about to tell Laws to return to his position when he felt a tug on the tablet. He paused, not knowing what was going on. Then he felt a harder tug, then a jerk, as if he were fishing and had a lunker on the end of the line. He gripped the tablet with both hands and pulled back, leaning with his weight to help. It came with him, and on the end, gripping the sniffer with both hands, was a homunculus.

The orange creature's eyes narrowed. It spit at him, and the liquid burned as it touched his cheek. Then the creature growled, adjusted its grip, and pulled so hard that Walker fell forward on his face. He tried to hold on, but his position didn't allow it.

Their technological superiority had just disappeared. He heard a chorus of growls coming from the other room.

"Wha—what is that?" asked the younger of the ICE agents.

"I lost the sniffer, boss," Walker said.

"You lost it? How?"

As Walker heard the growls, he got to his feet. "Draw your knives," he said, as if he were a Civil War general commanding his men to fix bayonets. The quarters was too close for ranged weapons. "They're coming." He drew his knife and shoved his pistol in his shoulder holster.

"What's coming?" the FBI agent asked.

"Homunculi," he muttered. "Fucking Freddy Krueger Chucky Doll Stretch Armstrongs all rolled into one, so your ass better be ready."

"Backs to the walls," Laws commanded.

Walker thought that was a great idea. With his back now to the steel door, he stood beside Ruiz.

The growls were becoming louder. They could hear an unidentifiable shuffling from the next room.

Ruiz cursed. "Cemetery Ridge," he whispered.

Walker recognized the reference. They'd all had the same classes in BUD/S. The West Virginian was talking about none other than Pickett's Charge—fifteen thousand men charging the defenses of Cemetery Ridge in Gettysburg. He'd always wondered how those men on the ridge felt seeing the force advance across the field toward them. He didn't have to wonder anymore.

"Fuck. NVGs," Laws yelled just as the creatures from the other room began to scream like howler monkeys.

Walker powered up his NVGs. Within seconds, the room was a placid green. A moment later that green was spoiled by a dozen scrambling figures with impossibly long arms.

Ruiz, Yaya, and Walker were in the best positions, with their backs against the walls. The wave of homunculi swept past them and onto the four agents who'd tagged along. Four beasts attacked each person, ripping and wrenching with claws, biting and jerking and pulling. The room was filled with human and demon screams, one in agony and the other in ecstasy.

The SEALs waded in.

Walker found himself assisting Agent Stephens, who had a homunculus attached to his face, chewing furiously at his nose. He grabbed the back of the beast and was astonished at its weight. Although it looked like a doll, it weighed as much as a pit bull. He stabbed it sideways with his knife, skewering it through the back.

It let out a shriek unlike any other sound it had made so far; then it died. His knife must have pierced whatever the damn thing had as a heart. But the shriek hadn't gone unheard. The other homunculi attacking Agent Stephens shifted their attention to Walker.

Out of the corner of his eyes he saw Agent Stephens fleeing back up the stairs. Walker backed away, waving his arms and kicking his feet in a furious imitation of the spiderweb dance.

But still they came on. One latched onto each of his legs while another leaped toward him.

Walker brought his knife up more in panic than skill and managed to skewer his second long-armed imp. He grabbed it by one of its arms and ripped it free from the blade. Then he used its body to hammer first at the beast on his left leg, then the one on his right. He stunned the one on his right and sent it flying with a kick. The one on his left leg still clung to his thigh, staring one-eyed up at him with a furious grimace on its ugly mug.

Kneeling, Walker let go of the dead homunculus, wrapped his left hand around the living one's neck, and peeled him off. His leg was bleeding from a dozen wounds, but there was nothing to be done about that now.

The orange creature spat on his hand, making the skin pop and sizzle, but Walker still held on. He brought his arm up, then down as hard as he could, slapping the beast into the ground over and over and over until it felt like nothing more than a sack of wet bones.

Once it was past dead, he tossed it aside and stood. He was breathing heavily. Sweat poured down his brow. He surveyed the living. Surrey was fine. The older ICE agent was fine. The younger ICE agent was on the ground, facedown.

Walker ran to him, knelt, and checked for a pulse—nothing.

That left the FBI agent. Last time he'd seen him, he was running for the stairs.

Walker spied his supine figure on the stairs. Atop it sat two homunculi. At first they seemed to be just sitting, but on closer look they were . . . eating.

"Aw hell," he said, over his MBITR. "Two left."

Walker reached down and grabbed a piece of wood, then advanced on the stairs. He was able to coldcock the one nearest him with a *thwack* on the back of the head. The other leaped free, dragging what could only be part of the agent's intestine behind him before dropping it. Then it rappelled down the stairs and onto the floor. It sped across the floor toward the pirates' cave, winding through legs, and leaping debris. Everyone tried to hit it or kick it, but it was just too fast. Just as it seemed as if it was going to make it to the relative freedom of the cave, a knife impaled it into the drywall.

Ruiz stepped carefully over the debris, ripped his knife free, cleaned it on the fabric of his pants, then replaced it into its sheath.

"Okay boys," Laws said, his breath coming heavy over the MBITR. "Everyone scream, this time as loud as you can."

"What?" Yaya asked.

"Just do it."

It took a moment, but finally everyone figured it out. Screams went up from six mouths, then howls, grunts, shrieks of pain and fear, as if they were being eaten alive by the homunculi. The clamor lasted for twenty seconds, then died to nothing.

All they heard was their own breathing as they stood and waited for their next command.

When it came, they were ready.

"Fucking charge," Laws whispered.

Yaya went through the hole in the wall first. Moving in a

combat crouch, he sped toward the back of the cave, double-tapping until his magazine was empty.

Behind him came Laws, then Ruiz.

Laws did the same and didn't spare any ammo.

Ruiz posted between the first and second caverns.

Walker came in with a bead on the first cavern.

On three, Laws and Ruiz took the middle; Yaya fired through the cot-built barricade and took the first.

Six enforcers were already in heaps along the floor. A single Hispanic woman, her mouth stitched, tears pouring from her eyes, stood in the far corner. Beside her, stretched on a bone-made frame, was a fully finished tattoo skin.

Walker put his hand on the back of her head and pulled her down gently but firmly. *"Tranquilo. Silencio.* Shhh," he whispered as he scoped the rest of the cavern. It only went back about thirty feet. The walls glistened with dampness. Green moss carpeted them in differing layers. The woman stared at Walker, the red ChemLights reflected in her eyes. He smelled the sea, urine, and the unmistakable coppery scent of blood.

He dragged the woman behind him and met Surrey at the entrance to the cave. He passed the woman off, then turned to help Yaya, who took two in the chest as he was running toward Walker. The first one punched him back, the second one knocked him down.

Walker had no time to check the other SEAL. He scrambled back to the cot barricade in time to see daylight from the end of the cavern. Even as he watched, a man was sliding into a circular hole in the floor. Walker fired. He caught the figure in the back, but the man kept going.

With the light streaming from the opening, his NVGs were no good. He slung them away and began to pull the cots down as fast as he could. He finally got enough of them out of the way to rush in. Four more enforcers lay dead, as was a woman. He checked the hole and found it was an access to a culvert that drained into the ocean. There was no sign of the man.

Walker jerked his head out of the hole and checked the woman. He could tell without touching her that she was dead. He slammed his back against the wall and held in place. Her eyes stared at him accusingly and seemed to ask, *Why me?* She'd been ripped open from chin to pelvis in a ragged cut. Her insides had all but slid free. Next to her lay the same bone-made rack, but in this case, the suit was missing. If only she'd been in the first cavern, she'd still be alive. Whatever fate put her here had something else in mind for her.

Within moments, Laws was calling the all-clear. Three more enforcers had been killed in the middle cavern, but the woman who was with them was unharmed except for the stitches in her lips.

Yaya rejoined them, grinning sheepishly as he knocked on his body armor. He'd be bruised, but he was alive.

There were two enforcers left alive. Both had been shot, one through the gut, the other through the chest. Neither would survive long without medical attention and they both knew it. So when Laws began to talk to both of them where they lay against a cavern wall, it was interesting to see their reactions. While the one on the left, a scar beneath his left eye, seemed relieved at the opportunity, the one on the right, who had a snake tattooed on his bald head, wanted nothing to do with answering questions. And when he realized that his fellow enforcer was going to answer, he tried to reach his hand into the other man's stomach and hurry the man's death along.

Ruiz grabbed him and pressed him to the floor with a boot on top of his wounded chest. "You should just leave that other bad Chinese man alone and let him talk," Ruiz said, with all the aplomb of one man talking to another as if they were on a main street waiting on a bus.

Walker paused to watch Laws in action, but soon tired of it. Unlike the previous interrogation, Laws wasn't taking the time to translate into English, so Walker had no idea what was going on. He moved on to the surviving women. Surrey had checked them and reported that they were unharmed, except for the stitching.

The ICE agent and Surrey helped the women out, then returned with reinforcements from outside, now that Laws had cleared the scene. Men came in disguised as a hazardous-materials team dressed in orange rubber suits with square enclosed headgear. They first disposed of the homunculi, cutting them into pieces and slipping them into double-thick black bags. Once they took those away, they returned with stretchers.

By then Laws had finished his interrogation.

Now that their part of the mission was over it was time to leave. Because the events were something that had surely garnered the attention of the local media, they'd planned for an anonymous extraction. One by one, the SEALs removed all of their military gear, lay on stretchers, and were carried out, a sheet over each of them. They exited into a triage canopy, which had ambulances pulled to the back. Two SEALs per ambulance, then it was taking off. The last thing Walker heard was a man bellowing through a loudspeaker about a gas leak and how everyone should stay away. Once they'd gone a block, the SEALs removed the sheets and sat up. But that was as far as they got. Corpsmen from the USS *George Washington* cleaned their cuts and scrapes and gave them IVs. But instead of heading to a hospital, they drove straight to the Mosh Pit.

34

THE MOSH PIT. MORNING.

Five o'clock came earlier than it should have. Upon their return from the mission yesterday afternoon, they'd had a mandatory debrief. This time it was Holmes who conducted it. He'd been cleared by the board and was his own stern self, acting as if nothing had ever happened, critical of each step of the mission. When he learned that they'd wasted time with the sniffer when they probably could have gotten the same result from the NVGs, he was initially angry. But as he railed against it, he conceded that the video-game solution Walker had devised had most likely saved the SEALs from being wounded. This concession surprised not only Walker, but Ruiz as well, who elbowed him in the ribs when Holmes wasn't looking.

When they got to the details surrounding the tattooed skin suits and the women, Ruiz interrupted. "They were using the women for sacrifices, weren't they?"

Holmes considered it. "It looks like it. Not sure how it works, but blood magic generally imbues a person or thing with the strength of the giver." Seeing Yaya's incredulous expression,

Holmes added, "Not the physical strength per se, but the spiritual strength."

Yaya had been silent through the entire debrief, but now he finally spoke. "I hear you talking, boss, and I understand the words, but I don't understand how they go together. Blood. Magic. Sacrifice. Homunculi. I mean W-T-F, over."

Walker offered Yaya a friendly smile. "I was sitting in your place just the other day saying the same sorts of things. Crazy, ain't it? And it's only going to get better from here."

"The suits worry me," Laws said.

Ruiz turned to Laws. "How so?"

"I get their use. It's a sort of blood magic used to create some sort of spiritual shield. The suit will protect the wearer. Looks like the same guy who owned the ship we took down ordered one." Laws, who had been staring at the floor the entire time, looked up. "So why all the other suits? Are they making an army?"

"Even *one* skin suit is bad news. Whether they're being made for an army, or the leaders of the world's organized crime, it suggests a broader knowledge of the supernatural and a desire to tap into it. Our job isn't going to get any easier anytime soon."

Holmes let the words sink in for a few moments. Then he crossed his arms and gave his full attention to the newest SEAL. "Think you'll be able to hack it?"

The other SEALs turned to Yaya as well, curious to hear his response.

"Oh, I can hack it, all right. It's just going to take some getting used to."

Holmes shifted his gaze to Walker. "And what about you, Walker? I heard you had another episode."

Walker felt the heat of embarrassment. He'd been trying to keep it in the back of his mind. Trying to think it never happened had been working so well until now. "I'm fine," he said.

"What I heard is that you were a deer in the headlights and

couldn't have moved if there was a train coming. Is that about right?"

Walker nodded. He licked lips that had suddenly gone dry. "That's about right."

"What are we going to do about it?"

Jack felt blood rush to his face. "I don't know. Why not ask Ms. Billings? I was her idea, remember?"

"Easy, Jack," Laws said.

"Hey, I didn't ask for this gig. I was asked *for.* This"—he was at a loss for words—"shit that happens to me is beyond my control. I don't want it to happen ever again, but I know it will and it scares the fuck out of me to think of what kind of danger I might put you guys in." Walker found that he was almost standing by the time he finished. He sat back hard in his chair, his eyes flashing with anger.

Everyone stared at him. Holmes was the first to speak. "You better hurry up and figure out a way to control it, then." Holmes uncrossed his arms and stepped up to the conference table. "Tomorrow morning we have a mission brief. Everyone needs to be ready."

They broke up after that. Although Fratty's room had been cleared, Yaya was still unwilling to move in. Instead, he pushed his bags into a corner of the immense room and claimed one of the couches as his own.

Later they ordered Chinese food, only afterward laughing at the irony of it. A few beers in their guts, then each of them made their way to bed.

The next morning, Walker forced himself out of bed at five. After a quick run on the beach and a breakfast of yogurt, juice, and a hard-boiled egg, Walker joined the others in the conference room. He'd tried to arrange a meeting with Jen last night, but she'd been busy. When he entered the conference room, she was taping several pictures to a board. She wore a knee-length dark blue skirt with a white blouse. He couldn't help but smile as he watched her work. Then he noticed Holmes staring at him with the same stern expression he gave to beegees or a Girl Scout selling cookies.

Walker went to his seat and sat. Everyone was there except Ruiz, who came in last, carrying a breakfast burrito the size of a Yule log.

When Jen finally turned, she gave Walker a quick wink that was lost to no one. He tried to use his tunnel vision, but he couldn't help but see Yaya, Ruiz, and Laws all winking dramatically at him. What almost shocked him senseless was when Holmes did the same. As subtle as it was, it was more extravagant because the man seemed to never joke around. Ever.

"Let's get started," Jen said.

Other than Jen and the members of SEAL Team 666 there were two other members of SPG—a young man who looked like he knew every episode of *Star Trek: The Next Generation* and a young woman who could have been either a candy striper or a porn star. Billings sat in back.

"I've brought along Peter Musso and Liz Lake. Peter's a specialist on the culture and geography of Southeast Asia, where you all will be going. Liz is new to our office. I brought her along to show her how these things are run."

"If y'all need a private tour, I'm sure that I can provide one," Ruiz said, true love in his eyes as he addressed the new girl.

"Chum in the water," muttered Laws.

The girl blushed and turned away. But the young man seemed more than pleased and grinned from ear to ear, as if he was hoping that he could get the same invitation extended to him.

"Let's get on with it," Holmes said, as if he were being forced to sit amid a room of fourteen-year-olds.

"Okay," Jen said. "First let's discuss the telemetry information we got from the hard drive you brought from Macau. There were two significant findings. One was the GPS history of the ship. It originated in Rangoon and is owned by an export company with nineteen other ships. Now that we have their international identification codes, we can track them once they pass near any of our subsurface tracking buoys. Until then, we believe they're still in their home-station harbor."

"Why don't we know this for certain?" Holmes asked. "Where's their harbor?"

Jen turned to the SEAL team leader. "Yangon. You would have known it as Rangoon, Burma. The country is now called Myanmar. As far as why we aren't sure? That directly relates to a lack of assets in the area. We can't do a physical eyes-on, so we've requested an NRO overflight, but right now all satellites are operationally deployed to support CENTCOM in Afghanistan-Pakistan. We're expecting a pass tomorrow morning. At that point we'll know for certain."

Walker thought about the creature they'd encountered in the hold of the old cargo ship. They'd lost Fratty and if it hadn't been for them rocking and rolling the ammo until they were all but dry, it would have had them, too. Put that beast inside of a mall or on a busy downtown street and it would end in a bloodbath. The enforcer in San Francisco had alluded to a threat to America. If the threat had to do with the chimeras aboard twenty ships sailing to America, then people would be dead in the streets from Los Angeles to New York.

As if reading his mind, Jen continued. "If each one of the ships has the same sort of crates as the first one, and we truly are the target, then our red, white, and blue is in trouble. The CDC assisted us in projection modeling, and if each of these ships has fifty creatures, and if each one lands in a different port, there's a seventy-six-percent chance that it could be the end of life as we know it within the continental United States. Based on your observations, we think we know how they transform from stone to flesh, but there's too much missing data. Some of the variables are that we don't know how they're controlled, we don't know how much they can eat, and we don't understand how they can metabolize their energy."

"Frankly, we don't need to find this out," Billings said from her place at the back of the room. "We'd prefer that the ships on this manifest be destroyed in place. Wherever they are. Regardless."

"That's clear," Holmes said. "We'll wait for reconnaissance, then launch."

"Can I get a printout of all the documents?" Laws asked. "I'd like to check and see if there are any clues you missed."

Musso's eyes narrowed. He frowned as he said, "It's in Chinese."

Laws just looked at him. "That's okay. I know Chinese."

"Which dialects?"

"All of them . . . basically. But that doesn't matter with the characters, now, does it?"

"We'll get them to you right after the meeting," Jen said, shaking her head subtly at her assistant.

Musso stood and made his way to the front. He gave Laws a wary eye. "All of them?" he asked again.

"Yep," Laws responded. "I also speak Spanish, Italian, French, and half a dozen other languages."

This gave Musso pause. Finally he turned to a map that had been taped to the wall. "Myanmar. It used to be Burma, but that was a colonial derivation of colloquialization of *Bamer,* which is the written word for the country. Rangoon is now called Yangon. Basically, all the names have changed."

"What's their military like?" Holmes asked.

"They've been embargoed since 1990, but still get support from rogue nation-states such as North Korea and Syria. Previously, they received support from Equatorial Guinea and Libya, but with the advent of the Arab Spring, we believe that these relationships will be changing, if they haven't already."

Walker found himself staring at Jen, who'd taken a position beside Musso. She was leaning against the wall. With three-inch heels, her legs seemed to go on for days. This evening they had plans. Dinner in the Gaslamp Quarter and maybe dancing at one of the clubs catering to upscale tourists. He could almost feel her in his hands.

He felt someone kick him under the table.

He returned his attention to the briefing. Musso was saying something about someone named Karen, or something like that. He listened dutifully for a moment, then noticed the way Jen had her hair pulled back and how a few stubborn strands fell across her eyes.

35

FORT ROSECRANS NATIONAL CEMETERY.

Zagat-rated translated to freaking expensive. They ate at Monsoon Indian Restaurant in the Gaslamp Quarter of San Diego. Lemon chicken, roghan josh, and fish were piled high on their table. After a bottle of wine, the curries and gingers and Far East spices mingled admirably in their palate. Walker was thankful he didn't ordinarily have enough time to spend his money. The cost of that meal was nearly a week's pay, but the satisfaction of being fed and pampered reflected in Jen's eyes made it all worth it.

When they were done, they walked around the Gaslamp Quarter for a while. She wore an orange silk summer dress. He wore tan slacks with a purple Polo. As nice as the cobbled streets and retro-old feel were in the Gaslamp, it soon wore on him. It was like any other shopping district in the world, just polished to a gleaming faux-Victorian shine.

Soon they were in Jen's Corvette, cruising over to Point Loma and Fort Rosecrans National Cemetery. "This is what it's all about. This is why we're here. These people here," he said, pointing to the geometrically straight rows of white stones, "are the reason I go out and fight."

"So it's the dead who inspire you to help the living?"

"Maybe." They were walking hand in hand between the rows. A gentle offshore breeze spun the bottom of her dress and made her hug close to him. "Or maybe it's my deep regard for their service and for their sacrifice. Most of those people on the street don't know what sacrifice is. Going without television? One less trip to the gym? One less Happy Meal for their kid? Every one of these men and women put their life on the line at one time or another. Many of them sacrificed that life so we could go into a nice restaurant and eat mahi mahi with ginger and coconut."

"It was good mahi mahi with ginger and coconut. Thank you, sailor, for making the sacrifice for me," she purred into his ear.

He couldn't help smiling. He knew she understood him. This was just how she acted when she was feeling satisfied. So why wasn't he acting the same way? It was because his satisfaction manifested in the need to serve. He was convinced it was part of his DNA.

"Do you always take your dates to cemeteries?" she asked after a while.

"Only those who matter."

"Oh!" She stopped and placed both hands on hips. "And why am I just now mattering?"

"You've mattered to me for some time now. With SEAL training and my new command, I've been—" He stopped as he saw her shoulders shaking in silent laughter. "You're messing with me."

"I only mess with boys who matter."

They walked for a time, then stopped at a granite memorial to the USS *Wasp.*

"This was an aircraft carrier in World War Two. It was sunk by Japanese torpedoes supporting Guadalcanal on March 19,

1945." His finger traced the list of Killed in Action, then stopped. "This was my grandfather. He was an electrician's mate, second class. He and a hundred and ninety-three men went down that day."

"You never knew him," she said, reaching out to touch his hand.

"But I grew up with stories about him."

"Your father was in the Navy, too, wasn't he?"

"It's sort of a family tradition. My brother was in as well."

"Are they buried here?" she asked softly.

"My brother is buried in Manila, in Manila American Cemetery. He got special dispensation because my grandfather is buried there, too."

"This grandfather?" she pointed to the name on the plaque.

"The same."

"Why not by your father?"

"Because no one except the men who killed him knows where he is."

She remained silent for a moment, then asked in an almost imperceptible voice, "Then how do you know he's dead?"

"I don't, I guess. But they sent his hands to Fleet Headquarters along with a box of black butterflies." Jen's eyes shot wide and her jaw dropped. Jack continued. "The package was traced through military mail channels to Corregidor. My father was a supply chief. He made a lot of money dealing with the Filipino black market. Navy HQ believes that he finally crossed the wrong person."

It took a moment for her to speak. "That's when you and your brother were sent to the orphanage."

"Only me. My brother joined the Navy. Got an old friend of my grandfather's to get him in when he was sixteen."

"Which left you all alone."

A sparkling slice of empathy for the child he'd been on that dark day he'd first been sent to the orphanage jabbed through his thoughts. He'd never been more alone in his entire life.

"Come on," he said, grabbing her hand and pulling her away as if he could flee the memory. "I want to show you something."

They walked amid the darkness between the stones. Their way was lit only by the intermittent lights shining on the monuments and the lights of San Diego. After a brisk ten-minute walk, they arrived at a stone that also had the symbol of the Congressional Medal of Honor.

"This was the first SEAL I ever heard about by name."

Michael Anthony Monsoor. Died September 29, 2006.

"A grenade was tossed onto a rooftop where he and others were operating. He threw himself on the grenade and saved the others. He was awarded the Congressional Medal of Honor. He was from Class 250." He turned to Jen. "This is who I fight for."

Jen nodded. She held on to his arm with both hands and hugged herself to him.

"My brother died a hero, too," he said after a long pause. "Or so I always thought. Turns out he died because he wasn't following orders . . . using his heart, not his head." He turned to her. "I had it out with Holmes the other night. He told me what happened. It was an IED. One minute my brother was walking along the side of the road, the next he was trying to get some kids to stop playing in the street. Then the bomb went off."

"Were any of the kids hurt?"

"No. He saved them."

"Then he was a hero."

"Holmes said that he ordered Brian to stay in place. He told Brian not to go to the kids."

"So he disobeyed an order to save the kids. So what? You say you fight for the dead. Looks like your brother was fighting for the living." She touched his chest. "You said he was using his heart and not his head like that's a bad thing. You have a good heart, just like your brother. I hope that when the time comes, you go with your heart."

"Even if it kills me?"

"Could you live with the alternative?"

"No," he said, shaking his head. "I couldn't."

"Sounds like you knew it all along."

"It's funny. I think I took my brother's death harder than my father's. In some ways, he was more of a father to me than our father was. He used to send me letters every month. Then when he was able, he made sure I was adopted."

"How did he make sure?"

"He found a family who was looking for an older son. They'd lost their child in a car accident."

"So you were their . . ."

"Replacement kid. Yeah. I know. But we needed each other."

"Do you still talk to them?"

"At Christmas and birthdays I call them. They're good people."

She rubbed his arm. "You know, we've been dating for almost a year and this is the first time you've talked to me about your family."

"Might have been sooner if we'd had a moment to breathe."

She nodded, but the look on her face showed her doubt. They headed back to the car. The wind had picked up and she shivered against him. "Do you know what my favorite memorial is?"

"No. What is it?"

"The Homecoming statue. Not a memorial really, but it's one that has been copied all over the U.S."

"I've seen it." It was a statue of a sailor returning home from a long time away. He's holding his wife in his arms and his son is hugging him from behind.

"So you know what it represents, right?"

"No . . . what?"

"The living. Those people the sailor went out and fought for."

Walker couldn't help but grin. "You really want me to change my opinion, don't you?"

"I do. I think it's dangerous to fight for an ideal you can't see. I think it's dangerous to fight to impress the dead."

"That's a little bit of an oversimplification, I think."

"Is it? I just want you to know that when you leave for wherever you're going on this mission you'll have someone to come back to besides a few old graves and a statue."

"Is that so?"

Weaving through the stones, they came back to the parking lot from a different angle. Hers was the last car. She went to the passenger door. He opened it for her and let her slide in. He closed the door, and as he walked around the back of her car, he noted that something had changed in their relationship. He'd never told anyone else about his family, especially his father. Which only left one secret, and that one he wasn't about to tell her or anyone other than the members of his team. At least they had a frame of reference.

36

SUBIC BAY. 1985.

Little Jackie waited in the pile of trash. The liquid from banana skins, coffee grounds, and rain-soaked rags seeped through his clothes, making him shiver. His teeth chattered. Beneath the soft skin of his bare chest he felt what could have been gravel. A piece of rubber he'd seen thrown away by the hookers on Llollo Street in Barrio Barretto rested like a deflated sausage two inches from his nose. A wasp crawled inside, causing the skin of it to wriggle and jump. He felt rats crossing the backs of his legs. When they sniffed at his skin, he fought the urge to jerk as their whiskers tickled the soft underskin of his knees.

Feral.

Like a pig.

Or a dog.

He was wild and eager to gnaw on something that screamed.

Twice, old men shuffled by, coming home from a day spent at the dump.

Each time he screamed like a dying cat. *"Hoy! Hoy! Tanda! Halika. Sayaw tayo." Hey! Hey! Old man. Come and dance with me.*

Whenever the men would look over, he could barely contain himself with glee. Although they looked right at him, he knew they didn't see him. He was invisible. He was like the air.

But then came the old cripple, pulling himself along with one withered arm, a hand gnarled like the fingers of a twisted branch. His skin was the color of old chocolate. He had a few hairs on his face and even fewer on his head. His eyes were the colors of olive pits and were sunken into craters of wrinkles.

Jackie could barely contain his laughter as he leaped free of the trash and high into the air. Pieces of trash sprayed the cripple. Jackie screamed like a beast. He picked up an old hubcap and swung it as hard as he could. He caught the cripple in the side of the head. The cripple screamed. The slick metal slid off without doing much damage, so he brought it around again, this time coming straight down with the hubcap on the crown of the cripple's head. Blood exploded outward, the sight of it fuel for another swing of the arm. This time it came around in a flat arch, catching the old man beneath the eye.

"Hoy! Hoy!" he cried. "Dance with me, you fool!"

The cripple fell to his side, his mouth twisted into a curl of fear as he whined miserably.

Jackie growled and peed on the man's withered arm. Then he turned and ran, giggling all the way to wherever he was going, his bare feet slapping at the ground, all the way down La Union Street.

37

THE MOSH PIT. MORNING.

"Try that one. Feel anything?"

Walker didn't feel a thing. He'd kept from touching the long ratlike tail, but now let his finger graze it. Still nothing. "Are you sure this was from a chupacabra?"

"Positive. I was there. Damn thing almost took Hoover apart. Gave her over two hundred stitches."

"Then why doesn't it work?"

Ruiz shook his head and put a fist under his chin. He looked up and down their trophy wall. He'd had the idea during the briefing the other day. What had started as a joke suddenly started to make a certain sense. He'd called it a spooky meter—the way Walker reacted to the supernatural. If they could somehow train it, or figure out a way to use it properly, they could have their own walking, talking supernatural-warning device.

Ruiz spied the pinky finger of a banshee they'd fought on the Isle of Man. He'd had to improvise a mini fuel air explosive bomb to kill her, sucking all the air out of the vicinity to protect them from her wailing. All that had been left was this pinky and a few unrecognizable chunks.

"Here," he said, hurrying to the piece of wood to which the digit was affixed. The date and place they'd gotten it was on a little brass plate. He pulled the wood from the wall and brought it over to Walker. "Anything now?"

Walker shook his head.

"Really? Not even a buzz?" He held it closer to Walker.

Walker touched it with his hand. "None at all. Maybe it doesn't work if they're dead."

"That can't be right. We're always dealing with artifacts that some beegee gets his hand on with bad intentions. Fuck!" He threw the wood on the nearest couch. It bounced up and slammed into the ground. The banshee finger went flying. Hoover, who'd been snoring in a stream of sunlight, leaped to her feet and scrambled after it.

Both Walker and Ruiz ran to the couch to get to the finger before the dog ate it. What ensued was a scramble between three trained killers and a leather sofa. It was anyone's game for the first few moments; then Hoover snatched the digit from Ruiz's outstretched hand and trotted toward freedom—

Only to be caught by Holmes, who'd just come out of his room. He reached into the dog's mouth and removed the finger.

"Anyone want to explain why Hoover is eating something that's supposed to be up on the wall?"

Ruiz felt his face turn red. He hated it when the boss caught him doing something stupid. Ruiz's life was a lesson in what two steps forward and one step back could do to one's career. He pulled himself to his feet, eager to explain himself.

"I was testing a theory, boss."

Walker managed to stand beside him. He touched a rip in his T-shirt that probably came from one of Hoover's claws.

"What sort of theory involves feeding Hoover one of our trophies?"

"It has to do with these feelings Walker gets," Ruiz said.

Yaya joined them, toweling his head and shoulders as he entered the room. Holmes had since cleared out Fratty's quarters and the FNG had taken it over as his own.

"Okay," Holmes said, walking over to the couch and straightening it. "Explain."

"Right on," Ruiz said, bouncing over to the wall. "I figured if we can have some advance notice next time, we—"

"You mean to turn your fellow SEAL into an early-warning system."

Ruiz nodded.

"Like NORAD," Holmes added.

"Exactly. Except it's not working." Ruiz shook his head and walked the length of the wall. He spun and gestured toward the trophies—hands and feet and teeth and horns and all matter of body parts. "These are all artifacts and should work with Walker here, but he can't feel a thing."

Holmes started to say something, but thought better of it. He glanced at Yaya, then back to the wall.

"What is it?" Ruiz said. He tried to look Holmes in the eye, but the team leader wouldn't do it. In fact, he was beginning to look upset.

Holmes shook his head. "It's nothing. It's just . . . nothing."

"Wait a minute. What's going on?"

"You and your ideas," Holmes said, shaking his head. He walked over to the wall.

"What? It was a good idea. I was trying to help the team."

"'I was trying to help the team,'" Holmes mimicked. He reached up and mussed Ruiz's hair. "You're a good SEAL, but Jesus, man."

"What? What is it, boss?"

Yaya raised his eyebrows. "They're not real are they?"

Walker's and Ruiz's jaws dropped as they looked from Yaya to Holmes to the wall.

"Why is it that the newest member of the house figures out

what neither of you two, or the rest of them for that matter, ever did?"

"They're not real?" Walker asked, his eyes narrowing as he looked at the wall as if for the first time.

"Yaya, please explain to your team members why they can't be real."

"Because they'd stink," he said matter-of-factly. "All of these body parts rotting on the wall? This place would smell like Mogadishu."

Ruiz couldn't believe what he'd heard. "They're all fake?"

"Every last one?" Walker asked

Holmes shook his head. "Not all of them. Yaya is partially right. Some of them do stink, but we have taxidermists who take care of that. What concerns us most is the residual magic."

Ruiz flung himself into a chair. "So much for my bright idea."

"Actually, it was a great scheme," Holmes said, as if he'd just realized something. "We still have a piece of the chimera. I just haven't had time to mount it. Hold on a minute." He returned to his room. After a few moments, he returned holding a steel lockbox.

"A piece of that thing in the hold?" Walker gave a searching look to Ruiz. "You brought a piece back?"

"Several pieces actually. I had to. It's not only the job of the team to categorize all the creatures we encounter, but it's imperative that the Salton Sea compound get a sample of the DNA so they can trace its origin or project possible weaknesses if we're forced to confront one again."

Holmes sat on one of the couches and pulled a coffee table closer, then placed the box in the center and gestured at the others to gather around. "Walker, you sit here." He pointed at a spot directly across the coffee table. After everyone was situated, he pulled his dog tags out from under his T-shirt. Beside them rested a simple silver cross and a key. He grasped the key, inserted it into the lock, and turned the key.

He glanced around at the others.

Yaya sat on the edge of the seat cushion.

Ruiz, on the other side, dramatically raised his eyebrows to Walker, whose eyes were as round as quarters. When Walker saw that both Holmes and Ruiz were watching him, he laughed self-consciously and licked his lips.

"I grabbed three spines. Two were sent for testing. This third one will be sent too, but only after Mr. Kwan over at the Trophy House fabricates a copy."

"If the soccer moms only knew." Ruiz grinned and leaned back, imagining all sorts of terrible things that could happen. The devil inside him that liked to blow things up appreciated the chaotic potential of such an encounter.

Holmes opened the box. Ruiz could see inside and noticed the royal-blue felt lining. He leaned forward and watched as the team leader used metal tweezers with a screw on one end to hold a seven-inch spike in place. Black at the base, it ran through the spectrum until it was red at the tip.

Yaya whistled low. "And that came off of something the size of a horse?"

"More like a pony . . . with spikes."

"Is it poisonous?" Ruiz asked. "I never noticed the color before."

"We were too busy trying to destroy it. I didn't notice the colors either. I think they may be poisonous, but for obvious reasons I haven't personally checked."

Yaya laughed nervously and repeated, "Haven't personally checked."

Holmes gave him a hoary eye. "You gonna be all right, SEAL?"

The Egyptian-American's wide, expressive eyes flashed as he nodded.

"Okay, then hold still." Holmes held the spike out in front of Yaya until it was only a few inches away.

Holmes brought the spike back and then held it out to Ruiz.

"What's the big deal, Yaya? The homunculi were far more dangerous than this."

"Were they?" he asked, transfixed by the spike. "Kind of hard to take them seriously when they looked like buffed-out action figures."

"Fucking new guy," Ruiz said, as if it were the saddest thing to say in the world.

"Okay, Mr. Wizard," Holmes said, holding out the tweezers. "You get to test your own theory."

Ruiz was surprised that Holmes would let him take the lead like this. He grabbed the metal tweezers as if they held a vial of nitroglycerin.

As soon as Holmes let go, he leaned back and put his hands behind his head. He took on the face of a curious scientist about to watch an experiment.

Walker noticed this and narrowed his eyes. "What do you think is going to happen?"

"You tell me," Holmes countered. "Feel anything?"

"I felt something as soon as you brought out the box."

"Through the metal? Interesting. What does it feel like now?"

"You know how your feet tingle after you've been sitting Indian style for a long time? My whole body feels like that."

"What about now?" Ruiz asked as he quickly brought the spine within a foot of Walker.

The result was instantaneous.

Walker's entire body went rigid. His eyes popped to what seemed like twice their size. His teeth snapped together and began to grind like a meth addict's in the middle of the second day of a rock.

Holmes leaned forward and put his elbows on his knees. "How are you feeling right now?"

Walker grunted as he tried to get his face under control. He brought a hand up but it was shaking too violently to be of any use. He dropped it back to his lap, where it flopped like a dying fish.

"Does it hurt?" Yaya asked.

"Nuh—no." He managed to close both of his hands. They were now vibrating fists.

"Can you stand? Could you operate a weapon?" Holmes asked, frowning.

Walker couldn't respond. Instead, he merely stared back at Holmes, helplessness and fear shining from his wobbling eyes.

"Enough." Holmes reached out and took the spine back from Ruiz. He placed it in the box, closed and locked the lid, then took it into his room.

Walker sat back gasping. "Oh, my God." He rolled his eyes at Ruiz. "That was way stronger than the Stretch Armstrongs."

"Dude," Yaya said, standing up and snapping his towel. "That was badass! Can we do it again?"

"Not if you want to live."

Holmes came back out of his room talking on the cell phone. A moment later he snapped it shut. "NRO's going to conduct their overflight in twenty-five minutes. We're going over to SPG to see it live. Grab your shit and let's go."

38

SPG OFFICES. MORNING.

Both human and canine members of SEAL Team 666 climbed into the van. Fifteen minutes later, they were strolling into the offices of SPG. Past the reception area, they continued into the SCIF, where access was made through a safelike door. The SCIF, or Sensitive Controlled Information Facility, was especially suited for the transmission, reception, and creation of information at the top-secret level and beyond. Besides its offices, the centerpiece of the SCIF was the Strategic Information Center. A Navy lieutenant passed them through, not even giving Hoover a second glance. With a pair of floor-to-ceiling flatscreen monitors as well as a battery of computers, this was the place where SPG could render assistance to the special-operations community when necessary.

Watching the men and women working at their stations, Walker felt certain this was the location from which SPG had assisted them when they'd been on the ship. He'd known the SIC was in the building because Jen had spoken of it, but until now he'd never seen it with his own eyes.

And there she was.

She walked swiftly into the room. Dressed in a business suit with her hair pulled tight, it seemed hard to believe they'd lain together in her bed just a few hours ago. She met Holmes and shook his hand. When she saw Walker, toward the back of the group, she nodded, but smiled only slightly.

He mimicked her greeting.

"We'll be up in two minutes," she said. "We've already established coms with NRO command. We've sent them access to our secure node and are just waiting for the handshake."

"Handshake complete," said one of the men working at the computers in the room.

The image on the monitors scrambled and pixellated for twenty seconds as the information protocols were passed and synced between SPG and NRO. Then the image slid into focus. Both screens showed the subcontinent of India. To its east lay Bangladesh, Pakistan, Bhutan, Nepal, and Myanmar. The screen to the left remained fixed on this image, while the screen to the right began to focus down.

Dropping like the gaze of an intrusive god, their view went from one hundred miles to one mile in a single moment, then focused further until they were passing over land. Trees covered squalor and farms, barely visible beneath the heavy canopy. They passed from forest to pasture, then from pasture to ocean.

"Coming to the port," came a man's voice.

"Match left and right screens," Jen commanded.

The screens were again synced to the close-up.

"On my mark, capture screen at max resolution."

Boats began to appear in the view on the flat gray water. Warehouses and cranes passed in and out of view as the water returned.

Walker wondered if they might be too late. Had their delay put them all at risk? If the ships had sailed in the last twenty-four to forty-eight hours, they'd have to depend on their global array of subsurface tracking buoys to detect them. But that meant that the ships had to pass near the buoys. And although they were strategically placed in water bodies such as the Strait of Malacca and the Gulf of Aden, and along the U.S. coastline, they were an imperfect solution to a possible attack.

Suddenly a fleet of cargo ships filled the screen.

"Begin mark. Capture."

"That's it, isn't it?" Ruiz asked. "Those are the ships we're after."

As if to answer his question, one of the SIC personnel said, "Hull numbers and names match manifest."

Ruiz grinned as he turned to Walker. "Think we're going to see them get blown to bits?"

Walker wasn't sure. He was too busy watching Laws and Holmes, who were conferring quietly with each other.

Then the image was back to canopy.

"Please pass to NRO Command our regards. Capture and separate digitals of each of those ships so we can examine them." Jen turned to Holmes. "Give me a few moments, and I'll put together a targeting set."

"No need," Holmes said. "How soon can we get another pass?"

Jen looked taken aback. "You don't want to see the images?"

"We'd like to see them. There might be some intel that can help, but the ships are empty," Laws said, pointing at the screen. "Either the crates are loaded on different ships, or they have yet to be loaded. Either way, we're back to square one."

"Jim, can you verify?" Jen asked, approaching an older heavyset gentleman sitting at a computer nearby.

"He's right. See the watermarks and where they're riding? That watermark should be at sea level."

Walker looked from Holmes and Laws to the personnel in the SIC. They were at a sudden loss. No one knew where the creatures were. They could be in American ports as they spoke. All the money and technological advancement in the world couldn't give them what they wanted.

Frankly, he didn't know what they were going to do now.

39

THE MOSH PIT.

On the way back to the Pit, Holmes let it be known that everyone was on one-hour recall. They had to find out where the cargo was for those ships. SPG was going to coordinate with FBI to see if they could get access to the enforcer captured in San Francisco. Meanwhile, Laws was going to sift through the data SPG provided. They offered to mirror the hard drive, but Laws was old-school. He preferred paper and pencil. So it was that they left the SPG with two boxes of paper, covering every piece of data they'd ripped from the hard drive.

When they hit the Pit, Yaya went off with Hoover for a little bonding. Ruiz and Walker went to strip and to prepare weapons. Holmes went to brief Ms. Billings. Which left Laws as the sole sentient individual to try and solve the mystery. Just the way he wanted. He scribbled a note on a piece of paper, taped it to the conference-room door, then set about unraveling the unravelable. It wasn't half an hour before he exited the room, his gaze already screwed into a faraway place. He first went into his room and grabbed two Chinese-to-English dictionaries. Then he ordered a large anchovy and green chili pizza from Alexander's Pizza, along with a carafe of Starbucks coffee. After going over the papers and categorizing them into different piles, he realized that he was going to need his references. Even though he had an audiographic memory and knew how to speak Chinese, the characters were a much harder thing to remember. Although there was a method to the Chinese madness, it was a three-step process to determine the number of strokes, look up the radical, then figure out what the character meant.

Bottom line, it was going to take some time.

40

CORONADO BEACH. EVENING.

The only person who seemed to be enjoying the run more than Hoover was Yaya. Walker hated running. Ruiz didn't hate it, but he thought it was one of the most boring forms of exercise. If it wasn't so damn effective, he'd have given it up long ago. Holmes approached it with his head down and his gaze ten feet in front of him. Walker couldn't tell if the boss liked it or hated it. All he knew was that the run was Holmes's idea. He wanted to spend some time with his SEALs.

But Yaya was a completely different matter altogether. His enjoyment bordered on the insane. He was running around their little group with Hoover chasing and barking after him. The dog seemed thrilled to have someone who liked to run as much as she did. Ruiz had mentioned that Fratty had hated running. If he had to do it, it was on the treadmill while watching basketball on ESPN. The former SEAL would run the entire time the game was playing, then get off, shower, and go to the gym to play some real basketball.

Yaya began clapping his hands and singing cadence.

Four miles. No sweat.
Five miles. Better yet.
Six miles. You can take it.
Seven miles. Gonna make it.

They didn't need the cadence; it was just that Yaya seemed incapable of keeping quiet. He loved to run so much that when he wasn't on mission, he'd take leave just to travel to races. He was an ultramarathoner, which meant that he liked to run races more than fifty miles long. He especially loved running the Bataan Death March in New Mexico, the Bighorn 100 in Wyoming, and the Zane Grey Highline in Arizona. He'd even raced to the top of the Empire State Building twice and loved every second of it.

They'd traveled four miles and had turned around to return. Walker's legs felt surprisingly well. Although he'd only left training a few days ago, it was the first time in months that he'd allowed his muscles to repair themselves and it seemed to be paying off. His shin splints had only begun hurting toward the end. Now, with a picnic table loaded down with food and beer in sight, he was happy to have finished the run with virtually no pain.

When they finally came to a stop, even Hoover had had enough. Her tongue lolled long. Luckily, the support staff had brought a bucket of water for her. She plunged her entire head into the bucket and loudly began to lap up the water.

They'd also set the table up like a SEAL smorgasbord. Fried chicken, cold cuts, raw vegetables, hummus and pita, pickled peppers, stuffed olives, a cut platter of cantaloupe and watermelon, and five different kinds of beer on ice.

Holmes lit the bonfire that had been made ready, then ran into the surf to cool off.

The other SEALs followed, shouting in shock as the cold water smashed into their hot muscles. After about two minutes, they staggered out of the water, shivering.

They each downed a bottle of Gatorade before grabbing beers and huddling around the bonfire to get their warmth back and to dry their shirts and UDT shorts.

"Is Laws going to make it?" Yaya asked.

"He's locked himself into the conference room," Holmes said. He popped open a bottle of Longboard and took a deep draught.

"Didn't you see the sign?" Ruiz asked. "It said 'Come in if you are bleeding or if the place is burning down. Otherwise G-T-F-O.' "

"Laws is ass-deep in Chinese, trying to figure out what the SPG analysts couldn't," Holmes said. "If there's an answer to be had, he'll find it. Best we just stay out of his way." They ate in silence for a while.

Holmes finished first and stuffed his plate into a plastic bag. "Yaya, what do you think about all this?"

"Great food. Do you do this after every run?" he asked.

"Not that, the *team*."

"Ah, that. I kind of dug the homunculus. Little fuckers were easy to kill once you got a hold of them, but they're ferociously strong."

Holmes nodded. "The Triads like using them as servants for all sorts of things. They're good at stealing things, but even better at sweeping and cleaning the floors."

"Supernatural janitors," Walker said, laughing around a piece of cantaloupe. "Just crazy."

"You seem to be taking all of this in stride," Ruiz said to Yaya.

"Supernatural has always been a heavy part of Islam," Yaya said. "Not that we ever saw anything, but it was always understood that it could exist. Djinns have been around since time immemorial. I'm just sad I wasn't able to help you with that one."

Holmes shook his head. "You mean the mission from 2007? I see you've been reading the mission log. That wasn't a true Djinn. An oil executive was possessed by one that had become attached to a knife he'd been given by some Bedouins."

"You gave credit to SEAL Team 6 for that one."

Holmes shrugged at Yaya's comment. "We had to. We don't exist."

"And the other SEALs? What do I tell them when they ask me?"

"It's a SAP, plain and simple."

"Plain and simple?" Yaya drank his beer and shook his head. Doubt showed in his eyes.

"What about you?" Ruiz asked. "Did you know about us before you were asked to join?"

Yaya considered a moment. "I knew there was something going on. I knew there was no pest control service. I also knew that Holmes was involved in a SAP."

"And you never asked?" Ruiz raised an eyebrow.

"I never asked. Okay, I see your point."

"What about family?" Walker asked.

"What about them?"

"I mean do you have one?"

"A family?" Yaya laughed. "Sure, doesn't everyone?"

Ruiz and Holmes glanced at Walker. The look wasn't missed by Yaya. "What? Did I say something wrong?"

"They're worried about me," Walker said. "I don't really have any family."

Yaya's eyes widened.

"Long story," Walker continued. "I was asking you about your family."

"I have the usual—I mean, a mother, father, two sisters. They live in Philly. My father's a doctor there."

"What about a wife?" Walker asked.

"I had one of those. She didn't work out."

"Isn't that always the case?"

"Wasn't like that. She didn't care how much I deployed. She just wanted me to be more devout."

"How devout did she want you to be?" Walker asked.

Yaya held up the half-empty beer bottle. "None of this, for

sure." Seeing their expressions, he shrugged and added, "Listen, there's devout and then there's crazy. My father raised us as American Muslims."

Walker crinkled his eyebrows. He'd never heard the phrase.

"Think of me as a Methodist Muslim," Yaya said. He downed his beer, tossed it into the trash, and grabbed a new one. He twisted the top off and leaned back to rest against the picnic table so he could stare at the ocean.

"Okay. Now you have me interested. What the heck is a Methodist Muslim?" Holmes asked.

"Someone who believes in Allah and the Pillars of Islam. I pray. I fast. I give. I travel to the holy places. I believe that Allah is the one God. All the rest," he said, waving his beer absently to the universe, "is fashion."

Ruiz snorted. "What? You mean the burkas?"

Yaya nodded and got to his feet. "Absolutely. Ever look at the robes worn by a Catholic priest and an Aram mullah? Same damn thing except one is made from satin and the other from wool. It's all a circus after the word of Allah. A Pee-Wee Herman doodle time for the fashionistas to get us involved in pomp and circumstance of worshipping the right god the right way."

41

THE MOSH PIT. MORNING.

Pain lanced through Laws's brain from the sheer amount of concentration he'd exerted over the last twenty hours. Operating on energy drinks, espresso, and a secret stash of Jolt Cola, he was as wired as any meth addict. Still, he'd made progress. At first he hadn't seen it. There'd been so much data, he'd felt like the first IBM computer getting stuffed with the grammar rules of the Chinese language. Because it *was* about grammar. It was about grammar and the differences between characters as they appear in modern standard and the more ancient usages.

He'd started out by plastering every available surface with pages upon pages of Chinese characters. He'd walked back and forth, staring at them, looking for a pattern, reading here and there. Some of the documents were technical schematics of different pieces of ship's equipment. Once he discovered these, he ripped them free and threw them into a corner, only to replace them with new pages. He repeated this over and over until the entire floor and underside of the conference table was a graveyard of ship's schematics and maintenance logs.

This allowed him to concentrate on the remainder. One thing he couldn't do was read them. His ability to speak so far outweighed his ability to read that it might as well have been two different languages—which it was. It was no joke that the average high-school graduate in China couldn't read the newspaper. This wasn't an indictment of the education system. Chinese kids and young adults were smart and driven. No, this was an indictment of a language that after three thousand years of use had failed to create that single essential element that allowed the progress of communication: the alphabet.

Of course, he realized that their lack of an alphabet probably had little to do with their ability to create one. If the Chinese had wanted to create an alphabet, they could have created a dozen. But that wouldn't satisfy their needs. Chinese leaders had always been sensitive to the need to control one of the largest populations on the planet. Informing the populace would have kept the leadership at a continual disadvantage. By controlling the way their written language was represented, they'd been able to maintain a vise grip on the flow of information for thirty centuries.

None of this had anything to do with the problem at hand, but railing against the ineptness of Chinese characters kept him from going insane as he paced the conference room, ate anchovy pizza, guzzled caffeinated beverages, and tried desperately to see what kept eluding him.

Around midnight he changed tactics. Realizing he couldn't read everything and he wasn't succeeding in finding any relevant patterns, he began to search for characters applicable to the mission at hand.

He began flipping through his radical dictionary, which contained more than ninety thousand characters, expressed by the numeration of the strokes on the left-hand side of the character.

First he looked for "tattoo." This required the use of two characters, *wen shen*. The first character, *wen*, meant "to write," and had to do with language and literacy and contained four strokes. The second character, *shen*, meant "body" or "life," and had eight strokes.

He wrote the characters on a piece of paper, then kept that word in the front of his mind as he scanned the pages taped to the walls. He circled each iteration of *wen* and *shen*, but never found them in use together. This first attempt took an hour and left him feeling wiped out at one in the morning.

But he felt like he was on the right track. Remembering the creature that had killed Fratty, he decided to search for this. But what was it called? It seemed to be a chimera, but what was the Chinese word for such a thing? Try as he might, he couldn't figure out how to represent the word using Chinese characters.

Finally he settled on dragon. The character used to represent it was called *long*, which meant that it would frame part of the whole of the word that was used to describe dragon. The character was well known. It was used frequently to describe food and was a common character on business signs. Using the dragon was considered to be good luck. So he began to search for the five-stroke character and, using a yellow marker, soon had more than a hundred marks on the pages plastered on the walls.

Once he was finished, he stood back and stared. Happy to find evidence of the character, he was slightly aghast at the number of times it appeared in all the pages. Now came the fun part. With dictionary in hand, he looked up each combination of characters and wrote the definition on a yellow sticky, which he stuck on the papers beside each character. After three hours, he fell back in a chair and drank two Jolts.

An hour later he found what they were looking for.

After running to use the bathroom, he grabbed one of the portable whiteboards out of the common area and wheeled it into the conference room. Slipping occasionally on the avalanche of papers from under the table, he began to write furiously on the board.

42

CONFERENCE ROOM. MORNING.

Walker woke with a mouth as dry as the Sahara. Too much beer. He'd have to learn to say no next time they offered it to him. He caught himself smiling in the mirror. No sooner had the thought passed through his mind than he realized he could never say no to good beer. Instead, he'd have to try and achieve *beer mitigation,* as an old marine gunny sergeant had once described it. When asked what beer mitigation was, the gunny had responded with nearly maniacal glee that it was PT—physical training!

After brushing his teeth and running some water through his hair, Walker went into the kitchen, where he found Ruiz reading the newspaper.

"Any sign of Laws coming out?" Walker asked.

Ruiz shook his head. "I heard some cursing in there, but that's it."

Walker poured himself coffee, added one sugar, then carried it into the other room. He stared at the door to the conference room for several minutes before he made his decision. He went to the door, turned the knob, and cracked it open.

The room looked like some kind of hurricane had slammed into it. Paper was stuck to the walls in several layers from floor to ceiling. It was on the table and covered the floor. Beneath the table was a pile of paper so large it looked as if it had been used to cover the body of a dead man.

A whiteboard had been brought into the room. On this was a combination of characters and diagrams that could have only been made by the love child of Michio Kaku and Carl Sagan. It was either physics, algebra, or some sort of scientific notation he'd never seen before. Here and there he recognized some Chinese characters. Laws was sprawled in one of the chairs.

"You get us a clue?"

Laws turned his head. "I think so."

Walker's eyes widened. "No shit?" He stuck his head out the door and called for the others. While he waited for them to come, he found a seat and sipped his coffee. "Man," he said. "You look like crap."

"Thanks." Laws smiled weakly. "I feel like crap."

Ruiz and Holmes joined them, each with his own coffee. Holmes carried a folder with the familiar red cover sheet that proclaimed it as secret.

Finally Yaya and Hoover came in. They'd been running together and both were still a little winded. Yaya had a bottle of water. He made some room on the floor by pushing some papers away, put down a collapsible doggie dish, and filled it with water for Hoover.

Walker admired the skill with which Yaya had befriended Hoover. In the short time the new SEAL had been with the team they'd become all but inseparable. Even now, as the dog lapped at the water, she looked up at Yaya to see if he was there. In fact, it almost looked as if Hoover was grinning.

"I think we can start now," Holmes said as he snapped the file shut and laid it in front of him. "SPG didn't learn anything we don't already know. So what can you tell us that a whole platoon of college-educated CIA agents can't?"

Laws swiveled in his chair and stared at Holmes with tired eyes. The only thing that didn't seem exhausted about him was the grin he wore. "I can tell you who the bad guy is."

Suddenly he had their full attention.

Even Holmes seemed impressed. He leaned forward and clasped his hands together on the table. "So who is it?"

"First things first," Laws said, standing. "Let me show you how I got there." He stepped over piles of paper to get to the board. He grabbed a red marker and tested it to see if it still worked. When he was ready, he turned back to the assembled SEALs, poised like a seventh-grade math teacher.

"It all begins with the *long*," he said. Laws circled a Chinese character. "This is *long*. It means 'dragon.' When I finally figured out what I was doing, it was this character that started things moving. You see, Chinese isn't like other languages. There is no alphabet. No method of sounding out a word." He glanced at Ruiz. "You know, like you did with the word 'truck' last week when you first learned it."

Ruiz turned to Walker, who knew exactly what to do next.

"Tru—" said Ruiz.

"Uck," said Walker.

"Truck," they said together.

"Today's *Electric Company* is brought to you by the letters F and U," Laws remarked, unimpressed.

Yaya snorted.

"Come on, guys. Give him a break," Holmes ordered.

Walker glanced at Holmes, who hadn't taken his eyes off Laws the entire time, but under the table his knee bobbed impatiently. Holmes wanted to get on with it, but he was willing to let Laws have his day in the sun. After all, while they'd been drinking on the beach, Laws had been secluded in the conference room like a freshman preparing for finals.

"So," Laws continued, letting the sound carry on for a few seconds, "we were talking about dragons. Normally you'd see the characters *hong long* on Chinese restaurants or signs in

Chinatown. That combination is very common. It means 'red dragon.'"

He checked to see if he had everyone's attention. When he saw that he did, he resumed. "In Western mythology dragons are considered evil, but it's not the same in the East. Not at all. Chinese dragons traditionally symbolize power, good luck, and control over water elements. There's literally dozens of dragons in their mythology. From *shen long*, which means 'god dragon,' to *fei long*, or 'flying dragon.' What I found curious in the papers from this ship was that the only instance I found for *long* was for *chi long*. At that point, I thought I'd figured something out, but the Chinese are tricky that way. *Chi long* literally means 'demon dragon,' but it translates better to 'hornless dragon.'"

"That creature we fought was anything but hornless," said Ruiz.

Laws pointed toward Ruiz and nodded. "That's right. I thought the same thing. So I looked more closely at the character for *chi*."

On the whiteboard, he drew two characters side by side that looked almost the same, but the one on the right had more flowing script.

He pointed to the character on the left. "This character is *chi*. Now, most characters are comprised of two internal parts. The radical, which helps define it. This is usually found on the left side. In this case it's the bug radical, which is typically used for insects, reptiles, dragons, etcetera. The other part of the character is the phonetic and helps us know how it's pronounced."

He pointed to the character on the right. "This character is pronounced the same way as the first. We can tell this by comparing the phonetic portion of the character. But as you can see, the radicals are different."

Walker realized as Laws said it that he was able to discern the difference. Up until that point, it all looked like squiggles. But the more Laws explained, the more it began to make sense.

"This is the ghost radical. Note these two strokes that look like legs and this square with a cross in the middle to represent the large demon's head. The last part is a curl, which represents a demon tail." He added the character for dragon after this version of *chi.* "At first I mistook it for the other radical. Between my tired eyes and the sheer difficulty of reading all these characters, I read the phonetic of the character and assumed it meant hornless dragon." He shook his head. "Never assume. It's exceedingly common in Chinese to see character pairs. *Long* is no different. But the character *chi* with the ghost radical only pairs with the character *mei,* which refers to 'mountain' or 'forest demons.'" He faced them for impact. "When I say it only pairs with *mei,* what I mean is that in all of my dictionaries and on Internet searches, I couldn't find any instance of the *chi* with the ghost radical pairing with any other. We're talking about it not appearing in more than fifty thousand combinations. Not once."

"I think I'm starting to understand." Holmes nodded. "Continue."

"This goes all the way back to the Hanshu dynasty in 111 CE when *chi* first appeared with a ghost radical. In every instance it had to do with something bad. Something evil."

"If those characters never appeared together, then how can they be together in the text? What does that mean?" Yaya asked.

Laws pointed at him and grinned. "And that was my question once I finally figured out the etymology of the words."

Ruiz turned to Walker and mouthed *etymology.* Walker grinned, but he was starting to get into what Laws was telling them.

Laws circled *chi long* several times with the red marker. "One of the exceptions to the pairing rule has to do with a name."

"So you searched for Chi Long," Walker said.

"Yep! I searched for Chi Long, using the same ghost radical. I found a single occurrence when researching the *San Guo Shi Dai,* or Three Kingdoms period of China. This time was around 220 to 280 CE. There's not a lot of real history that's been saved, except the writings of Chen Shou. *Romance of the Three Kingdoms* was a novel written by Luo Guanzhong in the fourteenth century. It's provided much of the textual fabric for sinologists. The occurrence of Chi Long appeared in an associated text when referring to a great warrior that belonged to Sun Quan, emperor of the Kingdom of Wu, during the Three Kingdoms period."

He produced a colored picture, which he passed around. On what appeared to be a background of parchment paper was a Chinese warrior in flowing robes wearing ancient, dragon-influenced armor. His face and hands had been eaten away, leaving only bone, muscle, and sinew. If anything looked like a demon, this did.

"This was one of Emperor Sun's greatest warriors. It was said that he was shot with over a thousand arrows and lived."

"That would indicate an invulnerability to weapons," Ruiz said, serious for the first time.

"What happened to him?" Yaya asked.

Laws shrugged and sat down. "I don't know. He could have faded into history. He could have died drinking ancient Chinese beer. He could still be alive today as a demon. All I know is that the text I saw referred to Chi Long as a person, usually in the possessive, so clearly there's something or someone alive who is using the name Chi Long with the ghost radical."

"So we have the possibility of encountering an eighteen-hundred-year-old Chinese demon who's evidently been creating an army of chimera creatures." Holmes sat back. "That about right?"

"That sums it up," Laws agreed.

"Well, then," Holmes said, standing. "We'd better figure out how we're going to beat this thing if we ever encounter it." Then he grabbed his coffee and the file and left the room.

"I'll get right on it," Laws muttered. "Right after I find that volume of *Chinese Mythological Demons for Dummies* I misplaced."

Walker watched as Laws closed his eyes and fell fast asleep.

43

FROM THE DIARY OF LARRY WALKER.

It's day three of the exorcism. My heart has broken so many times in the last seventy-two hours I can't begin to tell you how much I hurt inside. One day you'll read this and know that all your pain, all of your agony, is my fault.

Sometimes I wish that it was your brother they did this to. He's older and stronger. I think he would have taken it better. Although I have to admit, you have absorbed so much self-mutilation and punishment to your flesh that I am amazed at what is survivable.

I don't know how damaged you will be because of this. But if you survive, I know you're going to hate me. So I leave this to you. After all, if you're going to hate me, I want you to hate me for the right reasons.

Your mother called me an asshole. Not because I wasn't a good provider, but because I was never there for her. I didn't change after her death, either. I was an asshole to Brian and I was an asshole to you. My defense, if I'm even allowed one, is that there was only one way I knew how to provide a future for my family. Sure, I could have stayed like the other Navy chiefs and lived hand to mouth until I retired. But that's no kind of life. That's subsistence living. That's one step above the poverty line and it isn't fair that you kids should have to live a life like that.

So I made deals.

Some people say I stole. I never did. Everything I dealt I bought from the DRMO at auction. I have the receipts for everything if anyone ever asks. I'd buy a surplus of chairs from DRMO, sell them to a guy in Subic for a hundred cases of beer, then sell those to resorts in Mindanao who were having trouble getting local vendors because of all the Muslim separatists. I'd triple my initial investment this way and a hundred other ways.

Making deals wasn't about what you were selling. It was always about who you were selling it to. It's a personality game. You have to know people who know people, and I knew everyone.

Maybe that was the problem.

See, in order to make money, you have to take advantage of someone. To make a lot of money, you take a lot *of advantage of someone. Most of the times people realize it. After all, they're still making a profit. Their problem was they didn't have the means or know the right people to make the kind of profit that I did. And that usually left them feeling pissed.*

But I wasn't a good guy all the time.

There were the occasions when I took advantage of a situation if I didn't like the people. And this is where you come in. I made a mistake in Corregidor. I was hired to trade for some penicillin. I got the penicillin, but got a better offer in Manila. A bar owner wanted to corner the market on the drug, knowing that the girls had to have clean bills of health on their red cards. He paid me triple what I was going to get from the Malay doctor on Corregidor.

I figured I'd be able to take the cash, buy some more penicillin, and get it to Corregidor after only a few days' delay. But I hadn't anticipated the supply would dry up. When I realized that I couldn't get any more, I tried to buy back what I'd sold at a loss, but the bar owner just laughed at me.

I wired my contact in Corregidor. The reply I got back told the rest of the horrifying story. The drug was to be used to halt an outbreak of meningitis at a local orphanage. They had to have it. Without it they'd all die. And they did.

Forty-seven children.

Dead.

Because of me.

The last line of the telegram I received in return said that I'd pay for this.

Two weeks later I noticed the change in you. I don't know how it got in you. I don't know who did it. All I knew was that one minute you were a happy-go-lucky kid having a great life in the P.I., and the next you were like a ravenous dog with the mouth of a sailor.

Then I lost you for four months.

I'm still trying to figure out what exactly happened to you. According to the woman who convinced the priest to rescue you from the garbage dump, you are possessed by a Hantu Kabor. Turns out that's some sort of Malaysian grave demon. It sucks out the souls of the dead, but can be harnessed to do the same with the living. As it was explained to me, as if this were something logical, the demon possesses you for as long as it takes to break down your internal defenses. Once that happens, it eats your soul and moves on. I've seen the sort of people they claim have been its victims. And Jackie, they scare me. They scare me worse than anything because I don't want you to end up that way.

They just sit there, staring at the world.

No, that's not right. That would entail some sort of interaction. They sit there with the world staring at them. *They're like rocks. Or clay. Or a hill. They are* nothing. *There's nothing left inside except for the elements that made them.*

They're empty.

But you were strong.

You kept it at bay. Through whatever hell you were in, you kept it from consuming you.

And you are still holding on.

You have more scars than any child should ever have. You have been bleeding from your eyes and ears for a full day now. Your arms have been trying to dislocate, so we've put you in a straitjacket. Your heart has been at a steady two hundred beats per minute. Your breathing is rapid-fire. Your eyes shine with the heat of the beast.

But I think whatever the priest is doing is working. Amidst your screams of terror and agony, I think the shine in your eyes is beginning to dim.

That has to be good, right?

That means you're getting better, right?

Oh Lord, please make it so.

44

SPG OFFICES. AFTERNOON.

They'd found them. Or at least they thought they had.

Walker sat with the rest of his team as Musso laid out more information about the target set.

"We'd originally believed there was a Chinese connection. Based on the hard work Mr. Laws conducted deducing the elements of Chi Long, and perhaps identifying the supernatural connection, we were further lured into the idea that this was a Chinese Triad–organized endeavor. But the events of the last two hours have dissuaded us substantially from that. The sinolinguistic association was merely a result of the language shift in an ethnically divergent group within Myanmar."

Walker glanced at Ruiz. Neither of them understood what the briefer had said.

Jen caught it and gestured toward Musso.

"Bottom line, we're now certain that the origination of the crates comes from the Karen. They trace their history back to the Mongols. They still use a version of Chinese, but they use many of the more archaic terms and characters. This would be the reason for the ghost radical appearing in the *chi* character. The Karen are currently indigenous minorities in Thailand and Myanmar. They have been waging a silent war against the military junta that has been in control of Myanmar for the last twenty years. They are separated both ideologically and politically from the Myanmarese and wish nothing more than to remove them from power and replace them with the Karen, who can trace their history back to a far earlier rule."

The briefer paused.

Holmes took the opportunity to ask a question. "How do you know specifically it's the Karen?"

"I've been mirroring Laws's efforts. While he searched the documents taken from the cargo ship for a Chinese connection, I searched for something else. What I discovered were Chinese literalizations—characters to represent sounds, usually for names—of a name that occurred several times in the documents we transferred from the cargo ship, *Saw Thuza Tun*." He glanced at Laws. "The only reason you didn't find it was because the radicals used in the literalizations were nonsensical."

Laws nodded but didn't say anything.

"So the name *Saw Thuza Tun* is clearly a Karen name. We know this because the Karen have an entirely different naming convention in Myanmar. Surnames are not commonly used. A person is usually known by a given name consisting of one or two elements. In this case they are Thuza and Tun, which mean 'success' and 'bright,' respectively. They're preceded by the title of the person. In this case, they give the word '*saw*,' which is the Karen version of the Shan title '*sao*.' Both '*sao*' and '*saw*' mean 'lord.' "

"Is that all you got?" Ruiz asked.

"Initial searches indicate that Tun is involved with the Karen separatist movement, but that's it. NFI," Musso finished, meaning "no further information."

The room was silent for a moment as everyone digested what they'd heard. Finally Holmes asked, "What does this have to do with us? Why are the chimera being shipped to America?"

"You're speaking to motive," Musso said.

"I am. Why us?"

"That's an excellent question, but one for which we can make only educated postulations. Here's what we think. If their intent had actually been to attack the U.S., they could have done it without our even knowing. We wouldn't be having this conversation. Frankly, we all might be dead."

"I've been thinking the same thing," Holmes agreed. "We almost have too much information."

"Precisely," Jen said. "Peter, show them the pictures."

Musso raised a hand and gestured to the back of the room. "Liz, please present the slides."

The room darkened and an image of a sprawling city was superimposed on Musso. He stepped to the side. "This is Rangoon, or Yangon as it's now called. It was the former capital of Burma and Myanmar. You'll remember that we found the ships in the harbor. They weren't hiding. They were at berth as if they weren't about to ship death to America. Next slide, please."

Another city appeared, this one not so sprawling.

"This is Thaton, located down the coast a ways from Yangon. You'll remember the circus name on the crates was the Suwarnabhumi Circus. It turns out that Suwarnabhumi was a semi-mythical kingdom of the Mon, which is believed to be the present-day Thaton. So we decided to search here. You'd think that a warehouse filled with crates should be immensely difficult to find. Next slide, please."

The next image was a truck bearing the logo of the same circus that had been painted on the crates. The quality of the photo was poor and it appeared to be taken from a low angle.

"One of our assets provided this photo twelve hours ago. He was able to follow it to a warehouse. Next slide."

An overhead of a huge building with several outbuildings flashed on the screen. The resolution was magnificent. Soldiers with AK-47s patrolled the perimeter. Several trucks with the same logos painted on their roofs were parked near what was probably a loading dock.

"Why does a circus need a warehouse?" Walker asked.

"Bingo." Musso grinned. "Anything else seem out of place?"

"Why did they paint the logo on the roofs?" Yaya asked.

"Double bingo. This whole thing is a lure. Let's go back to the Chinese tech smuggler. I think we've been led to this location since we got the original lead to take down the sweatshop. The cargo ship in Macau was in a secluded location with only a few persons on board. It was too easy."

"Easy?" Laws sat up as anger suffused his face. "We lost one of our own. That wasn't easy."

Musso held out a hand. "I meant no offense. I was just pointing out that if their intent had been to attack the U.S., they would have provided a more serious defense against possible intrusion. No one could have anticipated the ferocity of the chimera. Not you and certainly not Fratolilio."

Musso waited to see if his words had a mollifying effect. Walker watched Laws sit back. The fire had left his eyes, but his face still burned red.

"Continue," Holmes commanded.

"The ship provided us the logo, which we in turn sent to all of our assets. This circus has never had a show. It's never pitched a tent. It's never had a single flyer pasted to a Third World shithole telephone pole. This circus exists for one reason."

"To lure us in."

Ruiz rubbed his face. "Let me get this straight. They want us to come get them?"

"They want us to attack the Myanmar government. Look at the soldiers on guard outside the warehouse. They're wearing official military uniforms. The ships are present in Yangon Harbor. They want us to recognize the affiliation with the government."

"They want us to take down their military so that they can

rule," Walker said slowly, as he worked it out. "So what are we going to do?"

The door opened and Billings strode in. "You're going to go in there and find out what's going on." Seeing their expressions, she added, "I've been on face phone with Senator Brunson and the vice president. They're aware of the new information, but they're not convinced that this is a lure. As long as there's a potential threat to the United States, they want us to go in and see what we can see."

"Sounds pretty clear to me," Holmes said, looking at his team. "We have a mission. Transportation is standing by. We can leave in two hours." He turned to Musso. "Do you have a target package ready for us?"

"I do. I'll download it to your tablets."

"There's still the bit about Chi Long," Laws pointed out. "How does he fit into this?"

"And the tattoo skin suits?" Walker asked.

Yaya nodded his head slowly. "My bet is that you'll find them linked in some way. This Thuza Tun character is probably the mystery guy walking around wearing one of the suits. My guess is that we'll find the truth at the end of the trail of circus breadcrumbs, so we need to be prepared."

Walker nodded, but wondered how they were expected to be prepared for something they had absolutely no information about.

45

STARLIFTER. SOMEWHERE OVER THE PACIFIC OCEAN.

After two hours of discussing the targeting parameters, the other SEALs, including Hoover, curled up next to their gear for some shuteye. But Walker couldn't sleep. He'd tried, but had immediately plunged into a memory of when he was possessed. As if from a third person, he saw himself chewing off the heads of roasted rats, sucking out their eyeballs, and spooning their brains into his mouth with the crook of a little finger.

Laws and Holmes both believed that the skin suits could be used to protect someone from a powerful spirit, the idea being that the spiritual residue of all the people who made up the suit would keep the wearer safe from the demon he or she was channeling. How anyone could ask to be possessed, or channel a demon, was beyond his ability to comprehend. Clearly the lust for power was stronger than the need for self-preservation.

He'd been an American boy in the Philippines possessed by a Hantu Kabor from Malaysian mythology, a grave demon. If people weren't buried properly according to Malay custom, the demon would crawl through the graves and eat the souls of the dead. The Hantu was a collector of sorts. It had many souls within it. Walker remembered them and how at times they would scream at him, and whisper to him, an apartment building full of souls in a small boy's head.

During screening and selection they'd asked him how he'd known that he'd been possessed—what was the first sign? Walker had to think back on it, because he hadn't known he was possessed until it was too late. But as he delved into the memories he so desperately wished he didn't have, he realized that it had been the whispers. Whether he was walking down the street or alone in a room, he'd begun to hear the susurrations of faraway voices. It was like someone saying something right on the edge of his hearing. He remembered being infuriated that he couldn't understand, so he'd listened harder. By the time he did understand them, he realized that all along they'd been telling him to run. He just hadn't understood until it was too late.

Finally he couldn't take it anymore. He rolled over to where Laws was snoring gently. When he got next to him, the snoring ceased and Laws opened one eye. "What the hell, Walker?"

"I can't sleep."

"So you thought you'd share that affliction?"

"Sorry, it's just that . . . Never mind. Go back to sleep."

Laws sat up and grabbed a liter of water. "No. It's okay. Ask away."

"Okay, then. How are we going to take down Chi Long?" Seeing the judgmental look in Laws's eyes, he hastily added, "I know how to kill a man a hundred ways. I can disable anything mechanical. There's very little I don't know how to do because of the training we've received. But neither A school nor BUD/S provided me with even an infinitesimal crumb of information regarding ghosts, goblins, or ghouls."

Laws nodded grudgingly as he screwed the top back on the bottle. "Well said. Here's what we know. A suit of tattooed skin was sent to the Karen. Historically, there's only been one use for such a suit. Each piece of skin still holds an echo of the soul it once enclosed. Each piece of ink still holds an echo of the idea and thought someone put into it. When people get a tattoo, they usually expend a lot of mental energy planning it. Each one has its own special meaning. The wearer continuously looks at the tattoo and remembers why it was so important. This is akin to worship and imbues the ink with power. The combination of the pieces of skin and ink presents a problem set for a demon who was called to inhabit that body. Under normal circumstances, a demon's soul would quickly burn out a person who hasn't found a way to prepare him- or herself. And when I say burn out, that's exactly what I mean. Suits of skin are one way to allow the wearer to survive the internal forces exerted by the demonic soul, the power shared by all the echoed souls who so recently owned each piece of skin."

"So it's like a suit of armor for the soul. I get that," Walker said. "But how does one go about summoning demons?" When he saw the look on Laws's face, he shrugged and spread his hands. "You'll have to forgive me. All I know on the subject is what I've seen from movies, and for some strange reason I have the image of two young boys with underwear on their heads playing with Barbie dolls."

"*Weird Science.*" Laws chuckled. "Starred Anthony Michael Hall and Ilan Mitchell-Smith. They summoned a genie, Kelly LeBrock. Classic eighties movie. Bottom line is that there isn't one specific way."

"No specific way?"

"Well, there has to be a focus."

"A what?"

"Focus," Laws said more slowly. "Like a cross in a Christian ceremony."

Walker nodded. "Like the Barbie dolls."

"More like the underwear. Those would have been the focus for those boys. They wore them on their heads and used them to help them concentrate."

"So if we find the *underwear,* then we can do what? Sever the connection between the demon and the human? Short-circuit the summoning?" Walker held out his hands. "I don't know what I'm saying."

"Actually you do. I think you understand it pretty damn well. The focus might be a knife, or an amulet, or a ring. Very often it's a piece of jewelry. And yes. I think it might short-circuit the connection between the human and the demon, *if* we can find it and *if* we can remove it from the host. You should read the mission log. There are quite a few missions whose success was based on a team member first discovering, then removing a focus."

Walker nodded.

"Does that help?" Laws asked.

"Yeah. I think I've got it now."

"Good. Now roll back over and get some sleep."

Walker started to do just that when an alarm began going off in the cabin.

Holmes popped up and made a beeline for the crew chief, who'd also awoken and was already on a hard line to the cockpit. He spoke animatedly into the phone for what seemed like several minutes but could have only been a few seconds. When he was done, he addressed the team.

"We have weather. A cyclone is brewing and sending up thunderheads ten miles high. We have no choice but to fly beneath it. We're talking about two hundred feet above the water. It's going to be a rough ride."

"We gonna have enough fuel to reach our rendezvous?" Ruiz asked.

"Negatron. Air refueler was already called back. We'll be landing in the beautiful garden spot of Guadalcanal. NFI."

Walker shook his head. Murphy was with them already. It wasn't a good sign.

The Starlifter went into a forty-five-degree dive. Yaya and Ruiz fell on their rumps. The other SEALs managed to stay upright, although Walker's stomach felt like it was still a thousand feet above them.

They made it to the benches and strapped themselves in. The plane began to shake as it coursed through the outer edges of the cyclone.

Walker grabbed onto his straps and forced his mouth shut so that the vibrations wouldn't get his teeth chattering. Looking around, he realized that he wished there were windows. Not that there was anything he could do about it, but knowing that they were about to crash into the ocean seemed better than not knowing.

Ruiz, who was sitting beside him, pointed at his rucksack. The altimeter they would use for the HAHO into Myanmar was on top of it, the digital numbers rapidly running backwards. They were at twenty thousand feet and descending fast.

After a few moments, Walker closed his eyes. He decided it was better not to know. If death was going to claim them, he'd rather it be a surprise.

46

GUADALCANAL. MORNING.

As it turned out, they didn't die.

The wide blue sky made a lie of the fact that a cyclone had just blown through. But the tattered palm fronds and coconuts littering the ground were a picturesque testament to the angry winds that had buffeted the South Pacific since creation. Still, after a few days of wind and another of rain, the Solomon Islands would be back to normal. They'd survived far worse than a simple cyclone. They'd survived bombardment from the Japanese and Americans as this small hunk of rock and dirt had been battled over until tens of thousands of men had bled out on the sand.

Walker was cognizant of this and more as he stared out upon the island. He'd just gone to the monument and was in awe of the place, just as he had been at Gettysburg. There's a feeling at places where so much life has been lost, and Guadalcanal had it.

It also held some sort of magic. His skin was buzzing gently, as if a low current of electricity were running through it. But this was a benign sort of magic, perhaps created in the confluence of violence and death. A side effect of the battles, perhaps. Nothing like the malevolent ice pick he'd felt jabbing his psyche at the sweatshop.

He wiped sweat from his brow. They were essentially on the equator. The heat was stifling. He went shirtless above his cargo pants. He couldn't imagine how the U.S. Marines had fought in such heat while wearing old wool uniforms. Even as relatively cool as Walker felt, moving was a little slow-motion. Wearing full battle rattle and in uniforms with a steel pot on one's head had to be akin to walking on the bottom of the ocean in a diving suit. Fighting seemed an improbable occupation in this gloriously beautiful but terribly remote place.

He made his way back to the airstrip. The crew chief and ground personnel were talking off to one side, smoking cigarettes. Holmes, Ruiz, and Laws lay on their gear in the shade of the Starlifter. Down the runway, Yaya played with Hoover. This could almost have been a perfect moment. But it was the quiet before the storm. It was that single moment of peace before all hell broke loose. The Japanese had felt it before the marines landed. The marines had felt it as they huddled, wet and miserable in their foxholes, every morning that they held the island. And Walker had felt it aboard the USS *Tennessee* as he prepared his sniper rifle, with the sun, the wind, and the sea something out of a travel magazine rather than a Somali pirate sea adventure.

They were waiting for an agency jet. The initial infiltration plan had been High Altitude/High Opening—HAHO. They'd switched that to High Altitude/Low Opening—HALO. They'd changed it yet again to Low Altitude/Low Opening—LALO. The plan was for the jet to cruise in just above the jungle canopy east of the Thaton airport. SEAL Team 666 would jump out the back and land before anyone noticed their exit.

It was a simple plan.

But there were problems with it.

The United States had no diplomatic relations with the government of Myanmar. Among other things, this meant that no U.S. citizens or their conveyances were allowed into or around the country. Additionally, the government had made it known that they were pretty pissed at the posture of the United States against their regime and in support of the Nobel Prize winner Aung San Suu Kyi. In fact, a high-level minister was quoted as saying that he "wouldn't spit into the mouth of an American, even if he was dying of thirst"—translated, of course. The bottom line was that they were not wanted and the Myanmar government would be on the lookout for any sort of American intervention into their internal politics.

Another problem was that neither Yaya nor Walker had ever done a LALO jump—a jump of less than nine hundred feet. Since it took three hundred feet for the chute to deploy, that left six hundred feet to steer the chute to safety.

They also had the wrong parachutes. The MC-4s were designed for free fall. They were highly maneuverable and agile, because the parachute canopies were relatively small. After all, it had more than thirty thousand feet to scoop air. But now they had less than nine hundred feet. They needed a much larger canopy. They also needed something they could leave behind that wouldn't identify them as American.

The final decision had been to pair Chinese cargo chutes with drag chutes. The drag chutes would be deployed from an open air ramp. The wind would rip these back, thus drawing out the yards of material that composed the cargo chutes. Without the drag chutes, the cargo chutes wouldn't have enough time to open. But with them, opening of the cargo chutes would be simultaneous to the SEALs' exiting the aircraft. And when the cargo chutes deployed, they'd reduce their speed to almost nothing.

Then they'd flutter gently to the ground like a feather from the ass of an eagle.

Simple, Laws had said.

Piece of cake, Ruiz had said.

Deal with it, Holmes had said.

Walker watched Hoover play for a while. It was going to be toughest on the dog. Walker hoped the pooch was going to be okay. He had a feeling they'd need her before it was all over.

The sound of an aircraft reached him. He craned his neck and looked for it in the sky. Finally he spied it and tracked its approach.

Laws came up to join him. "You look nervous."

Walker shrugged. "Always nervous before an op."

"All the changes don't help, either."

"It is what it is," Walker said flatly. He knew he was nervous. Talking about it would only make him more so.

Laws seemed to realize this, because he shut up until the plane was coming in for a landing.

It was a big cargo jet, painted yellow with red stripes and letters. Walker recognized the logo. DSL—WE DELIVER WORLDWIDE. He chuckled and shook his head. Count on the agency to find the sort of plane that would be able to land at an airport in a country that despised Americans. Not only was DSL not an American-owned company, it was essentially the mail, and even the most backwater, right-wing dictatorships liked to get packages filled with sleek Western merchandise. It landed and taxied to a stop near the Starlifter.

"Okay, SEALs. Get your gear and load up. We got a delivery to make."

Walker did a double take. It appeared as if their fearless leader had just made a joke.

And you know what? It was almost funny.

47

KADWAN. TWO WEEKS EARLIER.

The city was theirs. Their power was unimaginable. No one could stand against them. They rose as one, two souls within one body, and stood amid the ruins of what had once been a church, a ridiculous symbol to one of the angry gods the meek insisted upon worshipping. A dead priest lay at his feet, unable to comprehend the reality of Chi Long even when he'd met him face-to-face.

A thrall came to them. He wore the suit of a policeman, but he was a Karen, one of their people. The thrall leaned back his head and knelt. "My lord, they are ready."

"Have they prepared themselves?"

"They have, my lord."

"You have done well." Chi Long reached out with jagged nails and sliced the man's neck from ear to ear. The man sighed and seemed to smile beatifically, then collapsed as his body bled out.

Chi Long and the soul known now as He Who Had Once Been Alone strode out of the church and into the street. Bodies lay in piles. Funny how they clumped together when they were about to die. If his people were to retake the world, they'd have to rid themselves of the bodies. Their rot would bring unneeded disease and pestilence.

He Who Had Once Been Alone recognized one of the dead. The man had been his doctor and had seen him through a fever that had killed many. Such a shame that he'd died. It wasn't his fault he wasn't Karen. Saw Thuza Tun's body had been transformed into something beautiful with the coming of Chi Long. Gone was his balding head. Gone was his growing middle. He was now tall and muscled and regal. He was a warrior from a time long gone. He was a leader who could capture the hearts of other Karen. He was a king waiting to take his kingdom.

Yet despite this outward change, covered with the suit of tattooed skin, he remained himself, sometimes able to exert control, always able to hide from the ever-searching souls Chi Long had captured before. Together as one, they moved through the city until they reached a wide-open space. His thralls were moving his beasts in place. It took four of them for each beast. The arrangement was predetermined and would allow them access to the most power.

When the time came, their deaths would be beautiful.

48

SKY ABOVE THATON. LATE AFTERNOON.

Walker crabbed to the edge of the ramp. Wind whipped around him. His head was ensconced in a Protec skate helmet. He wore a fishing vest, cargo pants, and black body armor over a black T-shirt. On his back was a chute so big it looked like the top half of a Volkswagen Bug. The Stoner was in its M1950 weapons case. This LALO jump, unlike his previous HAHO jump, he didn't require lowering. Instead, he held on to the case for dear life.

He was the first one out. Without looking back, he knew the other SEALs were stacked behind him. Once he jumped, the next drag chute would be deployed, then the next, etc. Unlike other jumps, they wouldn't be able to come down together. The operation of the drag chute necessitated the passage of time, and that meant distance as the jet moved over the jungle.

"Ready."

The agency crew chief wore black cargo pants with a black Marilyn Manson shirt. Black glasses completed his ensemble. He held the drag chute in his arms.

Walker gave him a thumbs-up and turned around. The other SEALs turned as well. Walker leaned forward as far as he could. When the drag chute deployed, he felt a hard tug as it began to peel away the loosely packed Chinese cargo chute. As the cargo chute gathered air, he felt an increase in the pull against him. Then he was jerked so hard, he was sure his lungs, eyes, and tongue had been left on the ramp.

He went from ninety miles an hour to zero in less than five seconds. When he finally opened his eyes, his feet were brushing the tops of trees. He had no hope of steering, but he still tried. Pulling the risers of the cargo chute gave it all the maneuverability of a Cadillac on an ice rink.

He struck the first limb with his thighs. It didn't hurt as much as he'd anticipated. Then he struck another, and another. Stomach, head, neck, head, arms, back . . . he was ricocheting to the ground like a human pachinko ball.

Then he was snapped up short so hard that he dropped his rifle. He hoped he was far enough above ground that the drop line would save it. If it hit the ground, his optics would be toast. He heard a crack from above. He craned his neck to see what it was. He saw the tree limb as it began to fall. Then he closed his eyes and scrunched his neck together in anticipation. A moment later, everything turned to night.

49

TREES ABOVE THATON. LATE AFTERNOON.

The dog whined.

"I got you, girl." Yaya was snagged in a tree. He could pull out his knife and release them, but he needed to see how high he was first. No sense in jumping out of an airplane with a parachute only to die in a fall from a tree.

He toggled his MBITR. "Ghost One, this is Ghost Three, over."

No response. Not even static.

He'd struck the tree several times on the way down. He'd have to check the system in his helmet, but if he was a betting man, he was sure he'd find a short somewhere. Hopefully it was something he could fix.

But first things first.

Above him the canopy was thick with twisted limbs and green leaves. Hoover was rigged to his chest, so he couldn't see beneath him. He kipped his legs to begin swinging so he could see the ground below. He gauged it to be about twenty to thirty feet. Just enough to break a leg.

He thought for a moment. If he'd been in an American chute, he'd have a reserve that he could deploy to use as a rope. Chinese cargo chutes didn't need reserves. After all, cargo couldn't activate them.

Looking around again, he spied a tree with sturdy limbs about six feet to his right. It only took him a moment to decide what to do.

"Okay, girl. This is what we're going to do," he said, looking into the soulful eyes of the Malinois. "I'm going to lower you down. You won't be able to reach the ground, but there's good reason for it. One, if I fall, you'll be that much closer to the ground. Two, I need to be able to use my arms to see if I can save us." He petted the dog. "Inshallah, we'll be down in a few moments."

The dog whined again, then seemed to catch herself. She licked Yaya on the cheek and resumed panting.

Yaya ensured Hoover was secured to the drop line, then unclipped her from the rigging. There was a moment of release when her weight left his chest, but he caught it with his arms.

"See you in a bit, girl. Keep your head down."

He gently lowered her to the end of the tether. The other end of the line was clipped to the harness on her back, so there was no worry of strangulation, although he was aware that when he began swinging toward the tree, she'd swing as well.

He felt her weight the way a boat would feel an anchor. To gain momentum with his hips, he kipped his legs and began to swing away from the tree, then toward it. Back and forth he went until his fingers brushed the bark of his target. Two more kips and he managed to grab a protrusion with the tips of his fingers. He felt himself slipping backwards and reached out for a vine he'd spied earlier. But as his hand grasped the slender green vegetation, he realized it wasn't a vine.

But it was already too late. He swung backwards and brought the object with him. The snake wrapped itself around his wrist, its head rising to appraise him. He wasn't a herpetologist, but he knew a tree snake when he saw one. Many of them were venomous. This one opened its pointed head and revealed a cotton-white mouth and two slender fangs.

Yaya did what any SEAL would do. He shook his arm furiously and screamed. The snake fell away and it was only too late that he realized that Hoover was below him. He squirmed to see the snake land squarely on the dog's back. Hoover snapped at it and shook her body, much as the SEAL had done. The snake fell to the jungle floor. Hoover looked up at Yaya, none too pleased.

"Sorry, girl!"

Yaya's pendulum movement had almost stilled. So he kipped again to get it started. This time as he gained momentum, he searched the tree for any more unexpected fauna. Thankfully, there was nothing. He was able to grasp a limb, cut away from his risers, and climb down the tree. Once Hoover's feet hit the ground it became easier, because Yaya no longer needed to hold the weight of the both of them.

Hoover began to growl and snap. But Yaya's grip on the tree was too precarious for him to look. He shimmied down as fast as he could. When his boots hit the ground, he jerked his 9mm free and swept the jungle. Then he saw Hoover.

The dog stood with the snake in its jaws. It strode to the SEAL, deposited the reptile at his feet, and looked up as if to say, *That's how it's done.*

"All right, girl. You done good. Now let's make the rendezvous." Yaya pulled out his compass and his tablet and oriented himself to the scrolling map. After a moment, he gestured in a direction.

"Point," he commanded.

Hoover took off like a shot.

50

CIRCUS WAREHOUSE PERIMETER. NIGHT.

When Walker had finally regained consciousness he had been upside down and about a foot from the ground. Beneath him raced a division of ants, making it seem as if the ground was moving. He'd puked, a sure sign of a concussion.

But he'd made the rendezvous with the others just fine. With the exception of the bad luck of their coms breaking down, the insertion went without a hitch. Of course, all hell could be breaking loose Stateside and a comet could be plunging into the Atlantic but they'd never know about it. He'd hoped that the twenty-four-kilometer trek through the jungle would clear his head, but it only served to make him feel worse. The faster his heart beat, the more his head throbbed. The fact was they were too deep in enemy territory for anything to be done about it.

Once outside the warehouse compound, the SEALs conducted reconnaissance using both infrared and night-vision devices. Their only thermal imagery came from the Leupold scope attached to Walker's sniper rifle. They hadn't counted on being out of coms with support. NRO had deployed a geosynchronous satellite above to provide the SEALs with real-time imagery intelligence across all visual spectrums. The SEALs didn't detect any evidence of habitation. The guards that had previously been stationed around the site were no longer there. It appeared to be deserted.

Holmes ordered Yaya to find a way to fix their coms. Both Laws's and Walker's ComTac headsets had been ripped and crushed in their descents. Holmes had his data mode and voice cables ripped free and his uplink wasn't functioning, although there was no visible evidence of damage. Ruiz's set had lost its cipher fill, which meant although it would work, it couldn't talk to anyone. And Yaya's receiver unit had been punctured by a branch. He had an ugly green and purple bruise beneath it to show how lucky he'd been.

They hadn't been prepared for the LALO. Had they had more time, they would have protected the equipment better. As it turned out, they were lucky the only damage was to the communications gear. Yaya was able to scrape together two complete systems that could talk to each other, but had no uplink capability. Holmes took one; the other he gave to Laws. There was talk about Walker taking it in his role of sniper, but Holmes was against that. He wanted to split the four remaining SEALs into two teams and he wanted to be able to synchronize activities.

Walker was reminded of the stories he'd heard about Camp Rhino. In the earliest days of the war in Afghanistan, a drug smuggler's outpost was chosen to become the coalition's first firm foothold on Afghani soil. Air Force special operators HALO'd in and secured a drop zone. SEALs arrived next to ascertain evidence of enemy personnel. Back then everyone in Afghanistan was an enemy, whether it be some poor trader with a camel or a fighter with an RPG. The SEALs were from Delta Platoon, SEAL Team 3. They were essentially one hundred nautical miles from friendly forces and experienced intermittent communications. Walker remembered talking to a guy about how when the coms went out they kept wondering if the mission might have been called off and they didn't know it. Back then the Task Force K-Bar commander was operating by the seat of his pants. The plan was to fly three hundred marines in from the Fifteenth Marine Expeditionary Unit by helicopter. The SEALs were to observe until then. The decision to postpone the insertion of the marines by twenty-four hours was made by the task-force commander, but no one informed the SEALs. During the last twelve hours of their mission, they had lost all coms and couldn't help but wonder what was going on.

But every SEAL knew that unless specifically told otherwise, they were to continue on with their mission. For the SEALs of SEAL Team 3, their mission was to observe and secure until the marines arrived. For the SEALs of SEAL Team 666, their mission was to try and discover the command and control network involved with the movement or nonmovement of the chimeras to America.

So it was Charlie Mike—continue mission.

The single-story warehouse was about seventy meters long by twenty meters wide. It had a tin roof and tin sides, which appeared to be affixed to a two-by-four frame. A dirt parking lot was in the front. It held several local vehicles and a five-ton cargo truck. The left side of the compound held several outbuildings that contained broken equipment and a small charcoal stove. The back, which had access to the front by a dirt road, had several open bays and a covered landing under which rested fifty crates identical to the ones they found aboard the cargo ship.

Infrared, night vision, and thermal all proclaimed that the site was deserted. But as they sat in the jungle, the noise of strange insects and animals surrounding them, Walker couldn't help feeling that the whole thing was too easy.

"It's Echo Platoon all over again," Laws said, mirroring Walker's thoughts. "This is a sensitive site exploitation, pure and simple."

"You were at Prata Ghar?" Yaya asked.

"I was."

"I was in Echo three years later. They still talk about the pucker factor on that one."

"I heard there were no casualties," Holmes said.

"Wasn't for lack of trying." Laws shook his head. "There were fourteen buildings. The Germans took the largest one and we took the remaining thirteen. We named each one after a major U.S. city. Washington, Chicago, Los Angeles—you get the idea. We had some Feebs, Air Force SOF, a pair of EOD boys, and fifteen SEALs. I don't mind shooting at bad people. In fact, I prefer it. And I don't mind CQB. But Jesus, Mary, and Joseph and all the farm animals, we cleared three hundred and fourteen rooms. There could have been a beegee behind each door, so we had to be ready. My ass was puckered so hard I think I shit Silly String for a week."

"Not many rooms here," Walker pointed out.

"And it looks like there are no beegees," Yaya added.

"Which makes it worse. Now we have to be ready for anything, all the time. Wired tight. Always on."

"Maybe you're getting a little too old for this," Ruiz said.

"Fucking hell," Laws snapped. "I'll give you too old. SEAL can't even bitch for a minute to get it out of his system?"

Everyone was silent for a while.

Finally Holmes asked Laws, "Is it?"

"Is it what?"

"Out of your system."

"Yes."

"Good. Then let's go."

They deployed Walker fifteen meters inside the tree line. He found a tree that provided him with a set of low branches to establish a nest. He switched his scope to thermal and watched as they progressed in two teams to either side of the structure. Worried about traps and IEDs, they left Hoover behind. The dog whined gently at the base of the tree, her eyes on Yaya's back as he departed.

Walker turned to scan 180 degrees. Other than a few monkey screeches and birdcalls in the trees, there was nothing living.

51

CIRCUS WAREHOUSE. NIGHT.

Ruiz moved stealthily behind Holmes. They'd reached the left side of the warehouse. Ruiz stared forward through the scope mounted on his Super 90. Infrared images were in black-and-white; the whiter the image, the more heat it was giving off. Right now he saw nothing but a field of gray. He wished he had access to a thermal scope like Walker had on his Stoner. Those handled more of the infrared spectrum and provided a color feedback, showing heat using the visible red spectrum rather than black-and-white. It was certainly more nuanced and had a greater degree of accuracy.

He'd once taken his thermal scope back to the woods of West Virginia. His hometown had a yearly possum hunt in the local woods. Sometimes there'd be seventy dead possum at the end of the day. He hated the hunt. What had been a sport had been turned into a tournament. But he'd fixed them . . . for that year, anyway. The night before the hunt, using his thermal imager, he'd tracked down every single possum and had relocated them to an abandoned farm. One hundred and forty-three possum. The night of the big hunt there wasn't a single thermal image larger than a squirrel in any of the trees. There were more possum lying dead on the side of the road than there were in the forest. For the first time in the history of the hunt, not a single possum was killed. Eventually he let it be known that it was him and that pissed people off even more. But he didn't care.

Holmes began moving toward the front, leading with his MP5. He checked the corner, then knelt. Ruiz knelt as well, keeping the boss in his peripheral vision while he swept the rear and side.

"Clear front," Holmes whispered into his MBITR.

Ruiz couldn't hear the response, but when Holmes turned and moved toward the back, he imagined Laws had it clear on the other side as well.

They made their way around the corner. Although it was dark, he could make out Laws and Yaya coming from the other corner. Both groups moved with care. Although there were no windows, they were approaching the area with open bay doors. Thermal imaging and infrared had its limits. If the steel was thick enough, a platoon of beegees could go undetected. Then there was also the fear of the chimera. They'd only encountered one on the ship, but they'd been well aware that the other crates in the hold had held hundreds of them . . . just as these crates probably did. They'd know soon enough. Part of the sensitive site exploitation would be to inventory the chimera and investigate their size, weight, and makeup. If there really was a threat to the United States, the information they'd provide could be critical to the defense of the country.

The wooden crates weren't arranged in any order. Some were stacked three high, reaching a height of twelve feet, while others were unstacked. It was as if a giant kid had just tossed his letter blocks on the floor. But before they could investigate the crates, they had to clear the building.

Holmes moved in fast. Ruiz kept on his six. The interior of

the warehouse was shrouded in darkness. Holmes and Ruiz checked their infrareds, but it was nothing but grays and blacks. They switched to night vision and the darkness was illuminated in an eerie green. They scanned the room. They could just see the opposite wall through the darkness. The center of the room was filled with more haphazardly stacked crates.

"Moving left," Holmes whispered into the MBITR.

They moved forward, hugging the outside wall as best they could. Here and there were smaller boxes, tables, and chairs. There was a spot where three couches were side by side. On the center one rested an old engine, rusted beyond recognition.

Ruiz continually scanned the room, his ears attuned for even the slightest sound. Not that he was trigger happy, but the longer they stayed in the room without being able to really see it, the more puckered his ass got. In fact, his skin began to crawl as he imagined a dozen fighters hidden behind the crates in the center of the room, just waiting to open fire on them.

They reached the corner and turned.

Ruiz remained in place, facing the center of the room as Holmes continued down the short side of the building. Moments ticked by as the SEAL team leader moved to the corner. When he arrived, he announced it into his MBITR, then gave Ruiz a hand signal.

Ruiz's chest tightened. If it was going to happen, it would happen here. He began creeping to the center of the room. He opened his eyes as wide as he could. He switched back and forth from night vision to IR, just to make sure that there were no heat signatures. When he judged that he was three meters away, he stopped and went to one knee.

Laws did the same to his right. Holmes was on his left. Which meant that Yaya was opposite him. They paused for a moment. Then both Laws and Holmes gave another hand signal. Ruiz closed his eyes tightly, but a moment later, even through his closed lids, he saw the surface of the sun simultaneously to hearing a tremendous bang. He opened his eyes and followed the flashbang grenade to the boxes, which were shoved together in a solid mass. Not even one beegee could have fit inside there.

"Turning on lights," Holmes said as he switched off the night-vision/IR scope and turned on the light attachment affixed to his MP5.

Everyone else did the same. Four spears of light stabbed through the darkness. The room was empty.

Not that Ruiz was trying to find things to worry about, but there should have been someone there. Where were the guards they'd seen on the imagery? Why wasn't anyone there guarding the chimera? Unless . . .

He moved to one of the crates and rapped against it. He was rewarded with a hollow thud.

"Boss, these are empty."

Yaya rapped on several as well. "These, too."

"What the fuck?" Laws looked around. "Think it's a trap?"

Holmes knitted his brows. "Walker would have let us know."

"Hoover as well," Yaya added.

"Still . . ." Laws gestured toward the empty crates.

"Come on, SEALs," Holmes said decisively. "On me."

The other three formed on their leader and they moved quickly out the rear bay. When they reached the door, he stopped and kneeled. Yaya did the same beside him. Ruiz and Laws stood with their weapons ready. They listened to the night. Animal screams answered them from the jungle. Then they heard another sound. Scratching.

They immediately looked at the jumble of crates before them. Maybe they weren't *all* empty.

"Spread," Holmes ordered.

The SEALs separated. They each went into a crouch, their heads on a swivel, weapons pointed toward the crates.

Something was worrying Ruiz as he crept forward. An image of the crate and the crazy Chinese captain flashed through his mind. Hadn't his blood been the catalyst for the chimera?

If so, where was the blood this time? There wasn't anyone else here and he found it unbelievable that Walker would have let someone approach the crates while the rest of the team was in the building. He glanced toward Walker's hide site. He heard the sound again, but it wasn't coming from the boxes. It was coming from beneath them. He was about to shout a warning when the floor dropped out from under him.

52

CIRCUS WAREHOUSE. NIGHT.

Walker saw them move out of the warehouse, then disappear. No, not disappear. They fell through the ground. He started to climb down from his perch, but thought better of it. An image of Holmes's angry face shot through his good intention. He remained where he was but stared through his scope, hoping to see something to shoot.

Hoover growled from beneath as if she knew something was wrong.

"Easy, girl. Let's see what's going on."

Suddenly the sounds of a firefight rent the night. He heard the distinct rapid-fire burps of the MP5, the angry barks of the shotgun, and the dull stutters of AK-47s.

What the hell was going on?

The sound of vehicles came from the front of the warehouse. Three five-ton trucks lumbered around the building. The firefight continued, but at a lesser rate. He saw Yaya crawl out of the hole and stagger to one of the boxes. He'd lost his shotgun. He pulled his 9mm from his thigh holster and in one move fired at the two men coming after him.

The trucks made the turn and rammed into the crates. Wood exploded into splinters. Crates tumbled. Yaya disappeared beneath an avalanche of broken and splintered wood. The trucks skidded to a halt. Men in uniforms poured out the rear of each vehicle. Walker tracked them through his scope. He wanted so badly to take a shot. But there were too many of them. If he fired, he'd only succeed in bringing attention to himself.

Damn!

As the soldiers surrounded the hole, the sounds of firing diminished to nothing. The soldiers cheered.

Walker bit his lip.

He watched as the bodies of Holmes, Laws, and Ruiz were dragged out of the hole and carried into one of the trucks. More bodies were pulled out. He was gratified to see that there were five dead soldiers for every dead SEAL.

His chest tightened at the realization that his team was dead.

The soldiers weren't messing around. Once they had the bodies loaded on the trucks, they climbed aboard and started the engines.

Walker felt helpless. He wanted to shoot, but he knew that someone had to survive the mission to tell Billings and NAVSPECWAR Command what happened. He pounded the tree with his fist as the trucks pulled away.

Hoover took off after the trucks.

Walker called out to her, but the dog was single-focused. What she'd do to the trucks if she caught up with them, Walker had no idea. But he shouted his encouragement. "Get 'em, girl! Chew their hearts out!"

He watched until the trucks and the dog were out of sight, and then he shouted to the universe. "Motherfucker!"

It took five minutes for him to compose himself enough to climb down from his perch. He slung the rifle over his shoulder and pulled out his pistol. He held it in a two-handed grip angled toward the ground as he walked morosely toward the killing zone. With the lights off, it was hard to see, but he didn't need the lights. The image of the location was burned into his mind and would remain there forever.

Sometime during his mini-breakdown it had occurred to him that Yaya was still beneath the crates—he hadn't seen them take him. The least he could do was to check the body and confirm what he already suspected.

When he arrived at the rear of the warehouse, he flicked the light on his pistol to On. He moved carefully to the hole. It was a rectangle, about fifteen by thirty feet. Judging from the litter of boards ten feet down, it appeared to be nothing more than a large animal trap. He could imagine its construction—a series of long boards down the middle, boards along the sides, all covered with dirt.

There were still more than a dozen bodies in the bottom of the hole. Many had been shot in the face by a shotgun, eyes, noses, cheeks, mouths obliterated into a single mush of blood and gristle. Even more were stitched with MP5 rounds. It had been a horrendous firefight. Blood covered every surface in the trap. By the litter of shells, he could tell it had been a shooting gallery. His brothers had really had no chance.

He turned and examined the avalanche of crates. There was no sign of Yaya. He tried to move a crate and found them only moderately heavy. Using both hands, he could move them one at a time. So began the project of moving and hoping. With each crate moved, he searched for signs of his brother SEAL. But it was as if Yaya had vanished. Walker moved eleven crates and still there was triple that amount.

Then he heard a moan.

It had to be Yaya. Walker waited until the sound came again; then he located the direction and began slinging crates out of the way as fast as he could. He didn't care where they went or even if they fell into the hole. His entire focus was on the sound of the intermittent moans.

He saw a booted foot. By the make of the boot—Hi-Tec—he could tell it was Yaya. The SEAL was faceup beneath a crate. Walker moved two more crates, then was finally able to lift the crate off his friend.

Yaya's face was covered in blood and his left arm was twisted at an awkward angle, but otherwise he seemed okay. Then again, there was no telling what kind of internal bleeding or organ damage he'd suffered.

Walker kneeled beside him. "Hey, wake up. Where does it hurt?"

"Ungh. Everywhere," Yaya answered, as if he were on Valium.

Walker began to compress the skin around the kidneys, lungs, and finally the pelvis. Yaya gave him a sickly grin. "Not even a bottle of wine, sailor?"

Walker grinned as well and grabbed the SEAL by the shoulders. "Maybe next time, Yaya."

53

CIRCUS WAREHOUSE. EARLY MORNING.

With Yaya's arm set in a makeshift sling and his wounds cleaned, they sat on one of the sofas inside the warehouse so that Yaya could relate the story. Besides a dislocated shoulder, he had a through-and-through in his calf and a bullet trail along the right side of his scalp.

". . . then the ground gave way." He wiped at his double-mashed mouth with a rag. "Must have been forty of them waiting. And don't get me wrong, the ground was firm. They must have activated it from below. Pulled out a support or something."

"It must have been hell with all the gunfire."

Yaya knitted his brow and shook his head as the events came back to him. "You'd think so, right? I mean it was, at first. We were firing at everything that moved and there was a lot of movement, let me tell you. But . . ."

"But what?"

"We realized they weren't aiming at us."

"What the hell does that mean?" Walker asked incredulously.

"Just like I said. They weren't shooting at *us*."

"But you were shooting at them."

"With everything we had. When my Super 90 ran out, I tried to climb out of the hole and draw my nine-mil."

"I saw that. They came out after you."

"And I popped them. What hit me by the way? A train?"

"Close. A five-ton crashed into the crates."

Yaya sipped water from the side of his mouth, wincing as a cut came in contact with the canteen.

"Back to the firefight. Weren't they shooting at you?"

Yaya shrugged. "I just don't think so. Mind you, I was only paying attention to those in my line of fire, and I'm telling you, they weren't firing at *me*."

"Then what were they doing?"

"A lot of them were firing into the sky, but some were trying to coldcock me with their rifle."

"That doesn't make sense. Unless . . ." Walker's eyes brightened as hope dawned in them. "Unless they didn't want to kill you."

"They wanted to capture us," Yaya said as the possibility hit him as well. "Are you certain that the others are dead?"

"I thought I was. I would have never believed that the men in the hole weren't trying to kill you. But now that that's a possibility, maybe they're alive. Maybe they're just unconscious."

"To what end?" Yaya wondered.

"No kidding. What are they going to do with them?"

"If Laws's idea of Chi Long is at all accurate, they might be facing a demon even now." Yaya turned to look at Walker. "You've seen demons before. You were possessed. What would it do?"

An image of himself chasing a cripple down the street with a bloody piece of metal slammed into his consciousness. It took a moment for him to shake it away. "I think this one is different. Mine was inside me. This one already has a host. A willing host if what we think about the skin suits is true," he added. "My guess is that it could do pretty much anything it wanted."

"And we have no idea where they are."

"Hoover might."

"That dog would chase them until it collapsed." Yaya made a face as he thought about the loss of the dog. "It should have done better by me. Damn dog should have stayed in place."

"I don't know. I think maybe she did. She did what I would have done if I'd been able."

"Well, unless Hoover comes back and somehow tells us where they are, it's like finding a virgin in Patpong," Yaya said solemnly.

"Know what they call a virgin in Patpong?" Walker asked.

"What?

"Oh, I thought you knew. I've never heard of one."

"Very funny. Is that your way of telling me we don't have a chance in hell of finding them or something?"

"Or something."

"If only our coms worked. We need SPG and support more than ever now."

"We could check the soldiers." Remembering Yaya's wounds, he hastily added, "I mean I could check them. We might be able to get something from their pocket trash. I'll bring you what I find." He gestured toward some of the boxes and containers along the walls. "Maybe there's something in one of these you can use to fix the coms."

Yaya stared morosely at the darkness, then hauled himself to his feet.

"Fine. You go check the dead and I'll see what I can find here."

Walker exited the building and began searching the bodies. They'd already started to smell. Offal and entrails were the worst. Neither were smells that should be outside the human body. Now, mixed with the humid Myanmar night, it created an olfactory cauldron from the bodies' unexpected excrescence. The smell and feel of the corpses was something new to Walker. As he worked among the dead, he fought to keep his stomach from crawling all the way out.

He'd killed before. But the pirates had been over a mile away and he'd been too busy to deal with the aftermath of the deaths of the Chinese Triad enforcers. This was something different. It was truly a butcherous job to check all the pockets. He found a lot of packs of cigarettes along with lighters and matches, but no wallets or identification cards. Several times he found a slip of paper with writing on it, but without Laws's facility with languages, he had no hope of knowing what they said. Still, he pocketed these in case he could use them later.

He found a strip of map on one soldier who had stars on his shoulder boards. Just a piece torn from something larger, but it showed a town on a coast, with the ocean to the west. Or was it the east? He turned the page upside down. It had Chinese characters, and remembering the shape of the characters Laws had showed them helped him determine which direction. He turned it back around so that the ocean was on the west. Here and there Xs had been made. What looked like a sporting field of some sort had been circled several times.

The sky was brightening by the time he climbed out of the hole. When he stood on the edge, he gratefully inhaled the clean air. As if the oxygen was capable of increasing his awareness, a thought came to him.

He hurried inside. He found Yaya on the floor amid a pile of odd cables and electronic parts. He held up a shredded wire and gave it a look of sheer disgust.

"They're coming back," Walker said with a certainty.

Yaya looked up. "Who's coming back?"

"The soldiers. They didn't finish their cleanup. And my guess is that they'll be looking for you. I think you got lost in their rush to remove the others."

Yaya's expression went from concerned to thoughtful. "If they come back, then we have a chance to find the others."

Walker nodded. "Exactly. And we need to be ready." He pointed toward the pile of electronics. "Any luck with those?"

"I don't even think the love child of Jules Verne and Guglielmo Marconi could make sense of these. Some of these cables come from World War Two." He tossed one aside and got to his feet. His legs were wobbly. "With any luck they'll bring back the MBITRs all fixed, shiny, and like new."

"Yeah, just don't hold your breath."

54

SPG OFFICES. CORONADO ISLAND.

The lack of radio communications was driving Jen crazy. All they could figure was that the roughness of the team's multiple-tree landing had caused some problems with the uplink. She'd hoped that Chief Petty Officer Jabouri would have been able to fix them, but the lack of contact told otherwise.

What was even more infuriating was watching the attack unfold. If they'd had coms, they could have warned the SEALs about the trap. Even though the satellite hadn't been in place to see them set the trap, once it was overhead, the heat signatures from the bodies beneath the wood were obvious. All it would have taken was one word and the SEALs could have dealt with the threat.

But as it appeared now, three of the five SEALs were dead. Guiltily, Jen was happy to see Walker alive.

They'd followed the convoy of trucks south to the town of Kadwan. A little research determined that it was the old traditional capital of the Karen and seemed as likely as any place for a Karen insurrection to be headquartered.

But a strange thing happened when the satellite tried to view the city. It couldn't. Not only was there an improbable and immobile cloud layer over the town, but there seemed to be thousands of fires that were keeping the thermal imaging system from correctly sensing.

Musso had been in contact with technicians at the NRO to determine what was spoofing the images, but so far they were at a loss.

Suddenly the door opened and Billings marched in. Jen had never seen her look so concerned.

"We've lost three," Billings said, more of a statement than a question.

"So it appears . . . although they could just be wounded."

"Do you have a copy of the firefight? I want to see it."

Jen turned to a workstation. "Liz, prepare this system to replay the firefight. Check the log for the time stamp." She gestured to the seat in front of the wide-screen monitor. "You can sit here, ma'am."

"I'll stand."

Liz dialed the video up on the screen. The view seemed to be from several hundred feet, although it was really a thousand times that. Still, the images were clear. They could see the layout and the surrounding jungle. The video began with the four SEALs leaving the wood line.

Liz pointed to a spot in the trees. "Walker is positioned here."

"Thank you," Billings said tightly.

Everyone in the room stopped working as the video played on the smaller screen. The silence gave the events a sad undertone. Billings didn't move a muscle as she stood with her arms crossed, watching the SEALs and their apparent demise. As the SEALs fell into the hole, her mouth tightened and her fingers began to twitch.

When it was all over, she said, "Again."

Liz looked at Jen, who nodded.

Within five seconds, the entire video segment was being replayed.

Jen glanced at the other images. Kadwan was still virtually invisible. There was no action at the warehouse. The surviving SEALs had gone inside. Musso was charged with informing her when they moved outside.

When the video ended, Billings turned. "They were firing into the air," she said.

"Muslim fighters do that frequently," Musso pointed out.

"But usually after they accomplish something. They even fire in the air at weddings. It's an expression of joy. Of accomplishment. These soldiers were in the middle of a firefight. Where was the accomplishment?"

Musso and Jen exchanged looks.

"Let's run it again," Jen said.

They ran the video again. Everyone gathered around the monitor and saw what Billings had seen. They also noticed that none of the soldiers appeared to be firing at the SEALs.

"What do you make of that?" Billings asked when it was all over.

"They weren't aiming at them," Jen stated as her mind began to work over that fact.

"Yet the SEALs were taken away."

"The action in the hole was too jumbled and chaotic," Musso said. "But I think there's a chance that they might be alive."

Billings nodded. "I think you're right." Once she'd said that, she seemed to relax a bit. She spied a free chair and lowered herself onto it. "Anyone have coffee?"

"You staying?" Jen asked.

"To the bitter end," Billings said. "Do you have anything else?"

"Musso has some additional information," Jen said.

Liz brought Billings coffee. She took a sip, grimaced, but didn't say anything else. She put the coffee down. To Musso she said, "What do you have?"

Musso rose from his workstation with a stack of papers in his hands. "We had Cyber Command scrape servers with known Myanmar access nodes, searching for all instances of Saw Thuza Tun. There's more than seven thousand hits. I know that's a lot, but through the process of disambiguation I was able to learn that the owner of the land upon which the warehouse—that warehouse—sits"—he pointed to the screen—"is none other than Saw Thuza Tun."

"So his name is connected to the cargo ship and the warehouse. Any other connections?"

"I checked the registries for the other ships in the harbor that we were concerned about, but none of them can be traced back to this individual."

"What does that lead you to believe, Musso?" Billings asked.

"That attacking America was a complete ruse."

Billings pinched the bridge of her nose and closed her eyes. "So we're back to this individual and his people trying to draw us into action. What else do we know about this Thuza Tun?"

"He has multiple holdings centered around Kadwan. He's also been active in the Karen separatist movement. I found several editorials he provided in the last ten years regarding the importance of international attention regarding Burma/Myanmar. He rants about the suspension of the constitution in 1974, about the confinement of the Nobel Prize–winning activist Aung San Suu Kyi, and America's willingness to go to every other corner of the planet except for their country. He definitely calls us out."

Billings nodded, deep in thought. "What else?"

"Then five years ago he dropped out of the limelight. He had a regular column and followers, but he disappeared."

"Any reason why?" Jen asked. She'd asked Musso this question several hours ago and was hoping he'd been able to find an answer.

"I'll let Liz answer that."

The young woman stood and approached nervously, picking at the file in her hand.

"Don't worry. I won't bite," Billings said with a flat smile.

Liz laughed, but it came out as a bark. She licked her lips. "At first we thought maybe that he'd been arrested for his politics, but we found no record of this. We did find, in a collateral search in the Drug Enforcement Agency database, that he's a known facilitator of cross-border drug transit through southern Thailand. He has links with several Triad figures, all who have been under investigation by the DEA."

"That might explain the connection," Musso offered.

"I was also able to track his major purchases over the past fifteen years, since the advent of the use of the Internet in Burma/Myanmar. Any older records haven't been added." Liz cleared her throat. "I have a record of all of his land purchases, including his substantial holdings around Kadwan. But what I found interesting is this purchase."

She pulled out a photo and placed it on the table next to Billings. It was a full-color glossy of an overhead of an ancient town that was still partially covered with jungle. The buildings looked like they were shaped like immense pointed bells. Billings leaned forward to study the photo, but made no move to pick it up.

"This is Wethali. It's the birthplace of Pyinsa Kalayni, who was the mother of King Kyansittha of the Pagan dynasty circa 1040 CE. It was a tourist site until the mid-nineties. The government reallocated their resources to the military and shut this down. Thuza Tun bought the town from a Myanmar general."

"They can do that? Just buy towns?" the admiral asked.

"They can in Myanmar," Musso said. "Tell them about the archaeological site."

Liz's eyes brightened. "Yes, of course. Wethali dates back to the fourth century. It was said to have been founded by a great warrior who couldn't be killed. Sound familiar?"

"Chi Long," Jen said. "He was around two hundred years earlier, right?"

Liz nodded. "There's not a lot of information about Wethali, other than the place was destroyed by an earthquake in the eighth century. Until then, it seemed to be the center of the region, possibly even the capital."

"Do you think Chi Long retired to live the good life in Burma?" Jen asked.

Musso shrugged. "He could have. We just don't know. The data we have is so sparse that we have to stitch it together with supposition." He glanced at Billings. "But we're pretty certain of our analysis."

"Wrap this up for me," Billing said. "What's your hypothesis?"

Musso stepped forward. "We think that Thuza Tun got a line on an artifact, probably having to do with Chi Long, buried in the ruins of Wethali. We think he bought the land, searched for the artifact, found it, and is now a host for Chi Long."

"That's a lot of supposition," Billings said. "What benefit would he have for hosting Chi Long?"

"A couple," Liz answered. "Such a figure could become the center for a more active separatist movement. Chi Long was a general and was used to leading people. Also, if he can't be killed, he can spin that anyway he wants, including that he's divine."

"You mean a god?"

"Or the son of one," Musso said with a shrug. "Sure."

"Okay. I buy it. It sounds right." Billings stood wearily. "Get me to a secure phone. I need to contact the Sissy and let them know what's going on."

"Certainly," Jen said, hurrying to a side door.

55

CIRCUS WAREHOUSE. EARLY MORNING.

They set the trap well. Walker had opened one of the crates and laid it to one side. Yaya now sat inside, with several airholes in the top and firing ports made from slits cut into the wood. They'd used steel plates they found to retrofit the walls with armor. Walker left Yaya with his 9mm pistol and ammunition, which meant that the SEAL now had two pistols.

Walker moved back to his original location, then thought better of it. He was too far away to come to the aid of his friend. He needed someplace closer, with as much cover and concealment as he could have.

He moved back into the warehouse, where he arranged the crates in the center of the room so that a person could actually fit inside the grouping, then made it so he could escape easily if needed.

Being in the dark was smart. He could look out and see who was approaching, but until someone stepped inside and acclimated their eyes, they couldn't see him.

When he was finally ready, he settled in for a long wait.

But the wait wasn't as long as he expected. Forty-six minutes later, a five-ton pulled into the rear of the warehouse. Soldiers jumped down from the rear and dropped the metal door, which would make it easier to put bodies inside. They took their time. The first thing they did was smoke a few cigarettes. The five of them squatted in a circle as they talked.

Walker noted that each carried an AK hung rakishly across his back. They also all wore sandals, which he surmised wasn't regular military issue. Through his scope he could make out their yellowed teeth and their unshaven faces. These were the dregs sent to pick up the trash. He shouldn't have to worry too much about them, but he wasn't going to underestimate them, either.

He set up the shot. He could take out three of them without a problem, and if he could anticipate where the other two would head, he'd be perfect. Of course he wanted to keep one alive to interrogate. If they were lucky, the one he left standing would speak a little English.

He decided to take the shot.

Suddenly two new people entered his view. One was a soldier and the other must have been the driver. This new soldier wore boots, a pressed uniform, and a camouflaged baseball hat pulled low over his eyes. Where the other soldiers looked more like refugees, he was all spit and polish. He gestured into the hole and said something in a rapid-fire local tongue. The soldiers grudgingly got to their feet, argued a moment about who was going in the hole, then three of them went down and two stayed at the edge. By the wrinkle of their noses, they weren't pleased about the smell. All the while, they were watched by Spit and Polish.

The driver was another matter. He looked like he'd stepped straight out of an American mall. He wore white-and-red Reeboks and faded jeans and a T-shirt that said MADE IN AMERICA.

Walker put his aiming point between the crosshatch and the top of the letter A in AMERICA. If he pulled the trigger now, he could blow out the young man's spine.

The guy couldn't have been more than twenty-five years old. He had the look of a city kid. He held a cell phone in his hand and was either texting or watching something in the universal way of inattentive addiction that every kid in America had mastered by the age of eleven. His nonchalance spoke volumes.

The driver entered the darkened warehouse, walked unerringly to the couch holding the engine, and reached deep between the cushions. He came out with a plastic bag. He opened it and removed what could only be a joint. He had it lit in a moment and was leaning back on the couch, inhaling the sweet leaf.

Meanwhile, the soldiers were working fast. One by one they handed bodies up to the soldiers waiting at ground level, who in turn rolled them into the back of the truck. When it looked as if they were done, Spit and Polish put the soldiers in a line and called out to the driver.

Walker glanced over at the driver, who was halfway through his joint.

He shouted something back, pocketed the bag, and stood. He inhaled deeply, looking around as he did. His gaze stopped on the boxes in the center of the room. He stared right at the spot where Walker was hidden. But did he see him? Or was he noticing that the boxes had been moved?

Walker was ready to fire, but the driver turned away, dropped the joint on the floor, and wiped it away with his feet.

He strode a little unsteadily toward the opening.

Spit and Polish said something nasty and slapped the driver, knocking him to the ground.

Walker took his shot.

Spit and Polish's head jerked back and he fell.

Walker fired twice more, each shot taking down a soldier.

Yaya joined the fracas, double-tapping the remaining three, which left only the driver, who was crouched at the entrance, screaming. He started to run out the door, but Yaya was there, a 9mm pistol in his hand. The driver spun and ran back inside, straight toward Walker, who slid out of his concealed position.

Walker stood tall, his Stoner notched into his shoulder and pointing directly at the driver's face. The driver tried to stop, but his feet went out from under him. He fell backwards, sliding to a stop at Walker's feet. Walker put his rifle into the center of the man's forehead and said, "Don't move."

The driver's eyes were wild. He looked as if he were about to bolt.

Good. Now to figure out a way of ascertaining where their friends had been taken.

Walker reached down and snatched the cell phone from the young man's trembling hands. "You won't be needing this anymore."

"You . . . you . . . you . . ." the man stuttered.

Yaya approached from behind. "I think this one speaks English."

"At least one word of it," Walker said. "Let's see if he knows any more words. Got a name?"

"Ed . . . Eddie."

"Okay, Ed-Eddie," Yaya said, kneeling next to the man's head. He pressed the 9mm hard into one ear. "Where'd you take my friends?"

"I can't tell you," he whimpered. "He'll kill me."

"Who? Chi Long?" Walker asked, hoping that Laws had been right.

As soon as he said the name, Ed-Eddie's face blanched. "You know?"

"Of course we know. We're U.S. Navy SEALs. We fucking know everything," Yaya said.

Walker couldn't help but grin at his friend's aplomb. "Almost everything. Where are the others? Where are the other SEALs?"

"I don't know."

"Bullshit!" Yaya twisted his face into something monstrous. "Total fucking bullshit!"

Ed-Eddie's eyes rolled toward Walker, who knew instinctively that he'd have to be the foil for Yaya's bad cop. They didn't have Laws's interrogation experience, but it would have to do. In conversations on the safety of American soil, he'd always proclaimed that he'd never resort to torture. Now he'd have to put that assertion to the test.

"No, Yaya. Maybe our friend here just wants to help. I mean look at him. He's not like those others." As he said it, Ed-Eddie shook his head. "He wears American clothes and American shoes. Hell, look at his shirt. For all intents and purposes, he might just be American."

Yaya stared at Walker for a moment, then smiled slyly. "He's the farthest thing from American. A shirt and shoes don't make you who you are. You know what we say, clothes don't make the man."

Walker shrugged. "You're right about that. You can dress the part, but you can't act the part. An American wouldn't let another American get hurt. In fact, an American would make sure he'd do anything in his power to help his fellow American."

"Why not let me take him out in the woods," Yaya said, digging the pistol into the man's ear. "He's not American. He's just a pretender. He's just a slave of Chi Long."

Ed-Eddie began to cry. "I want to be an American," he sobbed. "I want to help. I do, but he'll kill me."

"Who'll kill you, Ed-Eddie?" Walker asked.

The man sniffed. "It's just Eddie."

"Okay, Eddie. So who's going to kill you?"

He squirmed on the floor, trying to see both Yaya and Walker. "You know," he whispered. "Him."

"Him?" Walker pointed at Yaya.

"Or him?" Yaya pointed back at Walker.

"No," Eddie said, his voice going low. "Chi Long."

"Ahh," both Walker and Yaya said at the same time. "Him. Is that where you took our friends? To Chi Long?"

Eddie nodded.

"Are they alive?"

Eddie nodded again.

Walker felt an immense surge of relief. But he couldn't dwell on it. They needed to know more.

"I wouldn't worry about 'him,'" Walker said, using finger quotes. "Yaya has a magical device that makes us invisible. He can't see us."

Eddie's eyes narrowed.

"No, really. That's how the other soldiers couldn't find us. Just as 'he' has magic," he said, using finger quotes again, "we have magic, too."

Eddie craned his neck to look at Yaya, who until that moment had been looking imploringly at Walker. Walker shrugged and grinned at his friend.

"Go ahead and show him the concealment device," Walker urged.

Yaya looked around, then reached into his side pocket. He pulled out the old cable he said was from World War II and held it up. "You mean this old thing?"

"That's it."

Eddie looked at it and narrowed his eyes. "How does it work?"

This time it was Yaya's turn to smile. "You put it in your mouth. Here, Walker will show you."

Yaya handed the cable over to Walker, who reminded himself that Yaya needed a good asskicking. Walker took it, grinned at Eddie, then placed an end in his mouth. It tasted like tar, cigar ash, and an old wig, but he kept it in his mouth.

Eddie looked from one to the other. "But there are two of you."

Yaya nodded in agreement, and looked at Walker. When Walker's grin grew even larger, Yaya's nod turned into a shake.

Walker pulled his out of his mouth momentarily and said, "We both have to have it in our mouths."

He put his back in and offered Yaya the other end. Yaya put it in his mouth and frowned only a little at the taste. The cable was almost at its limit as it stretched between the pair. Yeah, revenge is a dish best served with old cable.

"But I can see you," Eddie said matter-of-factly.

Walker removed it from his mouth. "Of course you can. You aren't a demon. This only works on demons. You know, like *him*."

Eddie stared at Yaya, who still had his end in. After a moment, he narrowed his eyes shrewdly. "Not as good as a suit."

Walker and Yaya exchanged a look.

"What kind of suit?" Walker asked.

"You know," Eddie said, touching the skin of his arm. "One made from people."

"You've seen this?"

Eddie glanced toward the dead soldiers. "I've seen one."

56

SPG OFFICES. CORONADO ISLAND.

The barbarians were at the gates. If it hadn't been a variation on the usual, Billings would have been outraged. They finally had eyes on and CENTCOM wanted to retake control of their satellite, citing their priority. *Their priority my ass,* she thought. If it weren't for the fact that SEAL Team 666 wasn't as highly classified as it was, they wouldn't even be having this conversation. After all, which was more important, hunting down someone's cousin they believed to be a member of the Taliban, or supporting an elite unit that was ascertaining whether America was being threatened with destruction?

That the four-star general at CENTCOM knew about SEAL Team 666 and requested the shift in priority anyway was an indictment on his status as Head Asshole in theater. He knew she couldn't drop the bullshit flag and point out which was more important. He knew that she'd keep the team's existence a secret no matter what. In fact, she would bet that he was counting on it.

But there was nothing to be done at this point except to try and make something from nothing.

She stared at a map of the world. Her eyes found Myanmar, then drew down the coast until she reached the spot where she believed Kadwan to be. It was so far away from anything. They had assets in Thailand, but they'd have to invade sovereign airspace to get there. Because Kadwan was on the coast, it would be so much easier to bring help across the sea. They could go virtually undetected until the last moment.

She grabbed her phone and put in a call to the SOCOM J3. He owed her a favor for fighting on his behalf for funding, during last year's congressional free-for-all after the budget cuts.

She explained her situation.

"I'd love to help, Alexis, but it looks like there's a big operation building along the Pakistan border. CENTCOM intends to conduct a series of airstrikes to root out some of Haqqani militant leaders in Northern Waziristan. C-130s have begun dropping psyop leaflets as part of an information campaign warning the militants that they're going to be bombed."

"If we warn them, won't they flee?"

"Doesn't work that way. Muslims are used to being threatened. It's part of their culture to ignore it. Psychological Operations was hugely successful in Desert Storm One, responsible for upwards of three hundred thousand defections."

"I've seen some of the leaflets they used portraying Saddam as a devil."

"Those weren't the successful ones. SOCOM had C-130s dropping leaflets on targets, calling them out by name and warning them that they'd be bombed the next day. Then they did exactly that. After the third or fourth time the C-130s dropped their leaflets, the Iraqis got the message. They'd take off running. It got to the point where they didn't have to drop conventional bombs, just paper."

"Nice. And they intend on using that in Waziristan?"

"Yeah. Only they're going to drop GBU-43s. We call them MOABs."

"I'm not up on my bomb nomenclature. What's a MOAB?"

"Stands for 'mother of all bombs.' Like the BLU-82, a fuel air explosive used to clear landing zones, it requires presidential approval for release. It's a twenty-one-thousand-pound bomb containing nineteen thousand pounds of H6 explosive. It vaporizes everything within a square mile, then continues its devastation, gradually diminishing to nothing on the farthest edge of its effective range."

Billings realized her jaw had dropped. She closed it as she thought about the absolute devastation one of those would do on downtown Washington, D.C., or any major city for that matter.

"I know. We haven't used it very often. The Russians have been using thermobaric bombs since their turn in Afghanistan. In addition to doing damage, they suck the air out of caves and anything within the blast radius. MOAB has a tremendous thermobaric capacity."

"So the intent is to drop leaflets, then the MOABs?"

"Yep."

"How many will they drop?"

"No one knows. They brought seventeen of them into theater yesterday, though."

Billings took a moment to process the information. Finally she turned back to the map. She thanked him and hung up. She had probably one more call to make. She went into the other room and spun up the video feed. It rang twice before it answered.

"Good afternoon, Mr. Vice President. I'm engaged in an issue here and need permission to reach across the pond to our friends in Whitehall."

He had a face that was Hollywood handsome and a voice made for politics. He was a moderate. He was a consensus builder. He would have been president had it not been for information surfacing about how he'd arranged for an abortion for his girlfriend in college.

"Why can't we handle it?"

"Operation PUFF DRAGON."

"That would do it." The vice president leaned back in his chair. Behind him was his desk in his working office on the grounds of the Naval Observatory. Pictures of his wife and Great Danes rested in silver frames. Paperwork was scattered on the desk's surface. "Is this regarding what you briefed me before?"

"It is, sir. Triple Six has found the locus of the problem and needs some support. We're losing priority as we speak."

The vice president shook his head and frowned. "This is bad timing. PUFF DRAGON needs those assets. As much as we need Triple Six, I can't change priorities."

"I realize that, sir. But I have another option. HMS *Victoria* is operating in the Indian Ocean en route to resupply at Diego Garcia. I might be able to convince the admiral aboard the vessel to send a sortie or two in support of our men."

The vice president made an expression halfway between impressed and perplexed. "How would you go about doing that?"

"Long or short of it?"

"Short."

"SEALs rescued him from North Vietnam in 1971. I think I can appeal to his sense of gratitude."

The smile of the vice president was one that any other politician would kill for. He used it now. "Sounds like a good time to collect, Alexis."

"It does. This mean I can make that call?"

The smile dropped. "Make that call, but know this. The administration has deniability. If this becomes a cockup, you'll be on your own."

"I expected nothing less, sir."

57

ON THE ROAD TO KADWAN. AFTERNOON.

Walker and Yaya sat on the bench seat of the old five-ton truck as it rolled down the Yangon-Mandalay road, or Highway 1. Eddie drove. He had the magic cable on his lap. Twice, Walker had to order him not to stick it in his mouth. It was bad enough that they were on a civilian road. They didn't need any more attention given to them.

Walker sat in the middle, while Yaya sat near the door. They both wore caps, pulled low over their eyes, from the soldiers they'd killed. Yaya could pass with his skin color, but Walker was the whitest thing on the road, so he sat in the middle scrunched down as best he could. He kept his 9mm in his lap, pointed at Eddie.

Yaya kept busy with Eddie's cell phone. He had it apart and was checking the SIM chips.

They'd removed the bodies from the back of the truck and left them in the hole. They cleaned the truck bed as best they could, then reconnoitered the way to Kadwan. It was less than two hundred kilometers south of Thaton. Plus another ten kilometers, because they still had to get through the city, and they should be there within three hours, give or take, depending on traffic, which as it turned out was the definition of congestion. Motorcycles were the most popular vehicles by far. White mini-pickups seemed to be the cargo haulers of choice, although they passed several motorcycles balancing boxes stacked ten feet high.

Eddie worked the horn like a New York cabbie. He knew just how close to get to the other vehicles and how fast to go without killing anyone. At first it had been a fearful onslaught of sight, sound, and motion, but once Walker decided to treat it as an amusement-park ride, it became much easier.

Walker had realized early that they'd need money for gas, food, and bottled water. If he'd been an Army Special Forces soldier, he would've had a Rolex to trade. The SEALs didn't issue Rolexes like their Army SOF brethren, but he and Yaya each had a hundred-dollar bill as part of their escape and evasion kit.

When they reached Mudon, the largest city south of Thaton, a promise that they'd give him the other hundred convinced Eddie to get a dozen gas cans, fill them and the truck up, and get some food and water for the trip. He got more than ninety dollars in local currency in change.

"Where's my phone?" Eddie asked.

"I have it safe," Yaya said, patting his pocket.

"I need to call my family. They'll be worried." He looked from Walker to Yaya.

"That doesn't seem so bad," Walker said. "We can make sure he doesn't call anyone else. What do you think, Yaya?"

Yaya shook his head subtly.

Eddie grinned like a salesman. "Walker is right. It's not so bad."

"He can't use his phone," Yaya said flatly.

Walker raised an eye, but didn't ask. He'd caught the other SEAL's nonverbal, albeit a moment too late.

"Why can't I?" Eddie asked Yaya. "Please, sir," he begged, turning to Walker. "Can't you make him let me use my phone?"

"Enough. Jesus." Yaya pulled out the phone, or what had once been a phone. It now had several wires attached to it, as if the Borg had come down and added pieces.

Eddie screamed. "What have you done?"

"Seeing if I can repurpose this for our use," Yaya said. He pulled out his 9mm and pointed it at Eddie. "Listen, Eddie. I think you forgot the process here. You drive the truck. We drive the guns."

Eddie looked from the gun to his ruined phone. After a moment, he put his head down and skulked to the driver's side. He climbed in and closed the door.

"Smooth move, Ex-Lax," Walker said. He climbed in the cab of the truck. Yaya got in after.

Within seconds they were once again part of the bumping, swerving, honking mass on the road. No one spoke for a good twenty minutes.

"Is it going to work?" Walker asked.

"I got it to interface with the MBITR and the base station, but it's a software problem. His phone isn't a real iPhone. It's a knockoff. It uses an old Android operating system."

"Can you make it work?"

"I'm not a software guy, but I remember some of it. All I can say is I'm trying." He pulled out the phone and began to type into it.

Eddie glanced forlornly at what had once been his phone. Walker watched the man's face for a moment before turning away. Fake or not, it had probably cost the man a good chunk of savings. It was also probably a status symbol and the SEALs had taken that away from him.

Then Walker reminded himself that Eddie was part of the crew who had killed and/or captured the other SEALs. In fact, it was time they talked about that.

"So Eddie, let's talk about your military friends."

Eddie shifted in his seat.

"Who are they and where are they from?"

"Karen," he said, only pronouncing it as *kayin*. "From Kadwan."

"Are they from the Myanmar military?"

Eddie shook his head.

"Then where did they get the uniforms?"

"We made them."

"So they wanted us to think it was the military. What was the plan—for us to get mad and attack?"

Eddie shrugged. "I don't know plans. I know that *him* wants to rule again. He wants to be king."

"I wasn't aware Myanmar had kings," Yaya said.

"We don't." Eddie hastily added, "Not anymore. Not yet."

"Tell me about Kadwan."

"Old capital of Kayin. *Him* has removed everything new." Eddie paused to swerve around a bike pulling a cart with a mound of old plastic bottles. "Everything is gone. My mother lives there and her home is gone."

"What do you mean gone? Was it bulldozed?"

"His *qilin*. They destroyed it for him." Eddie's jittery eyes glanced toward Walker. "Please, no more."

"Not yet. We need to know about the *qilin*." He described the creature they'd come into contact with on the cargo ship. "Is this one of them?"

Eddie nodded.

"How do you destroy them?"

Eddie gave a shocked look, then shook his head. "Can't be destroyed. They are messengers from the gods."

Walker and Yaya exchanged glances.

Yaya mouthed, *Messengers from the gods?*

Walker nodded.

"Which gods made the *qilin*, Eddie?"

"All of them."

Walker didn't like the answer, but he didn't feel that having

Eddie try to explain would help them much, so instead he asked, "What's their message?"

"It is said that they come when a new ruler comes. *Him* has come." Eddie looked down into his lap and grabbed the cable. He took it into his mouth and resumed driving. Clearly he wanted to be invisible for a time.

Yaya continued to work on the Android software as best he could. The bumping, jumping ride down the road didn't help, but there was nothing to be done about that.

Eddie laid into the horn to get around a group of men carrying baskets of vegetables on their backs. They wore sarongs on the lower half of their bodies. They were shirtless. On their feet were simple pieces of rubber with straps. He edged around them, and was once more at speed. But it didn't last. Suddenly, Eddie slammed on the brakes, stalling the engine. Had Yaya not put his foot on the dash, he would have smashed forward. As it was, Walker was unprepared for the sudden stop and slid from the seat into the front window. He struck with his shoulder, almost losing his grip on the pistol.

They slammed back into the seat.

In front of them lay an overturned vegetable cart and a motorcycle. Two men argued. The one in the motorcycle helmet was taller, but the other man seemed angrier, gesturing in great chopping motions at the produce. There seemed to be space to their left to drive around them.

A policeman approached and smacked the hood of their truck with a baton. He wore a black Mao cap and black fatigues. An orange reflective vest covered his torso. He struck the hood again and screamed in Myanmarese, gesturing angrily down the road. It didn't take a linguist to understand the international symbol for *get moving*.

Eddie hastened to start the truck, turning the lever on the dashboard. The engine sputtered and stuttered. He glanced worriedly at the policeman.

Walker noted the policeman had a walkie-talkie on his left

hip. A Chinese PM pistol rested snugly in a patent leather holster on his right hip. He held the baton in his right hand, so if he was to grab his pistol, he'd lose precious seconds either dropping the baton, or changing hands.

"Yaya," Walker whispered. "See that walkie? Can you use it?"

"Maybe. Not getting anywhere with this damned software. Using our tablets, I should be able to use the phone's SIM chip. I won't know until I try."

"Put that stuff away then. I don't want it to get smashed."

"What are you going to—" Yaya glanced at the policeman, and comprehension showed on his face. Then he hastened to shove his work into the extra-large glove box.

Walker reached out and put his hand over Eddie's to stop him from trying to crank the engine. "Remain calm."

The policeman's eyes narrowed as he shouted for the truck to move. Traffic had begun to move around them as if they were a boulder in a creek. Eddie shook his head in fear. The policeman moved to the door and stepped onto the running board. He shouted into Eddie's face. Then he noticed the others in the cab. His furious gaze focused on Walker as he took in the white skin. His baton hand disappeared. It was then that Walker made his move.

"Start the fucking truck," he yelled, as he gripped the policeman's collar and pulled him over Eddie and into the truck.

Eddie turned the lever and the truck began to sputter. But he couldn't see anything. The policeman's head and torso were in his face. The policeman struggled, kicking with his feet, elbowing Eddie in the face and chest.

Eddie screamed, but somehow continued trying to start the truck.

The policeman's eyes were wide with fear and anger. He screamed like a woman. Walker shoved his pistol into the man's chest and pulled the trigger three times. The man bucked with each shot, but stilled after the third. Walker pulled him the rest of the way in. At the same moment, the truck started. Walker and Yaya shoved the dead man into the space beneath their feet.

"Move! Move!"

Eddie's face was wet with blood. For a moment, Walker wondered if the man had been hit, but then he saw two exit holes in the metal roof of the truck. Each hole was surrounded by an oval of dripping blood and gore. The truck jerked forward, then jerked again. Once it found gear, it rejoined the flow of traffic.

Eddie nodded as he wiped his face with his left hand. He pulled it away and stared at it. Tears welled from his eyes as he began to sob.

"You got to suck it up, Eddie," Walker told him. "I didn't see you crying when you were loading the bodies in the back of the truck or when you thought we were dead."

The driver frowned, but didn't say anything.

The last thing they did before they entered the expressway was to shove a naked body out of the passenger-door window. It rolled and fell at the feet of an old woman selling cheap plastic jewelry laid out on a blanket.

58

THE ROAD TO KADWAN.

Yaya was starting to find some success. He had wires stripped and attached to different parts of the inside of his tablet and the walkie-talkie. Every now and then it would erupt in a fit of static. Once they heard Myanmarese voices. Still, he cursed the steampunk machination he'd created. He even shook it once. "You should work, damn it!" He was rewarded with the staticky voice of an Englishwoman who was delivering the news. It brought a grin to Yaya's face, but he didn't stop there. He stuck his tongue in a corner of his cheek and bent over yet again.

After ten minutes he leaned back and flexed his fingers. He stared at the rat's mess of wires and shook his head. "It should work. I've done everything I know to do. I just don't understand why it's not working."

"Did you drop it?" Walker asked. Seeing the grin on Yaya's face, he said, "I remember my father once telling someone that if it didn't work, to give it the 'three-foot drop test.'"

"No." Yaya wiped his face and cranked his neck. "I didn't drop it. I'm afraid to. I have so many wires and connections, there's no telling what would happen. I'm close now. I don't want to step backwards."

"So now what?"

"Now I stare at it until I figure out what the fuck is wrong with it."

The truck slowed. Walker glanced out the window. By his estimations they'd reached the southern edge of the city of Dawei. All traffic had come to a stop. A roadblock up ahead had a dozen police and military. Their guns were drawn. They were turning everyone away. Evidently the road was closed.

"What do you think?" Walker asked Yaya.

"Doesn't look like they're searching for us."

"Just keeping people from traveling south."

He turned to Eddie, but saw that the driver's door was open. In the rearview mirror he saw their driver scurrying back the way they'd come, and Walker slid into the driver's seat.

"Looks like we have to go to Plan B," he said, shifting the truck into gear and turning off the road. He'd spied a side street, which he took for about a hundred yards until he noticed something. He backed up, then stopped the truck.

"I wasn't aware we had a plan B," Yaya muttered.

"I wasn't either until I saw that." Walker pointed to a vehicle parked in a side lot. He'd seen Indiana Jones ride one and could imagine himself doing the same. "I think we'll take that."

"That?" Yaya shook his head. "Hell no. I'm not going to let you drive me around like some sidekick."

"Fine then. You drive. I'll shoot."

Ten minutes later, after Yaya had successfully hotwired the Russian Ural motorcycle with sidecar, they were riding through a forested area at about three miles an hour. Yaya no longer needed the sling. His shoulder ached, but was otherwise fine.

Walker had his Stoner out and lying along the cowl of the sidecar. He also had two AK-47s and his pistol, as did Yaya. The rifles were crisscrossed on his back, making him look like a Rambo samurai.

They found a dragon-fruit plantation where the trees grew far apart. They used this to bypass the roadblock. After half an hour they found their way back to the road. There wasn't a pedestrian or vehicle in sight. Yaya cranked the engine and they were soon flying down the blacktop, swerving only for the occasional man-eating pothole.

The going was great until Walker started seeing things. At first it was movements out of the corner of his left eye. They were large and fast, but when he looked they were gone. Then it was out of the corner of his other eye, too. Soon he was able to make out some very large things keeping pace with them. He could never really see what they were, but every now and then he'd glimpse something through a break in the dense jungle.

"Can we go faster?" he yelled.

He pointed to the jungle. Yaya looked, and after a moment, his eyes widened. He leaned forward and twisted the accelerator. They soon outdistanced whatever creatures were following them. Although Walker couldn't be sure, he had an idea what they were.

They had traveled without incident for about a dozen miles when they crested a hill. Yaya slammed on the brake and they skidded to a stop.

In front of them was a *qilin*. This one was the size of a horse. Like the one they'd seen in the ship's hold, it had six legs, a thick body, and the head of a prehistoric cat. Spikes jutted from its body and head as if it were a punk-rock monster.

It stood in the middle of the road about fifty yards in front of them.

Walker jerked up his sniper rifle and stared through the optics. Green liquid dripped from its multi-toothed maw. Orange fire glowed in its eyes. It breathed deeply, its scale-covered chest rising and falling.

And then it roared.

That roar was joined by others not far behind them.

They only had a matter of moments.

Yaya pulled both AKs from his back. He held one in his left hand and rested the barrel over the handlebars. The other he laid across his lap.

Walker got his AK ready as well.

"You ready?" he asked Yaya.

The SEAL revved the motorcycle engine.

"Aim for the mouth and eyes," Walker commanded.

Yaya shoved the motorcycle forward, gathering speed dramatically.

Walker opened fire, catching the *qilin* in its green-dripping maw.

The creature howled, raising its head.

Walker held fire until it lowered it again, then began to fire as fast as he could pull the trigger. Beside him came the AK-47's signature dull *thunka-thunka-thunka*.

The creature broke into a run straight at them, shaking its head much as a bull would as it began to charge an opponent. The SEALs and the chimera were engaged in a life-and-death game of mythological chicken.

Walker found that when the creature was running at them, he had a better aiming point. Somewhere in the back of his mind he was reminded that it also meant that he'd soon be within chomping range, but he ignored that and kept firing. He depleted his twenty-round magazine and racked another.

The *qilin* stumbled, then lost its balance and fell over.

Yaya swerved around it and cheered. "Take that, you motherfucker!"

But as Walker turned to look over his shoulder, he saw it get up and begin lumbering after them. He waited to see how far it could follow them, but it showed no sign of slowing down. Finally he took careful aim and blew one of its eyes out. It fell to the ground, skidding to a stop on its shoulder.

He turned around. "Now you can breathe easy," he said. Then his words faded as he saw another *qilin* waiting for them much in the same manner as the first.

"Aw hell." He thought for a split second and made a decision. "Stop the motorcycle."

Yaya did, the violence of his stop throwing both of them forward.

Walker climbed out and kneeled behind the sidecar. He used it to balance the rifle.

"Shoot it!" Yaya yelled.

Yaya kept the engine running, but picked up the last AK-47 and sent a couple of bursts toward the creature. It began to trot toward them.

Walker took careful aim at its eyes. Although the mouth was a larger target, he'd seen what one shot to the eye could do. He fired and missed by an inch, the bullet clanging off the creature's scaled armor. He fired again, this one making the creature turn its head.

He was aware that with each miss the creature was getting closer and closer. It was only thirty yards away now.

Walker fired another round, then another, but it was as if the creature could see the bullet coming and moved its head at the very last moment.

"Walker!" Yaya cried.

He decided to aim to the right of his aiming point. He only had time for one last shot. He lined it up, then fired. Instead of seeing if it hit, he threw himself out of the way. Yaya gunned the motorcycle and almost made it, but the creature plowed into it, sending it tumbling.

Walker ran to the beast, shoved the barrel into a bleary orange eye, and pulled the trigger, careful of the flailing claw-tipped legs.

The creature jerked, then shuddered and died.

Good thing, because his rifle was out of ammunition.

Walker spun toward the wreck of the motorcycle. Yaya had been thrown clear. Walker had almost reached his friend when he heard a low roar coming from behind him. A *qilin* leaped toward him. Walker threw himself to the ground and rolled, wondering what he was going to use to defend himself. But instead of attacking, the *qilin* snatched Yaya by the leg and quickly limped into the jungle. It was the first one they'd encountered. He'd thought it was dead, but . . .

He hurried into the jungle, but there was no sign of Yaya.

Then came an improbable sound.

"Walker, this is SPG. Get away from the trees. Come in, Walker. Walker, go to the motorcycle."

It was Jen's voice. He ran back to the wreck and pulled out Yaya's contraption. It had been taped together and wrapped in a piece of the orange safety vest, the Velcro used to hold the entire thing in place.

He stared at it for a second like a pig looking at a wristwatch, then depressed the button on the side. "Jen, this is Jack. You there?"

"Jack!" Her voice broke.

"Jen, are you here? Can you see me?" He stared into the sky.

"We can see you. Listen, you have to get the motorcycle working. More of those creatures are coming."

Walker glanced at the wreck.

"Jack, I'm dead serious. Hurry!"

59

ALONE IN THE JUNGLE. NIGHT.

He'd picked up a limp sometime after the wreck, two hours ago, and now Jen told him he was less than thirty clicks from Kadwan. Somehow, he'd righted the motorcycle and managed to get it started. The wheel on the sidecar was blown and both wheels of the cycle were bent, but it ran, albeit like a circus-clown funnycycle. Still, it moved faster than he could have.

So while he'd wobble-wheeled down the center of the deserted road, wary of a *qilin* appearing around every corner, he listened to Jen as she provided what information she could. Much of it was old news, but other parts were incredible.

"We've been tracking Hoover for the last few hours," she'd said. "She's within ten kilometers of your location."

Walker had inadvertently slowed down when he'd heard that. "But how?"

"We have no visuals, but Hoover has an RFID broadcasting on ultrahigh frequency."

"She's following them?"

"Must be. By her direction of travel, she's heading straight towards Kadwan. Holmes must have activated her homing beacon when he was captured. We believe he and the others might be still alive."

"They are," Walker said, then briefly told them about the information he'd received from Eddie.

Then Billings came on the line. Walker felt his posture tighten as she took command of the mission from ten thousand miles away. She explained how they'd seen the attack on the warehouse and the ambush. Then they'd lost coverage for a time. It took getting the vice president involved, but now they had another satellite to use for a short three-hour window. Not that it was doing much good. They were totally blind to the events transpiring in Kadwan. Inexplicably the advanced optics on the NRO satellite were incapable of penetrating the cloud cover. All she could verify was Holmes's location, currently in the middle of a cricket field.

As he rode, they devised a way for him to intersect Hoover. The dog was moving at a steady clip, but traveling east of Walker's position through the jungle. By their estimation, Hoover should reach Kadwan within an hour. If he was able to continue traveling by motorcycle, even at its reduced rate because of the crash, Walker would be there half an hour before the dog, which was plenty of time for them to engage.

But ten minutes after that calculation, the motorcycle stopped for good. Not only was it out of gas, but the rear tire had lost its air. Walker was now on foot.

He hung the improvised radio around his neck. He had his Stoner and a single AK with three magazines. The Stoner and the AK both used 7.62mm, although the diameter of the AK's rounds was slightly smaller, so he tossed the AK and settled on the better rifle. Although the ammunition wasn't what he was used to, what he'd lose in cyclic rate of fire he'd gain in accuracy and distance. If the *qilin* were any indication of what he'd expect, then it didn't matter how many times he hit it if those shots weren't on target. With the Stoner across his back and the 9mm in his thigh holster, his hands were free and he began jogging right away.

He kept to the center of the road. He considered sloughing through the jungle, but the going would be slow and any attempt at speed would mean that he'd be heard well in advance. He kept his eyes and ears open for everything, lowered his head, and pretended he was back on the Coronado. For as bad as his legs had felt during his all-expense-paid vacation at the BUD/S resort, the stress and danger were nothing compared with this mission. On the island he'd been concerned with making it through each day. Here he was concerned about making it, period.

The image of Yaya's expression of surprise as he was hauled into the trees bore through his attempt at concentration. He felt his cheeks burn, but ignored it as best he could. He made seven kilometers before he was forced to rest. He kept walking, but he couldn't run until his breathing found a rhythm.

"You okay?" Jen asked over the radio.

"Sure." Cramps in his stomach and legs were already tightening.

"You've stopped running."

"Glad . . . glad you noticed."

There was a pause. "I have an update. You ready?"

"Sure." His breathing was coming around.

"In five hours Kadwan will be removed from the map."

"What?" He stopped, hands on his knees, and stared at the ground. "What does that mean?"

"The strange cloud above the city is spreading. People are finally starting to pay attention and they're getting worried. Nothing we have in orbit can penetrate it, which means we don't have a clue what's going on beneath. So, a squadron of Tornado jets are en route. After in-flight refueling, they're scheduled to deliver bombs on target at 0800 hours local time."

"So it's 0300 now?"

"Check."

"And how far do I have to go?"

"About ten kilometers."

It was doable.

"Jack?"

"Yeah."

"If for any reason you can't make it, don't get in the kill radius."

"What's the kill radius?"

"They're dropping GBU-38 JDAMs. Do you know what that is?"

Joint Directed Attack Munitions. Five hundred pound bombs. "How many?"

"Four bombs per plane."

Which meant forty-eight bombs—twenty-four thousand pounds of explosive on target.

"That gives you a standoff of five kilometers," she said, her voice breathless. "Do you hear me, Jack? Do you hear me? *Don't go if you can't make it.*"

"I have to, Jen. I have to." There was no way he could not try and save his friends. For too long he'd been fighting for the dead. Now he was fighting for the living and it had never felt more right. Wasn't it she who'd told him that?

It took a few moments for her to answer. When she did, she said simply, "I know."

"Going to go silent for a while," he said. "Save batteries. I'll contact you when I'm close."

Then he turned off the set. The silence was at once welcome and foreboding. He began to run faster. He narrowed his vision. He thought about everyone he'd lost, from Yaya to Fratty, to Holmes, Laws, and Ruiz, to his father, his brother, and that little boy who'd done nothing to anyone except be taken by a demon sent by someone keen on getting back at his father. Walker thought of all of them and created a fuel by which he could run.

He began to whisper cadence, using his breathing to propel the air one syllable at a time.

One mile. No sweat.
Two miles. Better yet.
Three miles. Beat the jets.
Four miles. Shoot the rest.

And on and on he sang his barely audible motivational cadence, letting the mindless motivation push him forward. It was all he had.

60

KADWAN. EARLY MORNING.

A small hill overlooked the flat plane of Kadwan, all the way to the sea. A long narrow city with rolling hills to the east and the Gulf of Martaban to the west, it had once held a hundred thousand people. But that had been before all the buildings had all been destroyed.

Musso had told them that a direct translation of the original name of the land of the Karen—Kawthoolie—was "land burned black." Now it seemed the only name this place deserved. Fire burned everywhere. A pall of acrid smoke gripped the length and breadth of the city, hanging low and thick. The occasional scream broke the silence, from what or whom Walker didn't know.

That this virtually unknown group, lost to the whims of history, could be so powerful was unanticipated by all the analysts. But it shouldn't have been. After all, it was the Karen who'd stopped the Mongols. It was the Karen who'd stopped Alexander. They'd once been as dominant a group as ever lived on the earth. But the centuries had taken their toll. Now they were a minority, scattered across several countries in the backwater of Southeast Asia, and it seemed that one madman was determined to bring them back to prominence. Saw Thuza Tun believed that for a new country to grow, the old one had to be destroyed. Their language was filled with double meanings. Kawthoolie meant both "land burned black" and "flowerland." There couldn't be one without the other. For the flowers to grow, the land of the Karen must be destroyed. And if Walker didn't do something to stop it, they'd fertilize the earth with the bodies of dead SEALs and fill the world with *qilin*.

Walker searched the horizon and spotted the cricket field, or pitch, as it was called. This was where the others were. He staggered down the hill into a street below. Cars were overturned. Pieces of rubble, parts of homes, and personal possessions lay upon the ground like they'd grown there. Doll heads and kitchen utensils jutted from the ground like vegetables in a mad hatter's garden. Pieces of brightly colored cloth whipped from the hard edges of scorched bushes. He'd seen the aftermaths of major attacks in Somalia and Iraq. He'd seen cities destroyed. But this was something more. This was as if the hand of an angry god had come down to sweep the city aside. The closest he'd come to this sort of devastation had been when Katrina had scraped entire communities from the Gulf Coast.

Walker limped down the center of the street. He held his Stoner in his hands. The holster on his right thigh was unclipped. He was past exhaustion, walking into a universe he'd never been in before. He felt alert, but like a great brooding animal, unconsciousness lurked just beneath the surface. He'd run farther and faster than he'd ever thought possible. He'd stopped only once more, when he'd crossed a stream. He'd fallen to his knees and had thrust his head into the water like a beast, gulping, then puking, then gulping some more.

He walked for perhaps three blocks. He wasn't sure. Here and there the streets had been wiped away. He saw a child buried in the rubble. He moved toward what looked to be a little girl, only to discover that it was a doll's head. Not just any doll's head, but the head of an Asian girl doll.

He felt a buzz beginning beneath his skin. He picked the head up gently, as if it were the head of a real child. Cradling it in his hands, he felt the buzz continue beneath his skin, but he ignored it. There were holes where the eyes had been. Its skin had melted in a fall of plastic tears. The buzzing increased. As he felt the seizure coming on, Walker squeezed the head in his fingers. He grunted and took several steps forward.

Then it hit him like an arcane fist.

His teeth chattered as he envisioned a taloned hand reaching into the doll's eyes, the finger so hot and horrible that its mere touch caused the plastic to melt. It was the hand of a demon. It was the hand of Chi Long. For a moment Walker felt what it was like to be so powerful; then he was able to let go of the head and free himself of its power echo.

Suddenly the world changed before him. Gone was the scorched earth of Kadwan. It was replaced by Washington, D.C. *Qilin* crawled up the vertical surface of the Washington Monument, their talons tearing into the stone and concrete. The White House lawn was filled with *qilin* ripping men and women to pieces. In flashes of a possible future, he saw thousands of the beasts in every city, on the sides of every building, eating and killing everything that he'd ever known and loved.

He fell to his knees and retched. With his stomach almost empty, there was nothing to come up. Walker dry-heaved until the feeling left. When he stood, a long string of drool hugged his chin. He let it hang as he took a shaky step forward. Now he knew who had destroyed the city.

He turned on the radio as he stumbled forward. When it was ready, he called in to home station.

"Where are you?" came Jen's voice immediately.

"In Kad . . . Kadwan," he croaked.

"What's wrong? Why do you sound like that?"

"Everything's gone. The magic is . . . so . . . strong." He stopped to grit his teeth. His body began to shake and he fought it back down. "Gotta . . . keep . . . moving."

"Jack . . ."

"How . . . how long?"

"Forty-five minutes."

"Hoover?"

"Almost there."

"Uh . . . good dog."

"Walker, this is Billings. I'm sorry I got you into this, but we need you now."

"You got me," he said, aware that his tongue had made it sound like *You goth me*.

"Listen closely. Musso discovered something. It looks like a man named Saw Thuza Tun ordered the tattoo suit from the Triad. Tun probably has a modicum of control. We don't know how much. But you might be able to get through to him if needed."

"Fuh . . . fuck that."

"Exactly. So you need to find the focus. Do you know what that is?"

As Walker stumbled forward he remembered the conversation he'd had with Laws about the use of foci to channel and control spirits.

"Fo . . . cus?"

"Yes, Walker. A focus. It could be a ring or a bracelet or even a necklace. It could be *anything*."

"Underwear. Bar . . . Barbie dolls."

"What'd he say?" Billings asked someone.

"I think he said something about Barbie dolls and underwear," he heard Musso say.

"Ceremonial," Walker said, the word sounding like *Theremonial.*

"What's wrong with him?" Musso asked.

"It's all the magic," Billings said. "It's affecting him like this. We can only hope that it goes away."

"Gothes away," he said, stumbling even farther forward.

Suddenly a *qilin* turned the corner and ran down the street toward him. Walker tried to raise his rifle, but he didn't have the strength. It was as though the buzz of magic had replaced everything.

The chimera ran straight at him.

Walker screamed in a cracked and broken voice as the beast slid to a stop in front of him.

But the creature didn't attack. Instead, it sniffed him.

Walker had never been this close to a live one before. He could see the reticulations on the beast's scales. Each one seemed to be intricately carved. Its eyes glowed a heated orange and its breath felt hot against his skin. Walker couldn't take his eyes off the spikes. The chimeric equivalent of a puffer fish's, they jutted out at all angles. One stumble, one bull rush, and he'd be impaled.

"Walker? Are you there?"

The *qilin* was startled. It jumped back and bared its teeth.

Walker reached up with a shaking hand and very slowly turned the radio off.

The creature sniffed his hand.

Walker didn't dare move.

Suddenly the chimera grabbed him by the leg and began to drag him toward the center of the city. The viselike grip didn't hurt, but there was no escaping it. Walker held on to his Stoner with both hands, hugging it to his chest, at the same time keeping his head from bouncing along the scorched earth.

They'd gone perhaps three blocks before a great horn sounded. The *qilin* stopped. It let go of Walker and raised its head. The sound came again. The *qilin* glanced once more at Walker, then took off at a gallop toward the sound.

It took Walker a few minutes to get his strength back. He stood unsteadily. Looking around, he realized that the streets were widening. Where were the cars? Where were the homes? Everything was gone. What was even more astounding was that he hadn't been eaten. Whatever had driven the mythological monster to take him had also freed him as it called the *qilin* back.

61

KADWAN. DAWN.

He stood, staring at the cricket pitch through the scope of his Stoner, for five minutes. There was nothing that could have prepared him for what he saw.

A thousand wooden crates rested on the pitch, aligned into grids. Atop each crate was a man, woman, or child, naked except for a dagger each held in their hands. The front row held three men he recognized—Laws, Ruiz, and Holmes standing on crates as well. Unlike the others, the SEALs were chained to the wood at each wrist and ankle, forcing them into the position of a dog. They'd been beaten. Blood was dripping from their faces onto the wood.

In front of them, looking ten feet tall, stood a man who could only be Chi Long. He wore chitinous medieval Chinese armor composed of green and silver scales. At his shoulders and feet were the heads of dragons in an aqua blue. They writhed upon his limbs, as if they were alive, but remained where they were. There was a red cloak beneath his armor. Tattered and scorched in places, it flowed several feet behind him like a battered bridal train.

But it was the face that transfixed Walker. Beneath a mane of luxuriously long black hair was the face of a dead thing. As if Chi Long had crawled from a barrow or crypt, the skin and sinew of his face was pulled back as tight as a drum. The skin had aged to the color of ochre, highlighting a mouthful of spiked teeth and fierce yellow glowing eyes.

Chi Long held a dagger in his right hand, and even as Walker watched, Chi Long pointed it to the sky that was beginning to brighten with the coming dawn.

Having seen what a sacrifice of blood could do to the contents of a single crate, Walker could only imagine what would happen if a thousand Karen did the same on the killing pitch.

Switching the selector switch to Fire, he took careful aim.

And fired.

A puff of dust exploded from the back of the demon's head as the bullet tore through it.

He fired again, confused by the result.

He was rewarded with another puff of dust.

Chi Long turned toward him. As he watched, the holes made by his rounds closed.

The demon pointed at Walker. He felt its power from a hundred yards away. Then the demon curled its finger in the universal gesture of *Come here.*

Walker tried to squeeze the trigger, but found that his fingers no longer worked. The Stoner fell from his now paralyzed hands. *Once again he was a child. The day was heavy with rain and he'd been walking home alone from school. It had begun with a whisper, one that he'd finally answered.*

"Who is it?"

"Please," came the low, soft voice from everywhere and nowhere at all.

"I can't see you," he'd said, such an innocent child about to be taken. "Who are you?"

"I am alone. I am lonely," came the voice, now not so soft, sounding more like the crunching of broken glass.

Little Jackie Walker had felt the fear then.

He'd thought about running.

Maybe if he had, nothing would have happened.

Maybe if he had, his father wouldn't have been killed trying to get payback.

Maybe if he had, he'd have lived the life of a regular kid with regular problems.

But he'd never know. He'd never know because he'd decided to be curious.

"Who are you?" he'd asked. "Where are you hiding?"

Then the words came in too many languages, sometimes all at once, sometimes separate. It sounded like a child. It sounded like a man. It sounded like a woman. It sounded like everyone and no one.

Then it said one word—"Jackie"—and everything went black.

Walker stumbled and found that he'd been moving toward Chi Long. He was less than a dozen feet from Chi Long and was unable to stop. He moved to within a half foot of the demon, who looked him up and down. He sniffed Walker, having to bend almost completely over to do so. Walker smelled the scent of hyacinth and death coming from the armor.

"Aaah, yesss," said the demon. "We knew you once. You were ours."

Walker's eyes rolled into his head as he fought against Chi Long's power. He didn't know what the demon meant, but he needed to free himself. He had a pistol on his right thigh and a knife on his left thigh.

"Take this." Chi Long handed Walker a long, wickedly curved dagger.

In Walker's mind's eye, he jammed it into Chi Long's face, but in reality he found himself raising the knife and walking stiff-legged to where Laws was chained to a crate. Walker felt the impetus of the knife before it reached its destination.

Run, Laws! he screamed inside. *Come on, man, please!*

But Laws couldn't move. He pulled himself to the end of his chains and made a furious face. "Snap out of it, kid!"

The knife came down slowly, piercing the skin of Laws's arm, sliding through it ever so slowly.

Laws screamed.

Walker screamed on the inside. But it didn't help. He walked around the other side of the crate and stabbed Laws in his other arm.

They both screamed again, inside and out.

Then he was forced to turn to Holmes. His knife hand rose, but then the control went away. Once again, he was his own. He turned to Chi Long in time to see a *qilin* spike buried in his chest and Yaya's other hand coming around to stab him with another. Just as the second spike penetrated the demon's chest, the demon screamed in outrage and flung Yaya away. Chi Long staggered.

Walker's paralysis gone, he leaped forward and plunged the knife into Chi Long's back. He started to yank it out and stab the monster again, but Holmes's shout made him turn.

"Hurry, Walker!"

Now free of Chi Long's influence, Walker shook his head to rid himself of the remnants of control, then hurried to comply. Each of the chains holding the other SEALs was held in place by a bolt, beyond their reach. But it was easy for Walker to release them.

They climbed down to the ground.

"What took you so long?" Ruiz asked.

Laws clenched his teeth as he ripped his shirt into strips to bind his wounds.

"Form a circle, SEALs. Here they come," Holmes ordered.

Walker handed Laws the 9mm pistol and drew his own knife. The thousand or so Karen, who until this moment had been prepared to sacrifice themselves in order to give birth to the army of *qilin,* were climbing from their crates and running toward the SEALs.

"You're fucking kidding me, right?" Ruiz asked the universe.

Then the first wave was upon them. The fact that they had to scramble around the crates made it so they all couldn't attack at once. But the SEALs were in the thick of it. They dispatched the first four opponents without much thought. But more came on, and more after that. Fighting back to back, the SEALs' only hope came from the fact that their opponents were completely untrained and simply threw themselves in their direction. One after the other after the other, they attacked and died, until the pile of bodies was higher than a man's height.

For a moment, Walker thought they might be safer behind the wall of the dead, then he realized that now their opponents could jump on top of them. The other SEALs seemed to realize the same thing at the same time. They climbed on the crates they'd just evacuated, and Holmes and Ruiz got stabbed for their efforts.

Suddenly Chi Long was back. The spikes remained in his chest. He seemed weaker, but he still had command of his people. He shouted and they stilled, all eyes going to him.

Walker felt the power descend on him once more. He felt his loss of control and the power of another take him over. He turned and raised his knife. Facing Holmes, all he had to do was jam the knife into the man's back and he would be irrevocably removed from the living. Walker took a step forward, then was launched sideways as a weight struck him. He fell hard to the ground, hard enough to lose the air in his chest and the knife from his hand. A growl erupted from the creature that had attacked him, but the growl wasn't for him. *Hoover!* The dog launched herself at the demon, ripping with her teeth and shaking her head.

The demon howled and made a swipe at the dog with a taloned hand. It caught Hoover on the front leg. Blood spurted as flesh parted. The dog howled miserably, but hung on, even as the demon clawed at her again and again and again.

Holmes and Ruiz saw their chance. They leaped on the

demon, grabbed the spikes, and jammed them over and over into any unprotected part of Chi Long they could find. He toppled onto his back, trying to defend himself against the naked fury of the SEALs.

Walker clawed his way to his feet and atop the fallen demon. He grabbed frantically at the creature's hands and torso, but he felt nothing. He didn't see any rings, nor did he see any bracelets. He had no necklace, no crown, nothing. So what was the focus?

With a roar, the demon surged to a standing position, throwing Holmes aside like a doll. Walker fell hard to the ground. Ruiz wasn't so lucky. Chi Long gripped him in two hands and viciously snapped his back, then hammered him into the ground over and over, screaming in frustration and rage.

It dropped Ruiz's body and turned toward Holmes; then a long *qilin* spike pierced the back of its head, the point coming through his left eye. Yaya! For that instant, the figure of Chi Long disappeared, replaced by that of a dumpy man in a tattooed skin suit. Anger laced his chubby face and bile flew from mad lips.

And a necklace encircled his neck.

Then he was once again Chi Long as he reached behind and pulled the spike free.

But that one glimpse had been enough to give the SEALs the direction they needed.

Holmes leaped onto the chest of the demon and clawed his way upward so that he could grab at the neck. His fingers searched for the necklace, but he couldn't find it. His hands scrabbled against the chitinous armor as Chi Long roared. The monster grabbed Holmes and threw him a dozen yards, where he fell, arms akimbo.

Walker leaped atop Chi Long's back. While one arm wrapped around the monster's neck, the other reached down and tried to find the necklace. Chi Long spun, reaching up and trying to dislodge the SEAL. But Walker had a death grip on Chi Long's neck, and used it to hold on, even as Chi Long spun again. Suddenly Walker's searching hand experienced the *pins and needles* he associated with magic. He concentrated, moved his hand several inches to the left, then wrapped his hand around something that burned with energy. He pulled, but felt resistance. He pulled harder, as he slid from the monster's back to the front. Now using both hands, he pushed both feet against the monster and heaved backwards, using his legs to push with every bit of his strength.

The monster grabbed him by the neck and squeezed. Chi Long's strength was staggering. Walker felt impossible pressure against his windpipe. It took all of his concentration to keep his hands on the necklace and not to try and pry the monster's hands away. Blackness began to invade his vision. Then—

Snap!

The necklace came free.

Suddenly he was falling.

As he hit the ground, he saw the demon replaced by a man—Saw Thuza Tun. The Karen man had started to shout something when one last spike pierced the back of his head and came out of his mouth. As he fell forward, Yaya stood behind him, grim determination and fury plastered on his blood-smeared face. Saw Thuza Tun was now merely human, and the spike's effect was permanent.

Walker stared at the necklace in his hands. Made of jade beads, it had five jade "fingers," carved like those of a person. Was this it? Was this the focus? He had an insane desire to wear the necklace. He felt his hands coming toward his own neck. He had no control. He could be powerful. He could rule the earth. But Yaya ran forward and knocked it from his grip. The necklace flew free and as it did so, Walker lost the urge to wear it.

He turned, ready to defend himself against the hordes, only to find them now milling around in stunned confusion, once again themselves, trying to make their way through an imperfect world. Then he remembered.

"Holmes, we gotta go. Bombers are on their way."

The SEAL team leader looked around. He spied Ruiz's broken body and hauled it over his shoulder. "To the water," he yelled.

They ran, climbing over bodies, pushing past the stunned Karen. They needed to make the beach and, with it, possible safety.

"Where's the necklace?" Laws asked.

Before Walker could answer, a cry went up behind him. He turned to see a young man standing on top of a crate, holding the necklace high into the air.

"Oh, hell," he said.

But he needn't have worried.

The young man put on the necklace and for a single instant was Chi Long. But the power of the demon was too much for his frail human body. It burned to ash in an instant, the necklace falling to the wood of the crate. No sooner had it landed than it was taken up again. And again. And again. As each Karen wore it, he burst into flame and died.

Laws pulled Walker away. "Come on—hurry."

Walker ran. His jerking fingers managed to switch on the radio.

"SEALs to the water," Holmes screamed as the sound of jets rent the morning.

The Tornadoes flew in formation out of the west.

The SEALs hit the water and swam furiously.

Laws spied more than a dozen skiffs tied along the water's edge and swam to one. He climbed in, shoved the fishing poles out, and got the outboard started on the second try. He revved the engine, then took off toward the SEALs in the water. He dropped the mooring rope off the left side so his teammates could grab on—first Yaya with Hoover in tow, then Walker, then Holmes, who was holding tightly on to Ruiz's body. They made it perhaps a hundred meters away from shore before the *land burned black* of Kadwan erupted in a ball of effervescent destruction as one bomb after another ate away at those beings who would be demon until there was nothing left except the memory of a tattooed skin man who would be king.

Epilogue

CORONADO ISLAND. NIGHT.

Walker stood in front of his mirror, examining all his new scars. His actions during the final battle had scared him. The demon had demonstrated a power over him it hadn't had over the others. Did that mean that there was some piece of the grave demon left within him? Was there a part of his soul that had been ruined and would remain forever stained because of it? If so, how much of a liability was he going to be to his team? Then again, if not for him, they never would have been able to stop Chi Long.

He found a T-shirt and pulled it on, then hurriedly tied his shoes. He went out into the main room, where Jen was waiting for him. When she saw him, she ran and threw her arms around him. He'd been back for two days and this was only the second time they'd been together. The first had been yesterday, when she'd made him meet her at the Homecoming statue. He'd arrived by taxi to see her standing in a summer dress, the wind picking up the hem of the orange and yellow material and the locks of red hair framing her face. He'd immediately felt a deep welling of pride and love as he strode toward her. She'd been right. Fighting for the living was much better than fighting for the dead.

"Hello, sailor," she'd said. "Glad you made it home."

She said the same thing now and kissed him on the cheek.

"Watch the PDA," Laws said, laughing as he came into the room. Both of his arms had been professionally sutured. He'd been angry at first that he couldn't get Purple Hearts for the wounds. He wanted to add to his collection, but was told that it didn't count if another SEAL stabbed him. Unable to explain that it was because the SEAL had been under the power of a demon, he'd had to accept the judgment.

Yaya entered next, with Hoover beside him. The *qilin* that had dragged him into the jungle had been all but dead when it had tried to eat him. Yaya had managed to stab it in an eye with one of its own spikes. He'd ripped as many of them free as he could, then set out determined to save his fellow SEALs.

"Are we ready to go to McP's?" Jen asked.

Laws nodded. "Holmes is already there setting things up."

"Ruiz would rather we blow shit up than drink," Walker said.

Laws smiled mischievously. "There might be some of that too."

Yaya slid his mirrored sunglasses in place.

As they strode out the door, Walker couldn't help commenting, "What worries me is that the spikes hurt Chi Long, but my bullets didn't."

"The spikes came from a supernatural creature. Maybe that's why—maybe it could only be hurt by something supernatural," Laws surmised. "But it's Charlie Mike. Don't dwell on something that's over."

"Sorry. I was just thinking. I mean, if my bullets didn't hurt it, what makes us think that bombs did?"

They all turned and looked at each other.

"But the bombs cause fire," Jen said. "Wouldn't the fire kill him? I mean, nothing could have survived all those bombs, right?"

They all started walking again.

"God," Walker said. "Let's hope not."

Suddenly they all stopped and turned. "Hoover!" Yaya shouted. "Get your ass in gear."

The dog ran toward them, eager and happy as only a dog could be. She wasn't bothered by her host of new scars, or the hundred sutures that banded her front legs. She was just happy to be home with her family, if only until the next mission.

As were they all.